JUICED

TED MULCAHEY

Other Titles in the O'Malley Adventures

Bearied Treasure

Teed Up for Terror

Little Dirt Road

One

It was one of those dark, rainy afternoons in the Pacific Northwest. Four-thirty, and already the headlights were bouncing off the slick, shiny freeway.

I was on my way back to Whidbey Island. Playing golf in Seattle in late November was not for the faint of heart. Bundled up with rain gear, umbrella stuck on the push golf cart, wet khakis tucked into even wetter socks, we had slogged through eighteen holes of betting and swearing.

Usually, the Wednesday round was followed by more swearing, drinking wine, and playing gin rummy, but today was different. Today was Jenne's birthday. It was the big one, double nickels. Well, sort of a big one.

Of course, she told me to stay, have fun and enjoy myself – no big deal. When you've been married more than once, you *absolutely* know for sure that birthdays *are* a big deal. Unless, that is, you don't care if your sexual activities are curtailed for, say, a month or two.

Well, not this husband. No sir. I managed to make the 5:30 ferry. And also had the foresight to stop at Walgreens and select a lovely greeting card. From Hallmark. I figured the card with a heartfelt message, along with the bouquet purchased at the Star Store when I drove through Langley, would put me in Jenne's good graces.

It should have been a wonderful evening.

But it wasn't.

I made the right onto Little Dirt Road. About five hundred yards up the hill, on the unpaved surface, I turned on the crushed gravel driveway leading to our tidy, shingled home. We live on a bluff that normally overlooks Saratoga Passage. Tonight it was dark and rainy.

And there were no lights on in the house or on the grounds.

This seemed odd. I negotiated the six steps to the porch in the dark. Emma was inside, barking as only a German shepherd can, when anything, and *I mean anything,* is perceived as a threat.

"Easy girl, easy. It's me." She quieted only slightly until I opened the door—it was unlocked—and she calmed down.

I flicked the lights on, rubbed behind her ears, and stupidly called out Jenne's name. *She's not here, you dope. She wouldn't be sitting in the dark.*

I walked to the kitchen counter. There was a note in her writing. "Went for a walk in case you get home early. Back around 4:30." It was followed by a little heart and a smiley face.

What the fuck? It was 6:45. Still not accepting reality, I dialed her cell. The sounds of "The Irish Washerwoman," her ringtone, came from the little nook with the fireplace, just off the kitchen.

This was strange. Even though she always thought she had forgotten her phone, she seldom did.

I stood there, searching my mind but coming up with nothing. Her car was in the courtyard, her phone in the house. *Where the fuck is she?*

We didn't know that many people on the island. We knew our neighbors and a few others, but few were close friends. The only people Jenne was close to lived off-island. And they did not come up in this crappy weather.

One thing was certain, if she left around 3:30, she sure as hell wasn't still on her walk.

I walked across the dark, grassy area separating us from our neighbors, Tim and Raye. I knocked on the door, perhaps a little too forcefully.

"Kevin. Hi, good to see you." Tim was a gentle soul and a terrific neighbor, always there if you needed him, and highly considerate in every way.

"Hi, Tim. Have you seen Jenne? When I got home, the house was dark. She left a note saying she'd be back at 4:30. Do you know where she could be?"

"Geez, Kev, no, I don't. I did see her a little before five. She was headed down the street. I thought it a bit odd because it was getting dark, but that was about it."

"She was headed south?"

"Yes."

"She always goes the other way on her walks and finishes by coming up the hill. She says it feels good to stretch out at the end of it."

"Well, I don't know about that, but I'm sure she was headed down. Is there anything I can do?"

"Thanks. Not yet. Let me think about it first."

Tim's face showed genuine concern. "You know we're here if you need anything."

"I do, Tim. Thanks."

I went back home and stood in the kitchen. "Emma, what do you think? Where the hell is your mom?"

The ninety-pound black and tan animal looked directly at me and twisted her head to the left. "Ah, I wish you could talk, kiddo."

If Tim saw Jenne go back down the hill, maybe she was going to one of the homes on Saratoga Road. For some reason. To someone's house, she didn't know. Sure.

"Emma. Let's go. Get in the truck." Before I went entirely off the deep end, I figured a drive around the area might be productive. Maybe Emma could be of some help. Maybe.

We drove slowly down the hill, past Tim and Raye's house and past the Robinsons, who lived on the opposite corner. Most of the properties were well over an acre. As a result, there weren't many homes nearby.

After turning right on Saratoga, where there was no traffic, thankfully, we crept as slowly as possible. I rolled down the rear windows in case Emma caught a scent.

We passed three homes. Emma acted as though this was a simple trip to the store. Maybe even treats if she behaved.

On the left was a huge vacant field where sheep occasionally grazed. Beyond that was a long, straight two-track that served as a driveway for a home hidden by tall firs and cedars.

During our walks, we'd always speculate as to who lived there. Occasionally we would see an island car chug and sputter down the drive. Island cars are beaters that nobody would ever take on the ferry. They frequently break down, and hell hath no fury greater than ferry patrons missing the boat because some yahoo couldn't start their fucking car.

We passed the mailbox and then the driveway. Then Emma went batshit crazy.

It was close to nine o'clock when I pulled to the side of the road. I shut the engine off and turned out the lights, and tried everything to get the dog to quiet down, with no success. She had picked up a scent.

With no streetlights and only a rare car passing, the only light was a very faint glow from somewhere down the driveway. I managed to back up in the darkness and then turned into the drive. Very cautiously, I proceeded. After what seemed like an eternity, but was only about ten minutes, the road turned into a clearing.

A small cottage appeared, wood smoke rising from the chimney. The droning sound from a generator suggested the electricity for the place was homegrown. Whoever owned this lived off the grid.

Emma was even more agitated as if that were possible. I couldn't imagine why Jenne might have been here, but I could think of no other explanation for our dog's behavior.

I stopped a good hundred yards from the porch on the front of the lonely-looking house. Any closer and whoever was inside would think they were under attack by the *Hound of the Baskervilles.*

"Emma, stay here. I'm gonna check this out. Quiet." She did that head turn thing, and oddly enough, she shut up. I stepped out into the cold air, now filled with the scent of burning cedar, and quickly shut the door.

The generator noise was much louder now. If someone had heard us approach, I would have been surprised. There was no doorbell, just a small brass bell. The clapper had a piece of twine attached. I shook it loudly. No answer.

I knocked on the weathered wooden door respectfully. Still no answer. Then I banged on it with my fist. Nothing.

Fuck this. I thumbed the latch and pushed the door open. A blast of heat hit me in the face. It must have been ninety degrees. A scorching woodstove sat in the corner with a redbrick surround. Considering the size of the house, the relatively large room was neatly and tastefully furnished.

Two upholstered chairs faced a stylish sofa. A rustic, live-edge coffee table pulled the seating group together, and matched lamps and aptly selected artwork lent a comfy feeling to the room.

The only obstacle to the relaxing atmosphere was the curled-up, frail-looking octogenarian seemingly poured into the sofa. If she wasn't dead, she was either sleeping or unconscious. I gingerly approached and was able to discern the woman's very shallow breathing.

As I bent down to feel her head, the rear entry slammed open. I jumped. Now the generator sound was deafening. Standing in the doorway, soot on her face and splinters and wood shavings adorning her Carhartt jacket, with her arms full of split firewood, was my wife.

She kicked the door shut, dampening the sound, and looked at me with mild surprise. "Hey, Kev, don't just stand there looking like a doofus. Help me with this shit. It's fucking heavy."

The relief I felt was shocking. I was near tears.

"Hey, you. Help me," she repeated.

"Sorry, Jenne." I rushed over and took the firewood from her arms. But not before I kissed her.

She dropped her arms like a rag doll. She looked exhausted. Beautiful, but exhausted. I placed the wood next to the stove, took off my jacket and hat, and turned to her.

She went over to the sofa, felt the woman's forehead, and tucked the blanket around her. She then turned to one of the chairs and collapsed into it.

"Jenne? You okay?"

"Fuck no. I'm just so, so tired. Where's Emma?"

She was about to pass out, and she wanted to know where our dog was. *First things first, I guess.*

"She's in the truck. She's worried. I'll get her, and then we can talk."

It was almost a relief getting out into the cool air. I got the dog, then braced myself going back into the oven-like room.

"Honey, you gotta tell me what's going on. Why are you here? How come you left your phone at home? Who is this woman and, shit, I was *really* fucking worried about you!"

Even as worn out as she was, she still looked beautiful. She turned to me with that dazzling grin that always got me deep inside. "I suppose you're speculating what the story is here, eh?"

"Ya think?"

"It'll be easier if I start from the beginning. I went on my walk as usual; I left a note for you in case you got back early."

"Um, yes. I read it. 'Back by 4:30,' it said."

"Yeah, well, shit happens. Did you look at my car, by the way?"

"No. What's that got to do with anything?" I was getting a little anxious at the pace the conversation was proceeding.

She held up her hand. "I'll get there, Kev; I'll get there."

I looked down at Emma, who was curled up between us. Now that her pack was together, she was relaxed.

"Sure, sorry. Emma was worried as shit too."

"Yeah, I figured, but I couldn't help it. I'm sorry too. So toward the end of the walk, I turned to head up the hill. I went past this field out here, you know, where the sheep are sometimes?"

I nodded and looked over at the old woman. I couldn't imagine where this was going.

"There were no sheep today, but I saw Sharon here picking the few remaining apples on the tree out near the road."

"Sharon?"

"Yup. It's Sharon Waffle."

"Like the thing you put maple syrup on?"

She shook her head and looked at me as if I were a child.

"Yes. Like that. Anyway, I was walking by, and I looked over and smiled. I told her, 'Nice day, isn't it?' She smiled back and said she just hated to let the last of the apples go to waste. Said she was gonna get them before the deer did.

"I laughed and kept walking. Then I thought I'd ask where the sheep were. I turned to go back and saw her lying on the ground. I ran over to see what I could do."

"Did she pass out?"

"Nope. When I got there, she told me she had vertigo, and sometimes she fell. I got her up and managed to get her back to the house here. Then she almost passed out, and I got her to lie down on the sofa."

"Why not call emergency, get someone out here to help her?"

"That's what I told her. She said absolutely not. She was adamant about that. A definite no. She said she had some medicine for her vertigo and told me where it was. I got the bottle from the medicine cabinet in the bathroom, but it was empty. The prescription was for meclizine."

"Isn't that the stuff I took last year when I had the dizzies?"

"It is. I told her I thought we had some and could get it for her. I said I'd walk home and drive back with the stuff, and that's what I did."

"Only what?"

"Only when I went to drive back, I saw my goddamn car had a flat fucking tire. God, I was pissed."

"That's why you asked me if I had seen it?"

"It is."

"Okay. You ran back here with the drugs, and then what?"

"I got back, and she was in the kitchen. She was sitting at the table doing something when she fell to the floor. She was semi-conscious when I brought her in here and put her on the sofa. She said she was freezing, so I gave her a blanket and fired up the woodstove. As you can see, she's on a generator. For the last three hours, I've been putting gas in the generator and splitting wood for the stove."

"Jesus, hon, you should have called someone for help."

"Like who?"

"Like 911."

"She made me swear that I wouldn't call them. Something weird there, but what could I do? Besides, I forgot my phone. Remember? And she doesn't even have one.

"She's been shivering off and on, so I've kept it warm in here. Now, I don't know, but she's got more than vertigo."

"Here's your phone. I don't care what she wants; I'm calling emergency."

I made the call, although the cell service was spotty here. After finally making a connection, I was assured they would be there shortly.

South Whidbey Island is very rural, with the only hospital in Coupeville. As such, they have an outstanding cadre of emergency medical service technicians who serve the community tirelessly.

They were there in ten minutes.

Suddenly the darkness was pierced with flashing red strobe lights, and the sirens drowned out the sound of the generator. The medics were on site.

Three of them rushed through the door we had already opened. They immediately went to the old woman, all the while asking us about her condition. Then all we heard were vials being opened, the tape being torn off plastic bags, and Velcro ripping off various pieces of equipment.

"Got a pulse but very faint. BP?"

"Sixty over thirty-five and dropping."

"Get the IV going. Start the norepinephrine."

"Get her legs up. Let's get her out of here."

"We'll have to medivac her to Everett."

The two working on Sharon rushed her to the ambulance and strapped her in. They jumped in and slammed the doors. The third person addressed us.

"Your mom?"

"No, a neighbor. I just met her."

"Okay. Call this number and tell them what you know about her condition." She handed a card to Jenne. "I gotta go. We don't have a lot of time."

She flew off the porch, jumped into the driver's seat, and sprayed gravel as she shot down the driveway.

Jenne and I stood on the porch watching the dust settle, the red strobes and the siren now off in the distance. The only sound was the generator.

"I'll call this number and tell them what little we know about her. At least tell them about the vertigo and the meclizine." Jenne now showed her fatigue.

"Okay. While you're doing that, I'm gonna shut off the goddamn generator. I've got a flashlight in the truck, and I saw some candles on the kitchen table. We can use them until we leave. That noise is driving me crazy."

After first getting the flashlight, I went around to the back of the little house and mercifully shut down the noise machine. There was complete darkness, excluding the beam of the torch.

"Hey, I'm in the dark here, ya know?" I had momentarily forgotten Jenne was thrown into darkness.

"I'm coming. I'll get the candles lit for you."

I came through the back door to the small kitchen table. There were three candles and a butane lighter lying next to them. Candles were a must, with the generator providing the only electricity.

I lit all three and brought two of them to Jenne, who was still on the phone in the living room. Through the candlelight, her face looked gloomy.

"Sure. I will, and thanks for your help."

She disconnected and stared through me. "Sharon didn't make it. While they were on their way to medivac her, she just shut down. They are sure it wasn't just her advanced age. They think there was some underlying stuff with the dizzy spells and all.

"The tech on the phone said there would likely be an autopsy even though she was old. They are trying to find her next of kin."

"Sorry, Jenne. I know you did everything you could, and it sounds as though even a faster response wouldn't have mattered. Let's close up and get you and Emma back home.

"If you'll close the air off to the stove there, I'll put the candles back. You can hang on to the flashlight."

I returned to the kitchen and placed the two candles with the third one. Now that the tabletop was illuminated, I could see several pages of handwritten notes. There was a Bic plastic pen alongside them. Thing is, I couldn't read them. They were in another language.

I left them there and blew out the three candles. Whoever her relatives were would be left to read them. I joined my wife and my dog. We closed up as best we could and limped to my Honda Ridgeline. Going back up the hill to the O'Malley residence would be good. It had been a rough night.

Two

Sunday morning arrived with low clouds and drizzle, as do most late fall days in the Northwest. Living on Whidbey Island had many plusses and one major drawback. The positives were more important to us than the negative.

We received about a third less rain than Seattle. We still had the clouds and the wind, but the rain shadow formed by the Olympic Mountains spared us a good deal of the moisture.

There was no traffic. The town of Langley, where most of the locals shopped, didn't even have a red light. Traffic in the Seattle area had grown to make the list of the country's top five most congested cities.

The people on Whidbey Island either kept to themselves or were kind and friendly. Yes, politically, there were polar opposites. Even so, there was a tolerance for alternate viewpoints, if not necessarily respect.

It was unearthly quiet. At night the occasional screech of an eagle or maybe the hoot of an owl was the only sound. No road noise or horns or trains, or any other ambient echoes could be heard.

The downside was it actually *was* an island. Access was either from ferry to the south end, or the Deception Pass bridge to the north. Some folks thought it a terrible inconvenience. Now that we were retired, we thought it was just perfect. It did require a couple of trips a week for golf and the random Costco or Nordstrom excursion. Thing is, it was only a twenty-minute ferry ride to the mainland, and we got to pick our times. Not a terrible inconvenience.

We both slept until seven, a rarity, and only got up then because our German shepherd required it.

"Still can't believe all that happened just a few days ago, Kev. It was so surreal. It's almost as if I dreamt it."

I was thinking the same thing. Strange occurrences.

"I wonder if they found her relatives. I'm glad I was there for her, though. I can't imagine what would have happened if she had been all alone."

I thought that the same thing would have happened. She would have died. The difference was that she wasn't alone. She'd had the good fortune to have Jenne walking by at the right time. She was very, very lucky, as was I.

"Honey, I'm glad you were there for her too. It had to mean a lot to her."

We spent the morning doing household chores. We would have finished them too, but a sheriff's patrol car pulled into the courtyard just as I was taking the trash out.

"Mr. O'Malley?"

"That's me."

"Could I sit down with you and your wife for just a minute?"

This didn't sound good. We certainly weren't criminals, but it doesn't bode well whenever the law wants to sit and have a chat.

"I guess so. What's this all about?"

"I promise you'll know in just a minute, but I need to have your wife with you."

With little room left to negotiate, I invited Deputy Roger Willkie into our home. He was a stout fellow with thinning grayish hair, about five-ten or eleven. He looked to be my age, sixtyish, but had nowhere near my own cut figure. He was in much better shape than I was, with forearms like pistons.

Emma gave him the same reception reserved for all visitors. Extremely loud barking followed by a rapid approach left all but the seasoned shepherd fans with more than just a modicum of concern.

"Sorry, Deputy. Just stand there for ten seconds or so. When she sees you're not a mass murderer, she'll stop." And, sure enough, although it was a good fifteen seconds, she stopped, sniffed his hands, and went back to her bed.

"You have much trouble with break-ins here?" The officer had a sense of humor as well.

"What do you think?"

"Um, I'm certain you do not. Please call me Roger. Can we sit for a minute?"

Jenne had joined us, and she, too, looked concerned.

"That was nice of you two to help Sharon, Wednesday."

"I showed up late to the party. It was Jenne who did the heavy lifting."

"I know."

"How do you know?" Jenne didn't miss much.

"Sharon told me."

The two of us looked at each other, then over to Roger.

"Huh, how?"

"Not sure if you saw it or not, but there were several pages of handwritten notes left on her table."

"I noticed them when I replaced the candles we used after we shut the generator down. I didn't think much about them, except they were in another language. We closed the house up then and came back here."

Willkie looked at us both, shook his head slowly, and offered a sad face. "I've known Sharon Waffle for a long time. She was still a Canadian citizen when she moved here to Whidbey. She lived in Vancouver, B.C., before coming to the States. Said she read about Whidbey Island somewhere, and it seemed like a nice quiet place to retire, so she did.

"She was originally from Utrecht, in the Netherlands. Living in North America so long seemingly diluted her accent. Folks here just assumed it was some Canadian affectation."

I was a little puzzled about where the deputy was going with this story, and from the look on Jenne's face, she was too.

"When she moved to British Columbia, she was twenty years old, and it was just after the passing of her mother. Sharon was an only child who never knew her father. He volunteered for the army during World War II and never returned. Her mother told her stories of *her* father, Sharon's grandfather, who emigrated to Canada in the twenties.

"Not having a male figure in her life, Sharon corresponded with her grandfather in Vancouver. With no siblings and no other family left, she decided to join her grandfather in Canada. Sadly, he died while she was en route.

"She was lost when she arrived but had the sense to seek out other ex-pats. The Dutch community is significant there, and she eventually found her way."

"It's an interesting story, Roger, but what does that have to do with us?" Jenne was as anxious for Willkie to get to the point as I was.

"I'm sorry. Just another minute. It will help you to have this background.

"Sharon learned English quickly, went to UBC and aced their STEM curriculum, then took a job with Voltare."

"Roger, this is all mildly interesting, but why are you telling us?" I was losing interest in the yarn.

"I'm telling you because the papers on that kitchen table were Sharon Waffle's last will. She left everything she had to your wife."

Jenne stared at me. I'm sure my mouth was hanging open. I closed it and said, "Huh? What? Why?" I was always brilliant with clever comebacks.

"Are you sure, Roger?" Jenne wasn't near as clever, but she made a lot more sense.

"Mostly. Whenever Sharon wrote anything, it was in the Dutch language. When I got to know her a little better, I started learning some of it myself. Kind of like German, but different. I didn't read all of it, but I did go over the last page. I'm not fluent, and I miss some of the nuances, so we'll send it off to an interpreter to be sure."

"But I hardly knew her. I only met her the other day. I don't know much about wills, but I'm fairly sure they have to be witnessed."

"Sharon was a very private person. I may have been her closest friend on the island. And we weren't *that* close. About a week ago, I stopped in to see how she was getting along. A rookie recruit was riding along with me.

"She told me she was working on her will and could we sign as witnesses. I told her I didn't understand most of it, and she had left the beneficiary's name blank. She said she would make sure to fill it in later. So she signed, and then we did. I suppose someone could get all fussy about it not being complete. The thing is, I didn't think there was much of an estate, and she told me she had no living relatives, so I figured it didn't make any difference.

"According to her notes, you showed her a kindness she hadn't experienced since she was a child. I'm guessing she knew she was nearing the end of the road. She probably finished it while you were out splitting the wood.

"She lived very frugally and, as you saw, she lived off the grid. She was passionate about taking care of the planet. When she worked for Voltare, she spent one hundred percent of her time studying ways to mitigate the damage being done to the earth by its citizens. Voltare even loaned her to the PNNL Research Center in Seattle for the last five years of her employment."

Since I had never heard of them, I asked the sheriff to enlighten me.

"The Pacific Northwest National Laboratory is rarely in the news. They have campuses all over the place, a big one down in the Tri-Cities, and employ scientists from almost every country in the world.

"She always said if she told me what she was working on, she'd have to kill me." He said this with a hearty laugh. "I really liked her. I got the impression that whatever she was involved with wasn't as much dangerous as was its impact on commerce globally. She felt strongly that improvements in technology should benefit humankind, not just make billions for a few particular companies.

"Anyway, that's why I stopped. Jenne, you are now the proud owner of that off-the-grid estate down the road. I don't think probate will be an issue. All we have to do is file it with the county. They'll need an accurate translation, but I can get someone to do that.

"Feel free to go over there whenever you'd like. I think this is less a windfall than it is a headache. For whatever reason, Jenne, she liked you very much. You certainly made an impression on her.

"She was also particular about how her funeral should be handled. She wanted to be cremated and spread over the Saratoga Passage. That's it. No ceremony. Nothing else. She designated an account in a local bank for the expenses. I'll make sure it gets done, but I'll let you deal with the ashes."

Jenne looked shell-shocked at all the revelations. "That's good of you, Roger. Thanks."

"I'll leave you alone now. Please call me anytime if you have any questions or issues with the property. Here's my cell. Anytime."

Three

We hung around the house for a couple of days. I messed around in my workshop while Jenne spent time with TD Ameritrade on her laptop. Seems as though my financial acumen wasn't solid enough for her, and she vowed to learn all she could about stocks and bonds and whatever.

And then it was mid-week again. I took an early ferry to the mainland and went to join my friends for eighteen holes. Jenne decided to take a walk on the beach with Emma. The low mid-morning tide made for outstanding beachcombing treasures. Washed-up driftwood, mussels, seaweed, and parts and pieces of crab were examined in great detail by the dog. Her energy level was fueled by the prospect of such unique and organic smells.

I made it back to the house a little after three. Once again, there was a note. *I took Emma down to Sharon's just to putter around. Back around 4:30.* There was that 4:30 thing again.

Rather than wondering what "putter around" meant, I took off down the hill to see for myself.

As soon as I made it up the long drive, I heard Emma barking. I opened the door just in time to receive two muddy front paws in my lap. "Hey, girl. Where's Mom?"

Instead of answering, she turned and ran to the back of the house. I followed.

"Hey," I yelled as soon as I saw her.

"Hey yourself. Figured that was you when she stopped barking."

"Who else? You're the owner of this now."

"Whoopee. I think Roger was right. It's probably more of a pain in the ass."

"Well, it's not like it's worth nothing. There must be a few acres here."

"Five to be exact. I looked it up on the county website. At least the taxes are paid up."

"Anything here interesting?"

"The house is sorta cute. And, except for a little deferred maintenance, it's in decent shape. I can't say the same for the outbuilding back there, though. I didn't even realize it was there until I walked around the property's perimeter. I copied the map from the Island County site."

"What's in there?"

"All sorts of shit. Bottles and jars of stuff, chemicals all over the place. Lots of metal rods and reams of papers and notes. All in Dutch, by the way.

"Funny thing, though. I expected to see dust and cobwebs over everything, but that wasn't the case. If it was Sharon messing around in there, she had done so recently."

"It had to be her."

"I agree. It would be nice to know what she was working on."

"Maybe you should learn the language. Get one of those Babbel thingies."

"It's not a thingy, moron; it's a computer app."

"Moron? Who do you think you're talking to?" I approached her slowly, my fingers wiggling and grasping air.

"If you do anything," she shrieked, "I'll tell Emma to bite you."

"Go ahead. See how that works out for you." I advanced to within a foot before she reached into the pile of dead leaves at her feet and threw them in my face. Then she turned and ran.

"Okay, have it your way," I shouted after her. "You keep being nasty like this, and there will be no more nookie for a long while."

"Hah, promises, promises." She stopped, laughing too hard to continue.

She got serious for a minute. "Kevin, what do we do with this place?"

"I'm not sure yet, hon. Let's let the dust settle for a few weeks. There's no hurry to do anything. In the meantime, we should see if we can find someone who knows the language. I suppose we could ask Roger, but I think we need someone who speaks it fluently."

"Yeah, I agree. Let's pack it in. I'm hungry."

Four

Several weeks passed while we went about our daily lives. Jenne occasionally visited Sharon's, now Jenne's, property and had done an impressive job cleaning up the leaves and blown branches that were too much for an eighty-seven-year-old.

We talked about whether or not to put it on the market, and we were still undecided.

Jenne occasionally muttered something about ETFs and stop losses, which I chose to ignore. I fully supported her research; hell, at least one of us needed to know something.

About three weeks after Sharon Waffle's death, Deputy Roger Willkie came by the house. Emma again announced the visitor.

"Hi, you two, I came by with this." He handed us a bronze urn.

"Sharon?"

"It is, Jenne. I told you what she wanted, but just do with it what you wish."

"We'll dispose of her the way she directed. Thanks for bringing this by."

After Willkie had left, Jenne placed the urn on the mantel. "When do you want to do it?" she asked.

"Why don't we let her visit with us for a while. I think we'll know when the time is right."

She smiled at me and nodded. We were usually on the same page, and this time was no different.

The next day was a sunny one. Jenne took advantage of the anomaly and went for her walk early in the day. I got the call at 10:30.

"Kevin. Will you meet me at the Waffle house?" We had begun calling it that.

"Sure. Why? What's up?"

"Just come down here, please. Now."

Whenever she used the word "please," it was an order, not a request. I immediately left the house.

She met me at the edge of the driveway. "Someone's been here."

"How do you know?"

"Follow me." She strode purposefully back to the tiny yellow cottage. "Come inside."

I did. It was a mess. Cushions had been tossed aside and chairs tipped over. The small bookcase had been emptied, and pages were torn out of several volumes.

"Holy shit. What a mess. Stupid kids drinking, you think?"

"I don't think so, Kev. Sure, it's trashed, but it seems like they were looking for something. If it were just kids, they would have left bottles or butts or something. Whoever did this was pretty thorough."

"I'm calling Willkie. He should take a look."

She continued investigating while I called the deputy.

"Roger, will you come by Sharon's place? Someone's broken in."

He agreed to do so right away. There wasn't a tremendous amount of crime on the island. A few break-ins and burglaries sometimes but extraordinarily little violent crime. It was a safe bet that a call to the sheriff would be responded to immediately.

"I agree with you, Jenne. It looks like somebody was trying to find something." Roger finished surveying the carnage. "Have you checked out back?"

"No, we haven't. I completely forgot about the little studio or whatever it was. We should check it out."

The three of us walked single file along the narrow path leading to the small building near the back of the property.

"I can't see Sharon coming back here often. You can't even see the house from here." I looked back through the blackberry thorns and assorted underbrush.

"But remember when we were here last? It looked as though it had been visited recently." Jenne was correct. It had.

We opened the door to the eight-by-ten, cedar-sided structure. The interior was just as I remembered it from our previous visit.

“Whoever did that in the house never made it back here, that’s for sure.” Jenne directed this to the deputy.

Willkie nodded in agreement. “I guess they weren’t familiar with the property. If you didn’t know this was here, you couldn’t find it. I still can’t get my head around that old lady coming back here, though. It must be two hundred yards from the main house.”

“I was wondering about that too,” I said. “Whatever is in here must have been important to her. Jenne, let’s take all these notes with us, just in case. We can find someone who knows the language to tell us what they are. Roger, how about it?”

“I don’t think so, Kevin. I know only enough to be dangerous. From what I can see in those papers, I’d be out of my league. It appears to be something scientific. You need a Dutch scientist, I’d say.”

FIVE

Back home with the passage still shrouded in fog, I tried to get a better understanding of my wife's benefactor.

"Does the name Waffle come from the Netherlands?"

"You're asking me?"

"I am.

"The worldly person that you think you are, would know the answer." Jenne was certainly crisp with her comebacks today.

"A less secure man would be insulted by that comment. Thank goodness I'm not."

"When I looked up the name, there was surprisingly little information on it. I figured since she knew the language, then it would be a Dutch name."

I hadn't given it much thought. If we wanted to get a handle on whoever broke in, I suppose it would help to know more about the deceased woman.

"Maybe she was married to someone named Waffle."

"Nice try, Kev. We didn't see any pictures of family or husbands, did we?"

"No, dear. We didn't."

"How about we get in touch with Rob Aronson at UDub?"

"He teaches law, doesn't he?"

"Yeah, he does. But he knows people. There's gotta be someone on the faculty who knows the language. We find out what's in those papers that were out in the shed, then maybe we'll find out why someone broke in."

"Good idea, Jenne. I'll give him a call."

There had been boxes of documents in the little outbuilding, and it had taken the better part of the day to get most of them back to our place. We left the other equipment along with the chemicals there.

Roger assured us he would drive by every so often to check, and we secured the house as best we could.

"Rob told me that they don't have any courses specifically for Dutch at UDub. He did give me the name of a professor who teaches German, though. I guess the languages are very close. Anyway, the woman's name is De Groot. He said he'd contact her and say we might be calling."

"Let me know when you can get to see her, and I'll make the trip with you," said Jenne.

"Of course."

Alice De Groot was kind enough to see us the next day.

The University of Washington is consistently ranked among the best universities in the country. Its six-hundred-plus acres sit on the shores of Union Bay in the city of Seattle.

With the vaccine availability and better understanding of the disease, Covid was no longer impacting the campuses across the country to the degree it had. Now though, just a week before Christmas, there were relatively few students on campus.

Following Alice's directions, we made our way to a small conference room located in the rear of the Suzzallo Library. The gothic structure, resembling something out of a *Harry Potter* movie, was world-famous and the center of the campus.

We knocked on the half-closed door and were met by an attractive forty-something woman with short, dark hair. With her petite frame and diminutive stature, I would have been shocked if she tipped the scales at anything over a hundred pounds.

She put down what she was reading, removed the half-glasses that were perched on the end of her classic, if slightly crooked nose, and greeted us.

"You must be Jenne and Kevin. I'm Alice, and it's a pleasure to meet you. Rob tells me Jenne's a sweetheart and that you're a pain in the ass on the golf course."

Already I liked this woman. We greeted her with good cheer and handshakes.

"That Rob, what a card. Thanks for seeing us, Alice; we appreciate it."

"It's my pleasure. I have a little time on my hands with Christmas break and all. He said you had something written in Dutch that you'd like translated."

"Yes. An older woman passed away and left her property to me. Someone trashed her house as if they were looking for something; then we found these boxes of notes in a small outbuilding. We don't want you to spend hours on this stuff, but maybe you could look through it and give us the gist. Rob said you teach German?"

"Yes, Jenne, I do. I'm actually from Amsterdam, but I am fluent in German. The university offers German, not Dutch, so that's what I teach."

"We have a couple of boxes of notes and material out in the truck. Should I bring them in?" I hated to take advantage of this woman's kindness, but we needed to know what this stuff was.

"Tell you what. I'm off campus for the next week. Why don't I bring my car over to yours and we can transfer them. I'll take a look over the holidays and get back to you after the first of the year. Will that work? I'll be careful with the material."

"Geez, that would be very thoughtful of you, Alice. Are you okay with this?" Jenne was always considerate.

"It's no problem. I think it'll be interesting. I don't get to use my native language much anymore. I'd get back to you sooner, but I'm running the New Year's marathon, and there's training."

I hated people who were attractive *and* in good shape. Actually, I was jealous. "Marathon?"

"Yes, I try to do three or four a year."

"Three or four? That's all?"

"I think I can see what Rob was talking about," she said with a wide grin. "C'mon, I'll get those notes from your truck."

Six

It was New Year's Day, and we hadn't heard from Alice De Groot. I didn't expect to on the holiday, but I was curious to hear what she saw in the material we'd left.

"Hey, Kev, let's go see if we can spot Alice in the marathon." Jenne was always up for new adventures. Me, not so much.

"If we go into town, we won't be able to watch all these neat bowl games."

"Yes, you're correct."

It seemed like sort of a dismissal of my wishes, so I made another attempt.

"Maybe there will be coverage on the sports, and they'll have pictures."

"Yes, maybe there will. We'd better go if we want to make the 8:30 boat."

"Um, sure. I'll get my coat." You didn't survive twenty years of marriage with a dynamite woman unless you knew when to pick your battles. And this wasn't one of them. Besides, I kinda wanted to see how Alice did in the race.

The marathon was the biggest in the Northwest and drew over 15,000 runners. The pandemic had impacted the previous year, so this one was expected to be well attended.

It was a rare sunny day in January with the temperature in the low forties. The race began and ended at Gas Works Park. The former coal-gasification plant was decommissioned in 1956 and eventually opened as a city park in 1976, proving Seattle's ability to declare almost anything a public park. The former toxic site landmark was now listed on the National Register of Historic Places.

We arrived after the race was well underway and managed to negotiate our way through the throngs of race rooters up to just beyond the finish ribbon. I thought it unnecessary to mention to my wife that seeing Alice finish in the middle of 15,000 runners was not likely. But I did it anyway.

"Jenne, you do know that we probably won't see her in this crowd. Right?"

"Of course, we will, Kevin. Relax."

If only I had the woman's conviction.

We had been there only ninety minutes when the first runners began to cross the finish line. After some serious ciphering, I figured an average time would put Ms. De Groot across the line in about an hour. I resigned myself to smiling at other well-wishers and stomping my feet to keep the blood moving.

I was seriously off in my computing. After fifteen minutes Alice De Groot, wearing number 158, *sprinted* across the line. Her time was just *under three hours*, easily among the top 10 percent of racers in her class.

Jenne was screaming and clapping like she'd known the woman for years. Worse yet, Alice looked directly at us as she raised her arms over her head in sheer joy. She easily slid through the crowd to greet us.

"Hey, you. What are you doing here?"

"We came to see you. Fabulous race, by the way." Jenne was as excited as Alice.

"Thank you. It's my best time ever. It helped that we had such great weather."

"Are you meeting anybody else?"

For a brief second, she seemed a bit pensive; then her smile returned. "Nope. I just live up in Wallingford. I walked here."

"At least let us give you a lift home," I said. Finally, an approving glance from Jenne.

"I'd appreciate that. Thanks."

As directed, we drove up Wallingford Avenue and hung a right on Thirty-sixth. Halfway down the block, we arrived at a cute 1940s bungalow.

"Come on in, you two. I'll make some coffee, and we can talk. The notes you gave me are fascinating."

The inviting porch led into a surprisingly contemporary interior.

"This is beautiful, Alice. Have you lived here long?"

"We bought this about three years ago, just after I took the position at UDub."

A glance at Jenne confirmed she hadn't missed the "we" either.

"The first year, we gutted the place and did a complete remodel. Another faculty member referred me to the interior designer she used. He was wonderful all along the way.

"Rob told me you were designers. Had I known…"

"Whoever you used knew what he was doing. It's perfect." Jenne was fiercely competitive while we were in business. She was also honest and recognized excellent work when she saw it.

"No argument here. Well done, Alice."

"Thanks. It means a lot coming from you guys. Unfortunately, my ex couldn't deal with all the construction. Said it was too disruptive. He moved out, just until we were done, he said.

"About a month after he left, I ran into him at U Village. He was holding hands with a young woman. Much younger. That was enough for me. I keep kicking myself for ever getting married to the putz. Ah, fuck it, it's over."

"Sorry about that, Alice, but I like your attitude." After only meeting the woman, I felt reasonably sure that her selection process would be more discerning the second time around.

"Enough. Let's get some coffee, and I'll tell you what I've learned."

We both sat around the kitchen island while Alice busied herself in the kitchen.

"I started looking at the documents randomly because there was no particular order to them," she began. "The notes span over twenty years, and there are extended periods between the entries. She was working on something when she worked at the National Lab and continued doing so until recently.

"Most of the material deals with chemistry and physics and is way over my head. There are some personal comments having to do with the environment and how most folks just don't give a shit about it. Her words, not mine. She dedicated her research, her life really, trying to make an impact."

"Was there something, in particular, she was working on?"

She joined us, delivering a tray with steaming cups of coffee and what appeared to be pumpkin scones.

"Batteries."

"Huh? What about them?" I wasn't sure I'd heard correctly.

"Even though all the scientific stuff was beyond me, there was enough I did understand. Her research was all about batteries—some recent technology that was cheaper, more powerful, and longer-lasting than even the most advanced lithium batteries of today.

"According to Sharon, the impact on the planet would be substantial. Any more than that, and you'd have to talk to someone much smarter than I am."

"Any ideas?" I felt a little lost but knew of no other option but to keep pressing forward.

"She occasionally referred to a fellow researcher at the lab. His name was Seth Robbins. She referred to him as 'that kid,' so I guess he was younger. From what I could gather this fellow traded theories with her after she retired. They never worked together side by side, but evidently, they were of the same mind when it came to the planet.

"There were some letters from him, in English of course. I think he took over her project after she retired. He wanted to know all about her research. Evidently, he picked up the project as soon as he started there. There are several recent ones from him asking about formulas she was working on. The last one was dated a few months ago.

"She must have been a big deal there because she stayed on until she was seventy. I'm guessing here, but I'll bet Sharon and this Robbins guy started working together outside of the lab."

"You think?"

"I do. Early on, a few years after her retirement, was when the letters began."

"Let me see if I've got this straight," I said. "According to Roger Willkie, the deputy on Whidbey who knew her pretty well, she moved to the States about twenty-three years ago. She lived in Seattle during the time she worked at the National Laboratory. After five years or so, which she appears to have spent on some sort of battery research, she retires and moves to Whidbey Island. Then, according to what you've been able to discover, after some time, she's contacted by this Seth Robbins. They write back and forth and agree to continue this battery project. About right, Alice?"

"I can't speak to the time before she worked at the lab, but from then on, what you say seems to reconcile with my translation."

Something was bothering me. "Wait. Why these letters and written notes? Wouldn't it have been simpler to just email each other?"

"Simpler, maybe, maybe not. She lived off the grid, remember? If she only used the generator once in a while, she'd have no internet. The cell service isn't the best where she lived, so that wouldn't have helped; plus, we never found a cell phone." Jenne glanced over at me with a look that spelled trouble.

"Don't tell me. You want to track down this Robbins fellow and see what he has to say." Whenever there was an opportunity to unravel a mystery, she was like a kid in a candy store. I have found it much to my benefit to just agree and deal with the consequences later.

The look intensified until I offered, "Exactly what I was thinking, Jenne. Where should we start?"

Alice, observing our verbal and nonverbal jousting, seemed to get a kick out of it. "I can see why you two have been married so long. You run a business for a quarter of a century that requires you to spend twenty-four hours a day with each other. Then you retire, still get along, and still like each other. You probably still have sex."

When we turned to look at each other, Jenne had even blushed a little. On the other hand, I quickly accepted the compliment and the accompanying devilish smirk.

"And Rob told you *I* was a pain in the ass. Wait until I get hold of him and straighten him out about his colleague."

Alice laughed aloud at this. "Touché, Kevin. It's so refreshing to see a couple who are so obviously in love. You're incredibly lucky."

Jenne had finally recovered. "Alice, you seem like a terrific person. I'm certain you're better off without the ex. Maybe we could grab some coffee next week, get to know each other a little better—just the two of us. Kevin will be busy. Right, dear?"

"Um, yes, yes, I will be. Maybe you could show Alice around the island and your new spread."

Alice's eyes brightened. "I'd love to. Just tell me when; I'll make the time."

As we started to leave, I had a thought. "Alice, I'm going to try to locate Seth Robbins. I'm guessing he doesn't know Dutch either. Do you think you could help translate Sharon's notes for him if I can find him?"

"Of course. This thing is beginning to get interesting."

SEVEN

The Pacific Northwest National Laboratory, or PNNL, is part of a network of National Laboratories across the United States and run by the Department of Energy. The labs explore the boundaries of chemistry, Earth sciences, biology, and data science. Their mission is to discover innovative technologies to preserve the planet, address environmental challenges, and advance the quality of life.

Scientists from the world over are employed at locations across the country. The organization is responsible for a considerable number of environmental breakthroughs and has produced some of the most impactful technologies in furthering the quality of life on Earth.

I hadn't known any of this, actually not even their existence, until I began looking into Sharon Waffle's past.

The Seattle Research Center, located on the south end of Lake Union, is home to over two hundred PNNL employees. Rather than call some anonymous person, I elected to visit the place. This was undoubtedly the event that I was "busy" with.

The Dexter Avenue address revealed a modernish brick structure exhibiting zero signage. From the exterior, it could have been anything. Inside was a reception desk staffed by two capable-looking gentlemen. They were dressed in blue, button-down dress shirts with open collars and jeans.

They looked questioningly at me as I entered. Clearly, they were not expecting any cold calls today.

I put on my most earnest face and approached. "Hi. I'm, uh, looking for someone who either works here or used to."

They offered nothing. I guess they needed more information.

"The person's name is Seth Robbins."

Nothing seemed to register as they looked at one another. One of them finally spoke. "Sir, there's nobody by that name working here."

"Are you sure? Could they have worked here before?"

These gentlemen were not being particularly helpful.

"Not that we know of."

Flummoxed, but not ready to admit defeat yet, I tried another approach.

"A woman used to work here a long time ago. Maybe you'd know her name."

The older one answered. "I've been here eighteen years. What's her name?"

"It's Sharon Waffle."

The greeter showed a little recognition. "Waffles? Sure, I remember her. Lovely woman. A genius. At least that's what I'm told. Everyone called her Waffles. She retired a few years after I was hired."

Some progress, anyway. "Seth Robbins knew her, I think. I was sure he worked here."

"Doesn't ring a bell. Her supervisor, Marylin Pearson, is here. Maybe she would know."

"Could I speak to her?"

He made a call, mentioned Sharon's name, and nodded. "You're lucky. She'll be down in a minute."

A tall woman wearing a lab coat came down the lobby stairs. She was wearing glasses, her gray hair in a ponytail, and slightly overweight. Her generous features were stern until I introduced myself. Then her eyes softened.

"I'm Marilyn Pearson. You were asking about Sharon? How is she?"

"I'm sorry to tell you this, but she passed away over a month ago."

The woman's distress was evident. "Oh, dear. I hadn't heard. I know she moved up to Whidbey Island after she left. Other than a card now and then, I hadn't heard from her. She was a delightful woman."

"Have you ever heard of Seth Robbins?"

"The name rings a bell, but he hasn't worked at this facility since I've been here."

"Can you tell me what Sharon was working on?"

"I can't. Until we pass a discovery on to the public, it needs to be kept secret. If word got out about a new product or process, private or public companies would attempt to corner the market. There is an incredible amount of money at stake with some of these things."

"I understand." I was reluctant to tell Marylin about the notes we had discovered.

Before I could speak, she asked, "Have you checked with Richland to see if this Robbins is there?"

"Richland?"

"Yes. Our headquarters. They have over four thousand scientists."

"Yikes? In Richland?"

"I know it's a small town, but they have an unbelievable facility there. You should check it out."

"Can I just call and ask them?"

"You can, but their policy is not to give out any information over the phone."

"How about you call for me?"

"Sorry, Mr. O'Malley. Can't do that."

"I know, I know, policy, right?"

"Yes, sir."

Rather than head back to Whidbey, I drove across Lake Washington to meet my good friend Bill Owens. The head detective of the Bellevue Police Department was my golf buddy and confidant, even if grudgingly at times.

I had called after my visit to the PNNL, and he agreed to meet for lunch. In short order, I made it to the grille at Kelsey Creek Golf Club and was already seated when he arrived.

"Hey, Kev, good to see you. Since you moved up to Whidbey, we don't get to do this as often. I'm thankful for that."

Bill's sarcastic humor was legend. Many folks still weren't sure when he was or wasn't kidding.

"You're just being pissy because I'm not as available to help you out on your difficult cases."

The previous spring had seen all manner of shit hitting the fan on the island. The resulting fallout had witnessed the demise of a notorious drug kingpin along with a brutal killer. When the dust had settled, a two-year-old murder had also been solved.

For some reason, I always seemed to be in the middle of things, to my friend's dismay.

"Yes, that's it for sure. Nah, I miss your wife. You I can take or leave. Shelly misses her too."

Bill's wife, Shelly, was a dear friend of Jenne's; they spent time together whenever possible.

"What brings you to town on a non-golf day? Please tell me you're not stirring shit up again."

"I'm hurt when you talk to me that way. Nope, I came down to look for someone who works or worked at the National Laboratories. We seem to be involved with something on the island."

"Of course you are. Why am I not surprised? Whatever it is, don't tell me. Let those locals up there work with you."

"How kind of you, Bill. What do you know about the PNNL facility in Richland?"

"Only what I've heard. It's been there a while and they have scientists from everywhere working there. Most of what they do, at least from what I've read, has to do with sustainability. They're working on energy storage, new ways to clean the atmosphere of methane, all sorts of stuff. Once they've reached a critical point, they publish the reports, and private companies get involved. Some of the discoveries out of there are fascinating."

I told Owens why I was asking and proceeded to relay the happenings of the previous six weeks. To his credit, he didn't berate me until I finished.

"So, someone broke into the Waffle—now Jenne's—home, and you surmise that it had something to do with some Dutch notes that you had translated. Now you're trying to find a guy who happens to be mentioned in the notes. That about it?"

"Um, yeah, sort of. There were letters from him too."

"Maybe it was just somebody looking to steal stuff."

"We don't think so. The house was tossed badly. If they just wanted to steal valuables, they chose the wrong house."

Bill picked at his salad while he considered my analysis. "You could be right, but do me one small favor."

"What's that?"

"When this shit blows up in your face, as it inevitably will, forget you know me. I've got more crap here than I can manage, and my last trip to Whidbey is still fresh in my mind."

Bill was still sore about him and his wife almost getting killed last spring. "Bad memories, eh?"

He looked up with his sympathetic eyes and resignedly shook his head. "Listen, just tread lightly. If the excrement gets over your head, I'm here for you. Good luck on this one."

EIGHT

As I was already in Bellevue, I chose to continue to Richland. I texted a quick note to Jenne, letting her know what I was doing. She was entertaining Alice for the day, so I thought a note was best.

Heading east on I90 over Snoqualmie Pass was like driving through a tunnel. The snow was piled two stories high on both sides of the freeway when I crested the three-thousand-foot elevation. The pass received 375 inches of snow a year on average, making it a favorite ski destination for the Seattle area.

Coming down the eastern slopes of the cascades was always a treat. Regardless of how gray the skies were on the west side, the sun inevitably shone on the east. It was remarkable the difference in weather patterns in such a short distance.

I made it through Ellensburg when the road split off to I82, which would take me to Richland. The three-hour trip got me there at five o'clock, forcing me to get a room for the night. Fortunately, my carry bag with a fresh change of clothes was always in the back of the truck. There was no telling when a golf game would materialize, so it paid to be prepared when off-island.

The Holiday Inn Express was fine for the night. As soon as I closed the door of my room, I gave Jenne a call.

"Hey, what's going on?"

"I'm in Richland."

"Yeah, that's what your text said. How come?"

"I went to the PNNL in Seattle and spoke to Sharon's former supervisor. She was sad to hear about her passing, and other than that I didn't get anywhere."

"Then what the hell are you doing in Richland? Are you glowing yet?"

Jenne was referring to the nearby Hanford Nuclear Waste Facility, which had been raked over the coals in the past for negligence.

"No, not yet. I'm here because Marylin, her former boss, thought she had heard of Robbins before and maybe he worked here. I figured it was worth a drive. I'll find out more in the morning. How was your day?"

"We had a great time. We had coffee at the Donut Shop in Bayview and then I showed her around Langley. Alice loved the place. Said she had only been up here once but never really appreciated it before. She's fun to hang with."

"That's terrific, hon, glad it worked out. I'm gonna go try to get something to eat and I'll hit the sack early. I'll call you after I visit the lab."

"Wait, Kevin, I got a call from Roger Willkie. He said the autopsy on Sharon showed she had been sick for a while, and it wasn't vertigo. She had pancreatic cancer; probably had it for some time."

"Ah, shit. That's awful."

"I know. I'm sorry I didn't get to know her."

"At least you helped her at the end. You did all you could."

"I know. I love you, Kev."

"Me too, honey. Me too. Good night."

It was Wednesday morning in Richland, and, of course, the sun was shining on the east side of the mountains. I'd slept fitfully through the night since, regardless of how clean or convenient the hotel was, it was still a strange bed.

The Lab was a massive installation on the northside of town, about a block from the Columbia River.

The main building reception area was staffed by two similar-looking gentlemen to the ones at the Seattle location. The lobby was substantially more spacious, with several groups of people milling about.

I approached the desk and asked if I could speak with Seth Robbins.

"I'm sorry, sir, but he no longer works at this facility."

"Can you tell me where I might be able to find him?"

"I can't, sir, we don't have that information. Would you like to speak to his supervisor?"

This was beginning to seem like déjà vu. "Sure, that would be great."

I cooled my heels for fifteen minutes before I was approached by a small, owlish-looking man, seemingly in his forties.

"Are you the gentleman asking about Seth?"

"That would be me, Kevin O'Malley."

"Pleased to meet you. Mike Slattery. Can I ask why you're looking for Seth?"

I went through the connection with Sharon Waffle and explained that we were just attempting to close the loop on letting her friends know about her death. I didn't think it made sense to cover the break-in and all the notes we had found.

"Seth left here about four months ago. His research was making remarkable strides, but he ran into some issues with one of our outside contributors."

"What does that mean?"

"Much of our research results in paradigm-altering changes. Suppose certain national or international entities were to get their hands on our research before we made it public. In that case, it could result in tremendous increases in their stock prices or give them a leg up on bringing products to market. It's why we are so secretive about things."

"So, what issues are we talking about?"

"The project Seth was working on is of great interest to automakers and energy companies, as well as many other manufacturing enterprises. Somehow, one of these outfits got wind of his progress and attempted to discourage him from continuing his work. What we do here is to benefit *all* mankind, not just a few companies."

"So why try to stop him?"

"Evidently, this particular company perceived this research as a threat to their existing business."

"Can you tell me who they are?"

"No. We cannot do that. It's why we're able to be so independent. If we started pitting one company against another, we would fall apart. Our funding precludes that."

"Can you say how they tried to dissuade him?"

"I'll just say he reported threats and sustained physical harm. We informed the authorities and then things quieted down. However, Seth was determined to complete his work, and he was afraid to do so here. He left and continued his work elsewhere."

"Can you tell me where he is?"

"No, he wanted it to remain secret."

"Even if what we have might help him?"

"Sorry. His orders, not mine."

This thing kept getting odder and odder.

"You knew Sharon, though. Right?"

The first hint of affection I'd seen washed briefly across his face.

"Ah, Sharon. She was up in Seattle for only a half-dozen years or so until she retired years ago. Wonderful woman. I met her at one of our team meetings. I received an email from one of the teams in Seattle yesterday telling me she had died. A shame."

"Can you tell me what Robbins was working on?"

"I'm sorry. No, I cannot."

I thanked him for his help and turned to leave. Then I had a thought. "Hey, Mike, did it have anything to do with batteries?"

The man froze, a look of worry crossing his face, eyes moving rapidly from side to side. He quickly rushed over to me.

"Please, please don't say anything more." He glanced about the entire lobby area. "I don't know where you heard that, and I don't want to know. I can't impress upon you enough, though, how vital this work is. It could be life-changing for the planet.

"We're trying to pick up the pieces of Seth's work, but it's difficult. I'm certain he's still working on it wherever he is. I hope he succeeds. I just hope he does so before they get to him."

"They?"

"I'm sorry, Mr. O'Malley. I've said enough. I've got to go."

With that, the little man turned and hurried through a side door leading to the bowels of the enormous building.

My mind was now cluttered with more information than I could process. The long trip back across the mountains and into the rain might help me focus. If only a little.

Nine

"Welcome home, stranger. How was the trip?"

"Interesting. I couldn't locate Seth Robbins, but there's something odd surrounding the research he was doing. He left Richland a few months before Sharon died.

"According to the guy he reported to, he had been threatened by somebody who had a strong interest in what they were working on."

Jenne's newly styled gray hair swished to the side as her wide-set hazel eyes locked on mine. "So, Mr. Detective, what next? How do we find this guy?"

"I thought about that all the way from Richland. I'm not sure why I didn't ask about this before, but were there any envelopes in those boxes we loaded up from the little outbuilding?"

"There may have been. But remember, all we cared about were the letters. From what I read of them, most asked about chemical testing and analysis. Way above my pay grade. We never saw the responses that went to Robbins *from* Sharon."

"Did we get everything back from Alice?"

"Yep. She organized them by date as best she could. They're down in the basement."

"What about the boxes they came in?"

"When she pulled the notes together, they fit into only one of the boxes. I guess she still has the other two."

"Let's get her on the phone," I said. "I think classes start next week, so we should be able to catch her."

"Alice, it's Jenne."

"Wow, miss me already? It was only yesterday."

"Of course. Hey, Kevin tried to locate this Seth fellow, but I guess he went into hiding somewhere. When you were going through the papers, did you see any envelopes that the letters may have come in?"

"Maybe there were a couple, down in the bottom. I've still got the boxes in the other room. Hold on while I check."

Jenne put her hand over the phone and told me what was happening. I crossed my fingers and held them out. She nodded.

"I found two of them, Jenne. They must have been with the letters and fallen to the bottom."

"Hold on, Alice. Let me put you on speaker."

"Hey, Alice, it's Kevin. Thanks for looking. Can you make out the postmark on the envelopes?"

"Just a sec. I gotta get my glasses. Okay, better. There's no return address, but the postmark says it's from Northport, Washington. Hold on…same thing for this other one. Where the hell is Northport?"

"I'm not sure I've ever heard of it. Thanks a million this helps a lot."

"Please keep me in the loop, Kevin. You've got me hooked now."

"You bet. As soon as we learn something, we'll let you know."

"Well, Jenne, think this helps?"

"Can't hurt. Let's check out where this is."

We pulled up Google Maps and found that the tiny town was located on the Columbia River in the far northeast corner of the state. The information online said the total population was under four hundred souls.

"Man, tiny. Why there?"

"From what that Slattery said, Robbins was frightened. Looks like he wanted to disappear, but evidently, he was determined to keep going on the project. At least we know the town has a post office."

"It looks like it's pretty mountainous there, Kevin. There's probably any number of places to hide."

"Yeah. That's what I'm thinking too."

We needed to find Seth Robbins. But how? It's not like we could drive into the middle of Northport and start shouting the guy's name. Hell, there was no guarantee he'd still be in the area. We didn't even know what he looked like.

Just then "The Irish Washerwoman" began playing.

Jenne picked up her phone. "Hi, Alice. What's up?"

A moment or two passed, then Jenne's eyes opened wide.

"Shit, why didn't we go there first. Thanks a million, we'll do it now."

She had my full attention. "What, what is it?"

"Why, dear husband, did we not Google this guy?"

"Ah shit. Don't know, just got all wrapped up in the chase."

"Alice says there isn't much, but she found an old LinkedIn page that at least has some info on Robbins."

"Let's pull it up."

According to the posting date, the picture was at least five years old. It showed he started at the PNNL back in 1995—the same year Sharon retired.

"Looks like he was recruited right out of college. Undergrad and Ph.D. in chemistry from MIT. Top of his class. Sheesh, Kevin, he's almost as smart as you are."

"Funny lady. The picture's fuzzy but he looks like Will Smith with an Afro and Fidel Castro's beard. This doesn't help us much."

"We need to come up with a way to track Robbins down."

"Why? Maybe the people who trashed Sharon's are long gone. If they didn't find anything, they won't come back." I was just spitballing here, but maybe we were better off leaving this thing alone.

"If her notes were that important, they won't let it go. Besides, maybe there's something in the notes that could help Robbins."

"How would they know about Sharon Waffle and her notes? How could they possibly know she was still working on the project? Hell, she was ancient."

Jenne pondered this for a moment. "I don't know. But if this project is going to have a major impact on the environment and these notes will help Robbins complete his work, we need to do what we can."

"Of course we do." I hated it when she made sense like this. "I have an idea."

"And?"

"Let's get with Alice again, or at least talk on the phone. Maybe there's something in the notes, some material or chemical that he needs.

Something that you just can't go down to Ace Hardware and take off the shelf. If it's something uncommon, then we might be able to track down a source that delivers to Northport."

Jenne made the call and Alice thought the idea made sense. "She said she'd like to look the entries over again to refresh her memory. She's coming by tomorrow."

"There are lots of chemicals mentioned that are beyond my understanding." We were sitting at the kitchen table while Alice De Groot was sifting through Sharon's notes.

"The one word that keeps popping up is vanadium. Do either of you know what that is?"

Jenne and I looked at each other with blank stares.

"Is that a Dutch word?" I stupidly asked.

"I remember looking it up when I first went through these papers. It's the same in Dutch or English. It's an element." Alice was more tolerant of silly questions than I would have been.

"Why do I think we're already over our skis on this thing?"

"We are. I'm going to do a little research. Maybe you can do the same, Kev."

"And leave Alice all by herself?"

"I'll be just fine, Kevin." Her smile was infectious. "You two go to work. I'll hang out here and do my own investigating. Maybe we'll find something."

After an hour or so, and several cups of coffee, we reconvened to discuss.

"Who wants to go first?" Jenne looked at me expectantly.

"Why, I think I'll do it," I volunteered. "Vanadium is a chemical element. It's number twenty-three on the periodic table." I was damn proud of myself and looked to each of them for compliments. They looked at me like I was in the fifth grade. Not even an acknowledgment.

So I continued. "Okay, you guys probably know that." They looked at each other, shaking their heads as if they were tutoring a particularly slow child. It was time to step up my game.

"This stuff is used primarily as a steel additive to increase strength and hardness. In the 'other uses' notes, it said it was also used in a relatively older process, discovered back in the 1930s but not relevant until much recently. It's called a VRB, short for vanadium redox battery. The info said something about a flow battery, energy storage, yadda, yadda, yadda. I gave up after that."

This time I got nods of approval from both women. Surely a gold star was in the offing.

"Very good, Kevin." Jenne was the first to patronize me.

Alice was next. "Yes, Kevin, excellent job."

"I think I was reading the same Wikipedia page as Kevin. Alice, anything to add?"

"That's pretty much what I got too. They use it in these flow batteries, whatever those are, so the thing that Robbins and Sharon were working on was at least building on that process.

"I looked up suppliers for the element. There are only a few, a couple of which are from Canada. This Northport is only a stone's throw from the border, isn't it?"

Because she had several dozen study plans to put together for the next semester, Alice spent the next few days at her home in Wallingford. Jenne and I managed to get the contact information for the Canadian vanadium suppliers through their websites, but both were closed for the weekend.

The next day we phoned both Oswego Limited and Allison Enterprises, the two largest vanadium suppliers. We knew most of the stuff was shipped to high-strength, low-alloy steel producers, but our research showed a growing, though small amount went to battery research and production.

We got bupkes from both outfits, each citing the confidentiality of their customers.

"Why do they give a shit about revealing who buys from them?"

"Maybe it was the way you asked."

I wasn't sure I liked my wife's insinuation.

"You think I wasn't charming enough?" I asked.

"It's possible." Her smirk at least suggested it wasn't totally my doing. "I can't blame them for not divulging their clients to some yahoo on the phone. Is it possible you might know someone in an official capacity who could inquire?"

"You can't be serious." I knew what she was suggesting, and I also knew that Bill Owens would throw a shit fit if I asked him for help.

"Maybe if you bought him lunch and were genuinely nice to him. You might have to kiss his ass a little too."

"That's what I'm afraid of. I'll give it a try, but I think you might be able to help with this as well."

"Huh? How?"

"Call your buddy Shelly. Tell her what we're trying to do. You know, save the planet, solve a crime, et cetera, et cetera. I think if she suggested to Bill that he help, he certainly would."

"Now you're thinking, Kev. Good one. You try to catch Bill the next day or two and I'll talk to Shelly after he shoots you down."

"You sound sure of yourself about him refusing."

"Yes, I am."

She was.

I bought my police detective a fine lunch, laid out our reasons for trying to locate Robbins, and suggested it would be a boon for all humanity.

His reply was thus: "You think all I've got time to do is act like your private investigator? Maybe when pigs fly. I've got a desk full of crimes that are *actually* in *my* jurisdiction. I really don't have time to do any legwork for you."

I offered the standard rebuttal with zero success. At least, now that we had attempted a frontal assault, Jenne could try to get in the back door.

"So how did it go with Shelly?" I asked.

Jenne had made the call right after I got home from lunch.

"She said she'd give it her best shot, which, as experience has shown, is usually damn successful. I don't think we'll know anything until, or if, it happens."

Any progress on our quest was stalled for a few days. We either needed to hear from Bill Owens or generate another way to find Seth Robbins. Alice, still largely invested in the search, had called Jenne a few times to check on progress or the lack of it.

The following Monday, I got a call from Detective Julie Houser.

"Hi, Kevin. Remember me?"

I did recall the name. She was a rookie cop who tagged along with Owens the previous year during a murder investigation. Unfortunately, we were kinda in the middle of that one too.

"Didn't you work with Bill on that Navarro thing?"

"Correct. Good memory. Know why I'm calling?" she asked.

"No." *What is this? A fucking quiz?*

"Bill was grumpy the other day. He gave me a couple of Canadian companies to call. Now, do you know why?"

Bill was correct about this one being a smartass.

"Yes. Now I do. What did you learn?"

"I learned about vanadium. Weird shit."

If I didn't say anything, I thought she might eventually get to the point.

Nothing.

"Julie?"

"Yes?"

"Please tell me what you found out."

I could hear a deep sigh. "Okaaay, okay. Only one of them shipped to the U.S. They mostly went to steel manufacturers, but several smaller shipments went to a little town in the northeast part of the state. The name of the outfit is Oswego something."

"Northport?"

"How did you know?"

"Do you have the addressee?"

"The person's name is Steve Roberts. They've sent three packages already and one more that arrives on Saturday. Evidently, they use their trucks since they're not far away. They leave it there at the hardware store."

"Why?"

"I don't know. Maybe that's what he wanted."

Certain that no more information was forthcoming, I thanked her and hung up.

TEN

With only one arrow in our quiver, we had no choice but to take a road trip to Northport. We filled Alice in on the results of our inquiries, and she insisted on tagging along.

"If you do find this guy, you're going to need someone to interpret the notes from Sharon. I'm coming too."

"How can you just leave school?" I asked.

"I've got a ton of PTO accumulated. I'll just take a bit of it. They can always get one of the grad students to fill in for a few days."

It was hard to argue against her logic. We grabbed the notes and loaded up the Ridgeline on Friday morning. After squeezing Emma in with Alice in the back seat, we headed for Snoqualmie Pass.

The dead of winter always brought heavy snow to the Cascades, and this year was no different. We were fortunate to have clear but chilly weather, which made for easy driving. We planned to get to Northport late in the day, spend the night, and be ready to watch the hardware store the following day to see who showed.

It wasn't a foolproof plan, but it's what we had.

Eleven

The snow had finally stopped. If he didn't get this end of the road plowed, he wouldn't be able to make it into town to pick up the shipment. The storm from last night had *only* deposited a foot of fresh powder. It wouldn't be a problem for his 1966 Chevy C20 Timberliner pickup. The county road stopped a mile before the ranch property, and that's where the county stopped clearing things.

He'd purchased the truck, one of forty-four built and customized exclusively for Yellowstone Park, just before he left the PNNL. At the time he wasn't sure where he was going, but he was certain it would be a remote destination. The truck was perfect for lugging chemicals and vanadium shipments back to the ranch, and the Meyer Super Blade plow could easily manage the job in a single pass.

After the attack and the threats happened, it still took a couple of months before he left the lab. The collaboration with Sharon Waffle had been a godsend. The woman was a genius when it came to electrolyte construction.

He saw the three-hundred-acre ranch for sale in a Homes and Land flier that he'd picked up at the grocery store. The property had been on the market for several years and was vacant.

With a little research, he found that the owners had passed away and now their heirs were selling the place. Naturally, the property was enormously overpriced to the tune of several hundred thousand dollars, hence its continuing availability. The attorney overseeing the transaction was more than happy to offer a month-to-month lease at a bargain price. It seemed as long as the offspring were being greedy, the attorney could make a few bucks as well. The Northport location was home to the logging industry and little else.

Vanadium redox flow batteries were not a new concept. They had been around for several years, but only recently was their capacity for storing energy something that was valued. Improvements in electrolytes and various vanadium electrode combinations had produced batteries with 70 percent more energy density than a lithium-ion battery of comparable size.

Currently, they were very bulky and only made sense for energy storage for power plants and electrical grids. The opportunity for use in wind and solar farms could provide communities with constant power, almost eliminating substations.

Theoretically, these batteries could propel a car up to one thousand miles on a single charge. The possibilities were endless, and the environmental impacts were great. The difficulty was in developing the technology to the point where considerable downsizing of the battery was possible. With the help of Sharon Waffle, Seth Robbins was very close to achieving a solution.

Robbins had spent his first few years at the PNNL trying to make sense of the notes Sharon had left behind. Most were in English, but occasionally she would revert to her native language, leaving Seth in the lurch. He'd set them aside for almost a dozen years when he came across a paper discussing the addition of sulfuric acid to the electrolyte solution, thus significantly improving the battery's efficiency. He dropped the project he had been working on and threw himself into his work.

Unable to decipher many of her notes, Robbins sent a letter to Sharon's last known address in the hope of reaching her. A week later, a letter arrived in his box. Sharon Waffle was glad to see that he was continuing her work and offered to help him translate the portions she had written in Dutch.

Seth understood and respected Sharon's passion for the environment and her need to live "off the grid." Corresponding via snail mail instead of email obviously contributed to the slow progress, but this was offset by the sheer brilliance of Sharon's grasp of the science involved. Early on, she was convinced that adjusting the electrolytes was the solution to downsizing the battery.

For the last seven years, they have made remarkable advancements. That was until last June. Initially, when the Coupetek Battery Company contacted him, it offered him an executive research position. It was only upon further interviews that Seth realized they were not interested in any new innovations.

Because they already owned 70 percent of the lithium battery market, including most of those in electric vehicles and both laptops and mainframe backup installations, they had no desire to innovate.

Coupetek had worked closely with the National Lab on the early lithium battery development and still had a few old contacts at the place. Someone had leaked the progress being made on reducing the size of the flow batteries, which, in turn, led to them making a play for Robbins.

They resorted to intimidation when he refused to play ball to push his research to the sidelines. One night, while late at the lab working with Sharon Waffle's calculations, he was interrupted.

"Robbins? You Seth Robbins?" The gentleman asking the questions smelled of cigarettes and was well over six feet, with a ruddy complexion partially hidden by several days' growth of beard. His voice was raspy. A ball cap pulled tight over long, stringy hair couldn't distract from the very dark eyes darting from side to side.

Seth was nervous. The discussions with Coupetek had been discouraging, and somehow he knew that wasn't the end of it. "What do you want?"

Without a word the intruder grabbed him by the throat and slammed him into the wall, scattering notes, pads, and pencils about the place. Seth's head bounced off the wall, and his throat constricted.

"This is the only warning you'll get. Leave this fucking battery thing alone. No more work on it, right?"

He was frozen.

"I said, GOT it?"

He nodded yes, still not able to speak. The pressure on his throat lessened.

"Yes, I've got it."

The man threw Seth to the ground, his head banging into the steel leg of the lab table.

"If I have to visit you again, you won't hear me coming." With that, his visitor walked swiftly out the door.

Seth picked himself off the floor, ran his hand across his throat, and tried to shake the fuzziness from his head. He immediately called Mike Slattery and related what had happened.

"My God, Seth. Are you okay?"

"I'm fine, just shaken up a bit. Will you take care of reporting this for me? I think I'm going home to crash."

"Of course. I'll deal with it. You'll probably need to provide a description of the guy, but that can wait. Get some rest. Take a few days."

Seth was too amped up to sleep. When he got home, he sat down and tried to develop a plan to continue his work.

It took two months to gather everything he had worked on over the past seven years. He did it secretly, pretending to focus on other disciplines. He sent off letters to Sharon telling her what had happened. *Don't worry,* he wrote in one, *I'll contact you when I get settled. We've come this far, and I'm determined to get across the finish line.*

When he finally landed at the ranch outside of Northport, he reached out again to Sharon. She responded that working on her own, she had developed a new formula for an electrolyte that showed great promise.

There were a great many parts and pieces to the recipe, and she had taken copious notes to document the discovery. They went back and forth for several months. Then Seth saw the report on the PNNL newsletter that a former employee had passed away. It was Sharon.

He felt alone. Sharon may have been thirty years his senior and they had never worked face-to-face, but he felt a strong connection to her. They were teammates on a mission that would massively impact the world. Now, it was up to him to make certain that his associate's efforts would not be in vain.

Twelve

It was 4 p.m. and already starting to get dark. The drifts and plowed chunks of ice and snow piled high on either side were testaments to the efforts of the county to ensure its roads were passable.

We left I 90 at Sprague and headed north on Rt 23 to Davenport. From there, it was Rt 28 following the Columbia River until we got to Northport.

"It's at least a hundred miles to Northport from here. Let's see if we can find a hotel while we still have cell service."

I preferred not to spend the next two hours in the dark on a snow-covered two-lane road, but there wasn't any choice. While this part of the state didn't get anywhere near the precipitation that the west side of the mountains did, what they did get fell as snow, at least during the winter months.

"I'm on it, Kevin. I'll find us something." Alice was happy to oblige. Emma had taken to her, literally. Her pointy ears were barely visible with the rest of her head buried in Ms. De Groot's lap.

"Uh oh."

"What is it?"

"Looks like the closest lodging is in Colville. That's still a ways from Northport."

Jenne turned to face her and asked, "Are the places in Northport full?"

"Um no. There aren't any."

"Rooms?"

"No. Hotels or inns. It's a very, very teeny town. No accommodations. Like I said, Colville is the closest town with anything to offer. The Selkirk Motel. Sixty bucks a night."

"Anything else?" I wasn't a hotel snob, but sixty bucks didn't sound like the Ritz either.

"Um, that would be a no. That's it."

"Well, okay. Looks like we're gonna be spending the night at the Selkirk."

We had to detour a bit to get to Colville, but we still made it in under two hours. It was just as I pictured it—a fifties-style motel—but it was clean and friendly. And cheap too. Also, for fifteen bucks they allowed pets. Perfect.

After a dinner of gourmet burgers and fries, we hit the sack early.

The next morning, Alice was already in the lobby getting coffee—it was free, one of the amenities—by seven when Jenne and I made it there.

"Hey, Alice, sleep well?" It was the only thing I could think to say with a still fuzzy brain.

"Actually yes. Where's my girl?"

"Emma's in the truck," Jenne replied. "She just can't wait to snuggle with her BFF."

"Hah. Thanks, Jenne. She's a sweetheart. I'd love to have a dog like that."

"Thanks, Alice. She likes you too. I think you're now officially a member of her pack. Trust me, it's a small one."

"We've still got about fifty miles to Northport. Let's hit the road and pick up breakfast along the way," I said. It was illogical to think the vanadium shipment would get there any time before noon, but we'd come too far to take any chances.

We arrived just after eight-thirty.

"Now I know why there's no lodging here."

"Why?" Jenne and Alice asked in unison.

Obviously, both women had missed the sign. "We just passed the 'Northport, Population 375' sign. Little tough to support a hotel."

"Why do you think Robbins would come here?"

"I don't know, Alice. He probably wanted privacy and anonymity. This area is as good as any. It's certainly off the beaten track." I was thinking, *Yes and maybe he'd stick out like a sore thumb,* but kept it to myself.

We drove down the main drag, which was still Rt 25. In town it was known as Center Street, apparently the center of everything. Just as we neared the northern end of town, we passed Northport Hardware.

In a town of just over three hundred people, I assumed there could only be one hardware store. "Well, this is it. Any ideas of how we should do this?"

"What about the gas station across the street?" An excellent observation from my wife.

"What about it?"

"You could get gas."

"Yes. That will take ten minutes if I clean the windshield *and* check the oil."

Before my wife could offer a nasty retort, Alice jumped in.

"While you're fueling up the beast here, perhaps Jenne and I could take Emma for a walk. You can chat with the owner, say we're heading up to Canada, and ask about things."

"Things?" I felt just for a moment the women were ganging up on me. Even Emma had sided with them. I hated it when they made more sense than *moi*.

"Yes. Things. What's the crossing like since the pandemic? Any sights to see here along the Columbia? Ask about the town's history. I know you can do it, Kev."

Alice was becoming too much like a member of the family—complete with sarcasm.

I did what any intelligent person would do. I caved. "Okay, okay, I think I just may be able to do this. How long do you think you can walk the dog?"

"As long as it takes. Nah, probably an hour or so. Maybe the delivery truck will have come by then. If not, I'm sure Alice and I will come up with another plan."

"Did I ever tell you two how lucky I am to be in your company?" It was always prudent to offer praise, regardless of sincerity, when you were an idiot.

"Good one, Kev. C'mon, Alice. When he gets like this, it's best to leave."

Rather than attempt a useless comeback, I kissed my wife and waved as the three of them headed toward the Columbia River.

By the time I finished chatting with Ralph, the owner of the Chevron station as well as the town mayor, it was approaching mid-morning. It took little encouragement to prime the man, who was more than happy to extoll the virtues of small-town living.

I stole a glance at my watch and suggested I should try to find my traveling companions while edging toward the door. After a hearty good-bye and effusive "safe trips," I managed to exit the place. Just in time to see a box van with Oswego Limited posted on the door of the cab leaving the dusty dirt parking lot of Northport Hardware.

Except for my black Honda Ridgeline, there had been no other customers shopping for gas at the Chevron station. Ralph wasn't in for a busy day. I left my rig where it was and headed to the side road where my three traveling companions had fled, just in time to see them heading toward me.

They were chatting like old friends, and even Emma seemed to be in on the conversation. "Hey, you guys." They looked to me, exhibiting only mild disdain for my interrupting their conversation.

"The truck just delivered the vanadium to the hardware store." Now I had their attention.

"When?"

"The Oswego truck just left. Now, all we have to do is kill a little time while keeping the hardware store in sight. I gotta believe you have some ideas about that, right?"

They looked at each other, shaking their heads, almost as if I weren't there.

"Of course we do," my wife replied. "Alice, would you like to enlighten this fellow as to how we should proceed?"

"Well, certainly," she said, with a hearty chortle at my wife and a split-second later a patronizing one at me. "There's a small grocery store a block down the road. We drive to it and park in the lot. You wait in the truck and keep an eye on things while I buy some food supplies. At the same time, Jenne goes into the hardware store to find something she needs."

"What does she need?" Even as the question passed my lips, I knew it was a mistake.

Again with the looks at each other.

"As soon as she sees it, she'll know she needs it." Alice delivered this one with a kind look. At me, this time.

"I can see you've both thought this through."

"We have. If still nothing happens, then Alice will go into the hardware store and find something she needs. Then if still nothing happens, you'll go in. After that, we'll just wing it." Jenne seemed deservedly proud of her team.

"I like it. Let's leave Ralph here alone and head down to the grocery."

We parked, and Alice went into the small store to find something to buy. At the same time, Jenne walked the few hundred yards to the hardware store so *she* could find something to purchase. At this rate, the truck would fill up with food we couldn't eat and nuts and bolts or tools we couldn't use. I was beginning to doubt our game plan.

Emma and I passed the time listening to Sirius Radio and playing Words with Friends. She wasn't particularly helpful with the word game.

Alice made it back first, followed by Jenne ten minutes later.

"That hardware store has lots of stuff I'd never seen before." Jenne was carrying a brown paper bag.

"What did you buy?"

"A bunch of mouse traps and this really neat toilet plunger."

"Whew, and here I was worried you'd end up with some useless shit. At least Alice bought six bags of pretzels and a six-pack."

"I'm going to ignore that. Your turn for the hardware, I'll go into the grocery store, and Alice can sit here with Emma eating pretzels."

This got a fierce head nod from Alice. "Absofuckinglutely. I'm cracking one of these pale ales too."

Both Jenne and I guffawed, then left on our assignments. A little bell rang as I pushed in the divided pane door to the country hardware store.

The main area consisted of one room, about thirty feet by sixty feet, lined with tall shelving, making for very skinny aisles. Perimeter walls offered floor-to-ceiling pegboard and displayed every tool known to man. The register was on the side of the room. Behind the counter was a doorway that I assumed led to an office and maybe a receiving area.

Two other shoppers in the store plus the tunnel-like aisles allowed me to stroll about casually without being noticed. It was apparent that the man behind the register knew the others as they swapped stories about many of the locals.

While I was studying a collection of hummingbird feeders, I heard the tinkle of the silver bell attached to the top of the door.

"Yo, Stevie. That shipment you were waiting for came in just after I opened up. The damn thing was heavy too. Want some help loading it up?"

"Nah, I got it, George. How much I owe you for letting me have it sent here?"

"Forget it. You spend enough in here as it is. Anytime."

I managed to tear myself away from the bird feeders to take a peek at Stevie just as I got a text from Alice.

There's a good-looking guy in a shit-colored pickup with a plow on the front that just pulled up. Check it out. Think he's our guy.

She must've seen him from the truck.

Having only the unfocused LinkedIn photo for reference, it was hard to tell. If it *was* Seth, he was now clean-shaven with noticeably short hair. And he *did* look like Will Smith if the actor was five inches shorter.

I waited until Robbins had managed to get the heavy crate into the back of his pickup before I walked over to him.

"Seth? Seth Robbins?"

A look of fear and maybe resignation crossed his face. He quickly opened the driver's door and jumped in. I managed to grab it before he slammed it shut.

"Seth, wait. We're friends of Sharon's."

The declaration had its intended result, but he still was wary. "How do I know?"

"We know about what you were working on with her. We brought her notes with us."

The look of relief was palpable. "Jesus, I thought they were gone. How…who are you? How did you find me?"

"We'll explain everything. Is there someplace we can go?"

"Who's we?"

"I'm Kevin O'Malley. I'm here with my wife, Jenne, and a friend of ours. A professor at UDub. She knows Dutch."

"Goddamn, that's wonderful. Follow me to where I'm staying. Nobody knows me here and no one will bother us there."

"I'm just down the block. I'll catch up."

I hustled over to the Ridgeline while Robbins waited just ahead of us on the side of Center Street. Saying that the two women in the truck were excited that we finally had located Robbins was an understatement.

As soon as I opened the door, Jenne asked, "Is it him?"

"It is. We're gonna follow him to where he's staying. I think he's thrilled that we have Sharon's notes with us."

"Damn, that's an awful nice-looking package out there, and I'm talking about the guy behind the wheel, not whatever's in the back." That Alice had chosen another point of focus was evident.

"Easy there, professor, we're trying to save the planet. Remember?"

"Oh yeah, that's right. I forgot. A girl's gotta dream, though, right?"

"I have to agree with our interpreter back there, Kev, he's a hottie for sure."

I wasn't certain I even wanted to engage in the discussion. Sure, the guy was good-looking, but I was convinced he was no renaissance man like myself. "That may be, people. Just remember, though, he has a Ph.D. from MIT. He's probably just a science nerd, no real-world experience."

I felt better having stated my impression, but judging by the looks on my traveling companions' faces, they weren't buying.

We followed the old pickup for about six miles. The snow was deeper as we got farther from the river. Turning onto a freshly plowed drive on the right, we stayed behind the Chevy for another half mile or so.

A narrow pastoral setting appeared with peaks rising six or seven hundred feet on three sides. If Robbins had been looking for privacy, he'd found it.

The snow crunched under our tires as both vehicles pulled up to a long hitching post. It was hard to tell how long it had been since horses had been tied up here, but I felt sure that they had.

We could see several buildings close by, all with snow-covered, metal shed roofs. The ranch house in front of us was relatively modest compared to what we could see of the property. Its white shingled siding needed a coat of paint, but otherwise, it appeared in decent shape.

Seth had already exited his truck by the time we turned ours off. The three of us—actually four because Emma felt the need to join us—

all walked over to complete the introductions.

Strangely, Emma bolted over to the man without so much as even a tiny bark. He knelt in the snow, spoke in a soft voice, and nuzzled the dog's ears. Emma was putty in the guy's arms.

"Yikes," I said. "What did you do to her? Give her a sedative?"

"Nah. As a kid, we always had German shepherds. They take a little getting used to, but you'll never have anything else when you do. There's no other animal, or person for that matter, that's more loyal. Incredible animals."

I looked to Alice, who appeared to be melting where she stood. The dazzled look on her face confirmed her earlier observations of the man.

"Seth, I'd better introduce these other folks before one of them keels over. This is my wife, Jenne, and this is Alice, our interpreter, and a close friend."

Alice snapped out of wherever she was and rushed to shake his hand. Naturally, she tripped just before she got there, and just as naturally, Seth caught her. "Oh shit, I'm sorry. Hi, I'm Alice."

Seth stood her up and backed off a step. He removed a glove and shook her hand while holding her gaze. "Pleased to meet you. It seems we'll be working together."

"Um, yes. I do. I mean, yes it does. Seem so, that is."

It appeared necessary to step in before Alice completely lost it. Fortunately, Jenne was way ahead of me.

"Hi. I'm Jenne, Kevin's wife. How about we go inside where it's warmer."

It didn't seem like Alice could be any warmer than she already was, but all agreed. And we did.

THIRTEEN

The interior decor of the ranch house was vintage 1980s. The central room consisted of the kitchen and living and dining areas. A ten-foot-wide river rock fireplace took up two-thirds of the living area wall and still had glowing embers in it.

Butcher block counters and a large farmhouse sink were featured in the kitchen island, while Formica laminate counters dominated the back row of cabinets. Looking like an old Buick, a forty-two-inch Kenmore stove handled the cooking chores.

The floors were heart pine, and the walls presented pine wainscotting with a parchment-colored grass cloth wallpaper above. All in all, it was very comfy if not current.

"Love what you've done with the place, Seth." Jenne grinned. The woman knew how to break the ice.

"Yes, I've slaved over the house ever since I rented it." The man was no stranger to sarcasm as well.

Alice was still dazed and very red in the face, unlikely from the cold, so she missed the point. "You've done some work?" she mumbled.

Seth, to his credit, seemed to understand things. "I was kidding, Alice. This is just as it was when I moved in. I'm on a month-to-month here; the ranch is on the market. I guess it's tough to find a buyer for three hundred acres of timber and pasture in the middle of Bumfuck, Washington."

The guy didn't talk like any geeks I had ever run across. I thought it prudent to get to the heart of the matter. "Seth, where have you been working on the battery business?" I still wasn't sure what to call it.

"There's another small guest residence out back. They used it for visitors since there's no lodging anywhere nearby. I've set up shop in there."

"We know about the lodging thing. We spent the night at the Selkirk."

"Ah, beautiful downtown Colville. I spent a few nights there myself when I was looking for something to rent. Not bad, but not exciting either."

We all nodded in agreement.

"Before we get into things, can you stay for a day or two? I'm sleeping in the smaller house, and there's plenty of room in this one. There are two bedrooms in the back, each with its own bathroom. Don't worry, I may be a dedicated scientist, but I'm not a Neanderthal. I make sure to keep it tidy. I'm not certain about toiletries or towels, but I haven't explored a few closets back there. There's a good chance there are some supplies in them."

We looked at each other and sensed agreement. Alice, of course, was the first to respond. "That makes sense, Seth. It'll probably take some time for me to go over the notes and translate for you." Her earnestness was unmistakable.

"Can you take the time from school, Alice?" I hate myself sometimes, but I just couldn't resist.

She looked at me with eyes that could kill. "Well, of course, I'll just need to call and tell them I need a few more days."

"That's great, Alice," Seth said. "I think those notes are going to make a difference."

Alice turned to me and slyly stuck out her tongue.

"Okay, let's get you settled first. I'll run into town and get some food for us. There's not much here. You can bring your things in and look for stuff in the back. I won't be long," Seth said.

I knew we were helping the guy out, but it didn't feel right having him pay to feed us and all. "Hold on, Seth, let me come with you. You know how picky these women can be."

Seth laughed knowingly while the two women just glared at me.

We made small talk on the way to the store but eventually, I had to ask. "Seth, your boss told me about the threat you received, so I get why you've chosen to disappear. I was wondering why you chose this place. I would think not being a local would make you stand out."

"A local or because I'm Black?"

"Well, there *is* that too."

He chuckled before responding. "I don't have a good answer. I lived in Spokane growing up, and we took summer trips up this way. Sometimes we went across the border and sometimes camped up here. My dad was a big fisherman.

"The folks in the eastern part of the state are mostly conservative, but I've always felt comfortable with them. Sure, you always come across a few racist or homophobic knuckleheads, but the locals here won't tolerate their kind.

"When I saw this spot, it seemed perfect. Isolated, but near a small town where I could have stuff delivered. I did use a different name when I leased the place. They weren't too picky about legal documents. It's a month-to-month, after all. Anyway, George at the hardware is a peach, and he's been extremely helpful, plus they mind their own business."

We bought enough food for several days, and I picked up the tab, despite Robbins' protestations.

We continued our chat on the way back to the ranch. "Are you close to achieving your goal?" I asked.

"I'm closer. Sharon was a genius even in her eighties. I only wish I had gotten to know her on a personal level. I tried to pick up where she left off when I first got hired at the lab. I grew frustrated and put it aside to work on another project until five or six years ago.

"I got her address from HR and was told she had no phone or email. That's when I wrote her, and we started collaborating. She seemed particularly excited about what I had done with electrode research, and it dovetailed perfectly with her ideas about the composition of the electrolyte.

"After I moved up here, she became my only connection to the scientific world. I hated that I couldn't call or email her, but that was what she wanted. A couple of months ago, she told me she needed to work on a few ideas, and she'd get back to me. Then I heard she had died. I'm hoping that the notes she left documented her theories."

"How small can you make one of these flow batteries?"

"Right now they are big and bulky since the electrolyte is in a liquid state. There have been major advances in downsizing, but even the smaller ones are still several feet square. Sharon and I were working on taking the technology used in liquid flow batteries and converting it to a solid state. Once that could be achieved, the battery could be miniaturized for almost anything. Cars, computers, home energy backup units—the possibilities are endless."

"Sounds impressive."

"If you consider almost limitless storage capacity with the use of readily available elements impressive, then yes. It is. Additionally, lithium used in the most advanced batteries today is becoming more and more problematic to acquire."

"And you think the threats came from this Coupetek company?"

"It's my best guess. They offered me a job to keep me quiet, so it makes sense that they'd try another tactic."

"It seems a little over the top for a big public company like that." We had just pulled into Seth's snowy driveway.

"I agree, but it's all I can come up with," he said. "Here we are. Let's get the food inside and start dinner. I'm hungry."

After turning the ignition off, he turned to me and, in the quiet of the cab turned serious. "I appreciate you looking me up. I feel terrible about Sharon, but if her notes are what I think they are, this could mean a great deal. Thank you."

I clapped him on the shoulder and brushed aside the thanks. "C'mon, let's put those burgers together."

FOURTEEN

We had finished eating and were still sitting at the table, savoring the last sips of wine. As often happens with meeting new folks, we shared our backstories. We learned that although he was a science nerd, Seth was also an excellent high school athlete. He was a star point guard on the basketball court and had made all-state in his senior year.

He ran the mile for the track team, and while he spent most of his hours at MIT in the lab, he still found time to run a few miles every day. Alice was impressed.

I felt the need to let our host know that he was in the presence of a bona fide marathon runner. "Alice, have you told Seth about your best time ever in the Seattle Marathon?"

Alice, mesmerized by Seth's history, now turned bright scarlet.

"It wasn't anything. Lots of runners finished ahead of me."

"How many are lots?" Seth seemed to be enjoying Alice immensely and appeared to be genuinely interested.

Alice, still flustered, relented. "I finished in 2:58. It was the top ten percent."

"Yikes! I'm in the presence of a star. Seriously, that is fantastic, Alice. Congratulations."

I didn't think she could blush any deeper, but she succeeded. Jenne came to her rescue. "I have an idea, Alice. How about you and Seth take those notes over to his work area and start organizing things. Kevin and I will clean up here. It should help you get a running start for tomorrow."

Both of them looked relieved. Seth was the first to speak. "That's a great idea, thanks. I'm excited to see what Sharon was working on during her last few weeks." Then, with a grin at his interpreter, he said, "I'm certain Alice will be a tremendous help."

After the two smitten folks left, I turned and grinned at my wife. "Well, how about those two?"

"I'd say there seems to be a spark there, yes?"

"Can't argue about that. It's nice to see, regardless of what happens."

The following day saw Alice and Seth cooped up in the guest house poring over Sharon's notes. They retreated shortly after breakfast, and we didn't see them until just before dinner.

Jenne and I spent our time pondering other possible entities that might want to halt Seth's research. We spent most of the day, however, attempting to learn more about redox flow batteries. The research material was overwhelming and, in many cases, contradictory.

Finally, we both agreed that we'd leave the science up to our host and we'd do what we could to find out who trashed Sharon's house and who had accosted Seth.

We had started to assemble the ingredients for a grilled chicken Caesar when Alice and Seth were heard stomping the snow from their boots on the back porch. Emma greeted them with her customary GSD eardrum-shattering bark, which silenced immediately when she saw who it was. She bounded up to Seth, clearly expecting kind platitudes and a vigorous ear-nuzzle.

"Looks like you've got a friend there." I offered.

"I'm glad she likes me. I wouldn't want to get on her bad side."

Now that the four of us were together again, Jenne took the lead. "How did you two make out today? You know, with the notes?"

I was reasonably certain I was the only one who saw the quick wink from my wife.

Alice was as cheerful as we'd seen her. "We were able to translate everything Sharon was working on from that last month. Of course, I have no idea what any of it means, but Seth thinks it is a turning point. Right?"

"If you hadn't brought Alice along, none of this would have happened. She was able to translate and pick up little nuances in the language, which changed many of the meanings entirely. Going through them helped both of us get to know Sharon better. She was a remarkable woman."

After spending the day on the Internet trying to understand the technology, I was unsure how deeply I wanted to get into the discussion, but I asked anyway. "What was she working on? Just in lay terms, please. I'm only capable of absorbing so much."

This brought a chuckle from Seth. "I understand. A great deal of my work combined different formulas of vanadium electrodes with already proven electrolyte combinations. Sharon Waffle focused on reformulating the electrolyte and the membrane material to improve the VRB's performance. Just *this* is a significant improvement in existing technology.

"Even further though, she, at least theoretically, developed a unique electrolyte that would allow for miniaturization of a *solid-state* battery that combined vanadium with a small amount of lithium. This is what I was collaborating with her on just before I left the Northwest Lab.

"Her final collection of formulae and notes further defines what materials and in what combinations are needed to produce the results we're seeking. Does that make sense?"

"Um, sure. How about a nice chardonnay to start with?" I knew when I was in over my head. Jenne looked as though she understood what he was saying, but me, not so much.

They ignored me, and Alice excitedly continued. "This means if Seth can develop a prototype, several companies will be able to produce a recyclable solid-state battery of almost any size. It will be able to charge in one one-hundredth the time, produce ten times the power at an extended discharge rate, and last for dozens of years. Plus, it won't tend to burst into flames. It's remarkable." She was now sitting there beaming at her new hero.

"Seems as though you've become something of an expert on this," Jenne said, impressed.

"I was deeply over my head until Seth started explaining the science. Now I only know enough to be dangerous, but I can still talk the talk."

Somewhat left out, I felt the need to reassert my interest. "I think now I can see why someone might have an interest in putting a stop to your work."

"You're correct. Regardless of who it is, they have a financial stake in existing technology. The global market was over fifty billion last year, and it will double in the next ten years. It seems like it's Coupetek, but it could be lithium suppliers or any number of companies that are making money off the current crop of lithium-ion batteries. The best thing I can do is complete a prototype, present it to the Lab, and expose it to the public, hopefully before someone comes after me again."

Seth's declaration sobered us all up quickly. "What can we do to help?" I offered.

"You've done plenty. It would help me tremendously if Alice could stay a little longer, though."

"That works for us, but how will she get back?"

"I'm sure I'll be able to find a car rental place, or worst case, take a bus."

Alice seemed to have thought it through.

"It won't be a problem. I'll just take her to the airport in Spokane. It's a bit of a drive, but there will be no chance of anyone seeing me."

I was sure Alice would be helpful to Seth, and I was less certain that that was all there was to it, but I was happy for Alice.

FIFTEEN

Charlie Balducci was a thug. He'd been in and out of jail since his sixteenth year, when his first conviction resulted from a joy ride in a vintage '69 Mustang. Because he was under the age of seventeen, he was remanded to the state facility for juveniles at Medical Lake on the outskirts of Spokane.

Occasionally youngsters will run afoul of the law, whether because of falling in with the wrong crowd, being raised in an unfortunate family situation, or perhaps drugs or alcohol. In Balducci's case, it was none of these. His family was well known in the Spokane area. His dad was a lawyer, and his mom a nurse. They were churchgoing Catholics with three other children, Charlie being second of the progeny.

His older sister attended UCLA, and his two younger sisters followed her, all three now productive members of society. Many folks wondered if Charlie had been switched at birth, such was the deviation from his environmental influencings.

Alas, the reasons for his nastiness were never discovered. He was just a vicious motherfucker.

Following his stint as a juvie, he felt it unnecessary to maintain contact with his parole officer. He skipped the state of Washington for the lure of Las Vegas, where he immediately was arrested for stealing Christmas gifts off unsuspecting porches in a retirement community.

A six-month sentence—this time among the adult population—turned into a lengthier one due to continual fighting with other prisoners. He was always big for his age and managed only one discipline in his life: that of a gym rat. Even at a young age, he could hold his own with even the saltiest of prisoners.

Upon his release he was told the usual stuff: no consorting with felons, no guns or drugs, blah, blah, blah. Without even taking a stab at lawful behavior, he contacted an organization recommended by one of his few prison pals. The gentleman had seen firsthand what kind of damage Balducci could inflict on a human being and felt he was a natural for an old employer.

Rothwell and Associates was not a law firm, nor did it employ an army of CPAs. Their cards simply said, "Asset Preservation." Charlie discovered that, indeed, this was an outfit that could make use of his subtle array of talents. Rather than counsel people regarding their retirement programs, Rothwell approached challenges from a unique perspective.

The founders, themselves a duo of questionable integrity, figured there were plenty of companies that skirted the edges of acceptable business practices and might be interested in their services.

They did no advertising, relying strictly on a word-of-mouth referral basis. Essentially, if there proved to be a threat to a company or an individual's bottom line, Rothwell came to the rescue. Threats, intimidation, extortion, and even death in certain cases were their solutions.

Based out of Las Vegas, it was easy getting the company off the ground. After collecting IOUs from unlucky gamblers, they graduated to recovering drug money from unscrupulous dealers. It was a simple leap then to making certain an auto restoration outfit's competition was no longer able to undercut the other's prices due to a mishap with one of the partners.

They gradually moved on from the seamier side to many legit companies that saw a need for stifling the competition—one way or another. Rothwell's services required a special type of employee...namely one with an absence of conscience.

With a ready supply of ex-cons to conduct the required services, they had managed to expand to most of the western states. Charlie Balducci had been with them now for a dozen years, and because of his familiarity with the Northwest, he was based there. Had he just kept to his employer's wishes, he might have managed to stay out of the slammer, but the intermittent bar fights and petty thefts seemed to lure him there regularly.

He'd been on the street now for an entire six months, almost a record for him. When he was assigned the task of threatening some chemistry geek at the PNNL several months ago, he thought his employers were undervaluing his skills, but the pay was good, so he did the deed for them. Now there were rumblings about how he had not been assertive enough. There were rumors that the chemist was continuing his research at an offsite location.

He was casing the units at a new retirement community, his favorite class of target, on the west side of Spokane when an unwelcome text appeared: "Call me."

Balducci knew the number. It belonged to his direct supervisor at the firm. Stanley Johnston was a no-bullshit former number-cruncher who had managed to rise rapidly in the organization. Unlike Charlie, Johnston carried out his orders scrupulously. Not once had he done anything to cause the firm any negative publicity and was valued because of it.

When Balducci's boss called, nothing good could come of it. He hated to return the call, but without the firm, there would be no steady income. "Hi. This is Balducci."

"Charlie, are you keeping your nose clean?"

"Of course, Stan."

"Yes, I'm sure you are. We're getting reports that the chemist who was working on the battery thing is still at it. Our client is telling us he's holed up somewhere. I don't have to tell you that if he's successful in producing an alternative to the lithium-ion batteries that exist today, our client stands to lose millions. In case you didn't hear me, I said millions."

"I heard you, boss. When I left him he looked like a scared little rabbit. I can't imagine that he's still at it."

"Well, according to our client, he is. You need to resolve this, or we'll have to get someone who will. This is a valuable client, Baldy, get it done."

He hated it when people called him "Baldy." In fact, he hated Johnston, who had done a nickel for embezzlement somewhere in Idaho. He was a jerk-off who thought he was special just because he had people working for him.

"If the client knows he's still on it, then why doesn't he tell us where he is so I can take care of business?"

It was quiet on the other end, almost like the thought never occurred to his superior. "Um, yeah. Good idea. Let me check on that; I'll get back to you." The call disconnected.

"Fucking douchebag. Guy thinks he's so smart, and I tell him what to do," he muttered quietly to himself as he abandoned his quarry to await his master's return call.

At 6:30 the following morning, Balducci awoke to the tune of his buzzing phone. Before answering he took a swallow of water to clear the previous evening's cigarette-flavored scotch from his throat.

"Yeah," he rasped.

"It's Johnston."

Balducci snapped awake, wishing he'd ignored the call. "Hi, Stan, what's up?"

"The client says your chemist is in Northport."

"Great. Where the fuck is that?"

"I looked it up. It's west of Spokane and way up north near the Canadian border. How about you get your butt up there and do what you were supposed to do in the first place."

It burned his ass when people talked down to him. "Sure thing, Stan."

"And Balducci?"

"Yeah?"

"Do it right this time. No one gives a shit about this guy. If you can't be sure he'll let it go, then execute a permanent solution. Got it?"

"Yeah. I got it. Goodbye."

Balducci opened Google Maps on his phone and did a visual of all the towns near the border. *Fucking thing's so small it doesn't even show up.* Next, he did a search and finally saw it tucked just under the Canadian border. *Damn, that town is small*, he thought.

It looked like he'd have to hit the road to get there before it was dark. He hated to miss out on pilfering the old-timers, but they'd still be there when he got back.

After driving for what seemed like hours through fields of winter wheat covered in snow, it finally dawned on him that he had no address for Robbins. *Figures*, he thought. Goddamn Johnston told him where to go but not how to find out where Robbins lived.

As much as he hated to, he tried to reach his boss. Unfortunately, the cell service in this part of the state was spotty, and he was unsuccessful. He assumed the town was so small that any of the locals would know if anybody new had arrived recently.

He made good time and got to town while there was still daylight. The post office was still open, so he thought he would attempt the direct approach. The fiftyish woman behind the counter was leery of Balducci as soon as he walked across the worn vinyl floor.

"Help you?"

"I'm looking for a friend of mine." His voice was especially gravelly today, and the pack and a half of smokes he'd consumed, mixed with sweat and unwashed hair presented a disgusting mix of aroma and appearance.

Had the postal worker even considered breaking protocol to give out an address, this was not an individual she would give it to.

"Sorry, can't help you."

"I haven't even given you his name yet," he whined.

"Don't care if his name's Jesus Christ. I can't help you. Against the law."

Balducci may not have been the shrewdest hoodlum on the planet, but even he knew when it was time to vacate the premises. It was a damn good thing he did too because as he opened the door of his ten-year-old Toyota Camry, he saw Seth Robbins and an older guy getting into an old truck in the grocery parking lot.

Son of a bitch. He waited until the truck headed out of town and followed at a respectable distance. He'd been concerned about the snow-covered roads this far north, but so far his front-wheel-drive ride was handling nicely.

After a few miles, the brownish-yellow truck turned into a freshly plowed one-lane driveway that appeared to go on indefinitely. Luckily Balducci had kept his distance and, in the rapidly darkening sky, had yet to turn on his lights.

The good news was that he hadn't been seen. The bad was that Wilcox Road came to an end shortly after he passed the driveway. Wilcox was a county road and had been cleared the previous day, even though it accessed only two residences.

He drove to the end of the pavement where the snow was piled high. Because there were no homes or ranches beyond this termination, there was no turnaround. Balducci needed to either execute a twelve-point turnaround or back down the entire road.

He stupidly chose the former. The Camry, an excellent vehicle, comes with front-wheel drive with an option for all-wheel drive. His ride was the cheapest he could find, so the AWD version was out.

Because the road was very narrow at this point, Balducci managed to adjust the turn less than a foot for each maneuver. After fifteen minutes he finally achieved a perpendicular position across the single lane.

Assured he was in the home stretch, he was dealt a serious blow thanks to his impatience. In an effort to bite off just a smidgen more distance, he buried the nose of his ride into a four-foot mass of the plowed white stuff. With only the front wheels attempting to gain purchase, he quickly found that the hold the snow had on his front bumper was, for the foreseeable future, going to win this war.

The more he accelerated the more the snow under the tires melted and turned to ice.

To say Charlie had thoroughly prepared for his trip to Northport would have grossly overstated his foresight. A sweatshirt covered with an oil-stained Members Only jacket picked up at Goodwill adorned his upper torso. Torn Wrangler jeans and worn Reeboks anchored the ensemble, which included a sweat-stained Mariners ballcap to top off the entire mess.

The outside temperature was now in the twenties. Although his chariot delivered a copious supply of heat on the inside, it did nothing to assist the idiot outside as he attempted to claw the snow and ice gripping the front end of the car.

After ten minutes of absolutely useless effort, he hurried back into the warmth of the interior. *Motherfucker, what a shitshow. I knew I never should have come here. I was better off shaking down the old people. At least I wouldn't be freezing my ass off.*

He was in a terrible spot and his cell phone was useless out here. He couldn't walk back to town; he'd freeze his ass off. He supposed he could walk up the driveway to get help, but he was certain Robbins would not have forgotten him.

In his panic to resolve his dreadful state of affairs, the focus of his mission had temporarily escaped him, but no longer. Of course, he could stroll up to the house. He was here to deliver a message, and by golly, he would do it.

He grabbed his gun from the glove box and turned off the useless piece of shit of a car. He zipped up tightly the Members Only, pulled down his cap, and headed into the awfully dark and awfully cold night air. He was out of cigarettes too. *Fuck!*

After the first hundred yards, he could no longer feel his toes. His hands in his pockets did little to keep out the numbing temperatures, owing to the lack of insulation from the paper-thin polyester material of his jacket. The Glock, stuffed into the front of his belt, felt like a block of ice.

Mostly the snow crunched under his tennies, but he did come across the occasional icy spot. Two of them, actually, and he fell both times.

When the single-story ranch home finally came into sight, he was covered in snow and visibly shaking from the freezing temperatures. He had no plans beyond getting into the house and thawing his quivering body.

Sixteen

We finished eating early and started cleaning up since the plan was for an early departure in the morning. We were looking forward to hitting the sack soon.

Alice and Seth were seated on the sofa facing the blazing fire while Emma snoozed at their side. They appeared to be discussing matters of a more personal nature rather than anything about battery technology.

With the warmth and glow from the fire, I could already feel a case of the drowsies overtaking me. Then all hell broke loose.

With a rush of cold air, the front door crashed open. Standing in the opening was a shaking human form, covered in snow and ice, emanating a mixture of cigarettes and body odor, and holding a gun.

Several things happened simultaneously.

Both Jenne and I were startled and turned to the sound. Alice jumped up from the sofa as did Seth, who shouted, "Shit! It's him!"

Funny thing about GSDs. They're annoyingly loud and bark ferociously when they *think* something's amiss. It's different, though, when a very real threat to their pack is present.

When that happens, they don't bark at all. They act. They go from zero to top speed in one and a half seconds.

The intruder with the gun didn't seem to register the movement to his right. Only when ninety pounds of truly pissed-off German shepherd, traveling at thirty miles per hour, clamped on the arm holding his weapon with over two hundred pounds of pressure per square inch did it register that he was in trouble.

Then he screamed. Loudly. Seth quickly recovered the gun that had skittered across the room. Jenne and I were still stunned. All the action happened in slow motion.

Emma was serious about her duties and maintained her viselike grip on the unwanted guest's arm. Finally, Seth approached as did I.

"Emma, Emma, it's okay, girl. Off, off." I grabbed her collar as she finally relented.

While the gunman's screams lessened to whimpers, Seth held the weapon on him. I could see the vicious wound delivered by our protector.

"It's you," Seth shouted.

It wasn't hard to understand that this was the person who had accosted Seth four months ago. I was curious how he had found us and was still trying to understand his frozen countenance. If I was attempting to accost someone, I'd like to think I'd be better prepared.

"K-keep that goddamn dog away from me."

Emma was seated two feet from his face, now growling with fangs exposed. I couldn't imagine him moving an inch. And he didn't.

"My arm is bleeding. Please help me."

I grabbed a dishtowel and threw it to him. "Here, wrap this around it and keep pressure on it."

He did as he was told while we—Seth still holding the gun, although I was certain it was unnecessary—stood staring at the carnage.

I turned to Seth. "Where should we take him?"

"Nearest sheriff's office is in Colville. There's a landline here, so let me see if they have a unit in the area. I'd hate to have to drive this asshole all the way there. Hold on while I call."

We waited while Seth dialed 911.

"They have a deputy about twenty miles out. When I told them what had happened, they said they'd get him here as fast as possible."

"What about that arm?"

Alice had been quiet until now. "Let me take a look. I took a couple of first aid classes with the Red Cross just before I signed up at UDub. Any peroxide or bandages here?"

When Seth provided the needed items, Alice showed what she had learned. Emma still hadn't moved.

"What's your name?" I figured we might as well find out something about our attacker.

"It's Balducci." His voice quivered in terror. His eyes never left the dog, nor hers, his.

"Why are you doing this? Who do you work for?"

Nothing was offered.

"Do you know what she'll do if we leave the room and it's just you and the dog?" I was in no way a tough guy, but my dog sure was.

His eyes went from me to Emma, and his fear was unmistakable.

"Okay, okay. I work for Rothwell…Rothwell and Associates." He couldn't get the words out fast enough.

"And why do they want to stop this research?"

"I don't know. I just do my job. It's not them anyway; it's a client of theirs."

This wasn't making sense to me. "What does Rothwell do?"

"They fix things. Clients hire them to make sure the competition doesn't cause them grief. Sometimes I make threats and sometimes I have to hurt people. But it's not just me."

"What do you mean?" Seth had picked up the thread.

"Rothwell is a big company out of Vegas. They've got people all over the place. I'm just a small cog in a big wheel."

"So, who was the client on this job?"

"I told you I don't know. They never tell us. I'm sure my boss knows though. His name is Stanley Johnston. He's in Vegas."

Not only couldn't we shut him up, but it appeared he wasn't particularly fond of his boss.

Emma ran to the door and began to bark savagely. Balducci curled into a ball, petrified.

"Gotta be the sheriff," I said as I put a leash on her.

Jenne opened the door before the deputy had a chance to knock. He stood there, hand on his weapon.

"Come on in. This is the one we called about. Seems that he's afraid of the dog." I didn't even feel bad about rubbing it in a little.

The deputy relaxed some and removed his cap. A big grin came over his face. "Well, lookie here. Did the big bad dog hurt you?" He looked over at Emma, who had finally quieted down, but still, a growl rumbled deep inside her.

He turned to us. "I'm Deputy Sanchez. Call me Tommy. It's not often we get the culprit all trussed up for us." He turned to Emma, "Great job, sweetie. Wish I had a partner as good as you."

Sanchez was at least six-five and looked as though he could play strong safety for the Seahawks. His tanned, ruddy complexion suggested he spent more time outdoors than in.

"Looks like you did some first aid on him. How bad is it?"

Alice delivered the injury report. "It's bad enough that he should see someone. The bite is deep. I'm sure he'll need a tetanus shot at the least, maybe some antibiotics for infection."

"Boy, I wish all my calls were this easy. You folks need a job?"

"Not us," I said. "It was all Emma's show."

Tommy knelt and Emma padded over to him while Balducci squirmed even farther into the corner. "Hey, sweetheart, what a good girl you are." He reached into a pocket and handed her a treat while looking up to us. "Gotta keep the treat pocket full. You never know when you have to deal with man's best friend."

We spent the next forty-five minutes telling Sanchez what we had learned and the backstory on the threats to Seth. He was impressed at how much information we were able to gather and suggested that the scope of the extortion and thuggery by Rothwell would almost certainly be an FBI matter.

He helped Balducci up from the floor and slowly moved him out the door. Slowly, because the injured man was still terrorized and would not turn his back on Emma.

So much for the early-to-bed plan. We finally managed to hit the sheets just before midnight. We were still leaving in the morning, and Alice would stay on to help Seth with any translating issues.

Both of them felt a measured sense of relief now that the immediate danger had passed. We still thought it prudent, however, to maintain a low profile until whoever was paying for the threats could be discovered. Only then would Seth be able to return to the PNNL.

SEVENTEEN

The next day, the report from a sheriff's office in Stevens County in the state of Washington was received at Special Agent Matt Steele's office in Seattle.

It was immediately forwarded to the bureau in Las Vegas. An extortion-for-hire syndicate operating in half the country was too big a fish to be ignored.

Rothwell and Associates did not have a physical office. Edgar "Eddie" and Roberta "Bobbie" Fusco did not need one.

Their plan to organize a company for which there was an unlimited market, with an infinite supply of subcontractors supplied by the American prison system, had succeeded beyond their wildest dreams.

There was no overhead. There was no need for company health care or 401(k)s. Multilevel marketing had worked for cleaning products, cosmetics, and herbal supplements; the Fuscos had succeeded in making it work as a criminal enterprise.

Six years prior they had literally bumped into each other at their parole officer's office. Eddie was backing out of the office as Bobby, looking at a recent text, managed a face-plant on the back of a Valentino cashmere bomber jacket he had pilfered from Saks.

Excuses and flirtatious smiles were traded, and the two agreed to meet for coffee at the nearest Starbucks as soon as Bobby finished her mandatory sit-down with her probation officer.

"Thanks for meeting me. Call me Eddie."

"I'm Roberta...Bobbie. What were you in for?" It was the first question one con asked another.

"My brother ran a numbers game over in Phoenix. Sometimes people don't pay after they lose, and they try to disappear. My job was to find them and collect. A couple of times I had to get rough, and one guy didn't make it. I was in for ten years. You?"

The fortyish woman across from him looked down at her coffee. Her blonde, shoulder-length soft curls brought Marilyn Monroe to mind. Not the looks, the hair. Otherwise, she was reasonably attractive, even with that silly mole on her left cheek.

"I ran an autobody shop with my ex. A couple of Mexicans opened one a block over and offered prices that were half of ours. We started losing all our insurance business, so I had a talk with them."

"A talk?"

"Well, it started that way. Fuckers barely understood English. I thought I had convinced them to up their pricing to ours, but they didn't. So I had to have another meeting. When I left they decided to move to a different city." She grinned at the recollection.

"What convinced them?"

"I shot one of them in the foot. That was enough."

"That's why you went to jail?"

"Nah. I went to jail because we got caught chopping stolen cars and selling them for parts. They never got me for the Mexican. I only did a few years."

After several more dates, the lovebirds became steadies. They married three months later.

Bobbie tried to go straight, hawking Mary Kay cosmetics, but after a few weeks found that she couldn't stand the rest of the women in her territory.

Eddie hooked up with an Amway dealer, and he, too, tired quickly.

With no other source of income, they resorted to doing what they did best. Eddie began collecting bad debts from bookies and drug dealers. Bobbie made the rounds of the auto shops.

After three months of moderate success, they planned a celebratory dinner in their studio apartment on the east side of town.

"Eddie, nice score today." Bobbie looked over her skinny husband, with his bushy graying mustache, tanned face, and sun-damaged complexion. He was two inches shorter than her five-ten. She toasted him with her Cook's sparkling wine.

"Thanks, babe. I've been thinking though."

"Again?"

"Yup. Those jobs we had at first were bad, but I don't like risking jail time either. What if we could use the business plan from those companies and create our own service organization?"

"I'm listening."

"We hire, not hire like pay them but—I guess the word is contract—contract them to do what we are doing. We pay them a commission depending on the job and the client and how much we make. We'd be really careful about who we took for clients, and even if it ever went sideways, we wouldn't be on the hook for it."

"What would we do for customers?"

"To start, you could sign up a few of those garages you've been working with. Two other dealers want me to work for them, but I don't have the time."

"Sounds interesting, but who would we get to do the work?"

"You remember the cellmate I had for a few months? Stanley Johnston?"

"Yeah?"

"He's out now, looking for something to do. He became an accountant after school, even went to college. I guess juggling all those numbers finally got to him, and he relieved some of his clients of their dough."

"And?"

"And, well, we could hire him, on the come of course, and then he could bring on whoever made the most sense to do the implementation."

"You learn a new word?"

"I did. You like implementation?"

"Very much."

"Heard it on TV this morning. I've used it three times today, so now I own it. I saw that somewhere too."

"Okay. We hire Stanley, he hires the muscle, and we get the customers. Right so far?"

"Yes."

"Well, shit. You mean I don't have to travel the mean streets anymore?"

"Nope, we'll be executives now."

"Fuckin' A, I'm all in, baby."

Now, six years later, the Fuscos were indeed flourishing. From a five-thousand-square-foot villa in Summerlin West, they handled the day-to-day responsibilities that faced all CEOs.

Their client list had ballooned to the point where they weren't accepting any new customers. Along with Stanley, there were two other managers, one in LA, the other in Texas. Stanley had the lion's share of the geography because he was their first hire, and he was also better at managing things.

Bruce Hardaway oversaw SoCal from his Dana Point bungalow. A former actor in C-grade porn flicks, he was a natural for the territory. The supply of clients from floundering studios and the vicious fighting among D-grade actors provided fertile ground for the services Rothwell provided.

Based in San Antonio, Ruben Martinez had joined the firm only recently. Strangely, his time in the big house was limited to only two years. It wasn't so much that his career as a leg breaker wasn't well documented, but the small giant was simply clever when it came to avoiding the law. That and his daddy was a former state senator. At any rate, Texas was its own country, and the Fuscos badly needed a local to resolve the myriad complaints from their corporate clients headquartered there.

All told, the Fuscos had over twenty "field personnel" under contract, all of whom reported to the three managers. These operatives were substantially less dependable than the three managers, but they were also expendable. A cardinal rule of the organization was to never, ever disclose the identity of the client. It was what kept Rothwell Associates at the top of the food chain in the extortion and nefarious acts sector of the economy.

Stanley Johnston was not fond of, nor was he in any way confident in, Charlie Balducci. The man was a walking pigpen. Stanley's problem was that other than those Aryan assholes in Idaho and parts of Eastern Washington, there weren't many other choices. Sure Charlie was undependable and unpredictable. His preying on targets of opportunity for robbery was also worrisome. For the most part, though, Balducci delivered. When he wasn't back in jail.

Not having heard from his subordinate for twenty-four hours was beginning to be a concern. Ever since the research done by MDV Mining based in Vancouver B.C. had located Robbins, Johnston had been on tenterhooks.

MDV was a newcomer. After purchasing two lithium mines in Chile, they had exhausted the money raised with their initial IPO and needed to issue more stock to continue funding their market expansion.

The last thing they needed was for the world to discover a better, cheaper alternative to lithium-ion batteries. They had even gotten so far as to have an interview with Elon Musk. If they could make inroads there, then the sky would be the limit.

Then this shmuck from PNNL started making headway with the vanadium thing. The brain trust had considered looking into the vanadium research early on but cast it aside when the EV market exploded. The thinking was that lithium-ion was a sure thing, a proven technology. No sense in getting involved with some experimental battery technology.

Nikki Baker was the R&D chief at MDV. It was her decision to forego the vanadium development in favor of the more conventional wisdom. It was also her ass on the line if the shit hit the fan. Her stock options alone would make her a multimillionaire, assuming nothing happened to upset business as usual.

When a connection at PNNL told her about the progress being made on vanadium, she became interested. Then she began to worry. Her contact kept her up on the progress being made by Robbins and let her know, too, that he was consulting with a woman who used to work at the lab. A woman who was a genius with chemical compounds. They also told her where this old woman lived.

It was during a monthly board meeting, the one following notching the Musk interview, that the chairman and CEO had heaped praise on their director of research and development. She received another twenty thousand shares as a reward.

No way was she going to let them in on the news she had received from Richland. There had to be another way. And there was.

Nikki loved the craps tables. So much that a trip to Sin City every three or four months became mandatory. The nonstop from Vancouver was only two and a half hours, and besides, she could stay with her cousin for free.

It was during her last trip, when she and Linda, her cousin, were eating bagels with peanut butter for breakfast, that she began bemoaning her situation. Linda, she of little patience, interrupted her with "Then why the fuck don't you do something to make sure nothing happens?"

"Like what?"

"There was a guy who used to collect for some of the bookies here. He started this company that takes care of things just like this."

"What's that mean? Take care of?"

"I don't know. I just know what I hear—that he's really good at what he does. And he and his old lady are stinkin' rich now. They live out in Summerlin."

"Got a number?"

EIGHTEEN

After a late morning start and then a butt-clenching drive over a snowy Snoqualmie Pass, we finally debarked from the Suquamish at 7:20 p.m. Emma was asleep on the rear seat, Jenne had crashed as soon as we got on the ferry, and I was just happy to be back on the island.

I felt better about leaving Alice in Northport after Balducci had been carted away, but I felt certain there was much more that I didn't know. Someone out there still wanted the vanadium research halted, and Seth wouldn't be completely safe until that threat was neutralized.

We had postulated all manner of theories on the way home, but none seemed to fit. I knew my buddy Bill would be ecstatic to hear about our adventures and I couldn't wait to fill him in the next day.

The following morning brought unexpected sunny skies with temperatures expected in the low fifties. With the lure of a round of golf at Useless Bay Golf Club, I managed to convince Bill to trek up to the island. He made it just a few minutes before our noon tee time.

We had played there together a few times and always enjoyed the quirky yet challenging layout. I waited until the fourth hole before spilling the beans on our adventures on the other side of the Cascades.

"Hey Bill, remember when we were talking about the PNNL and the elderly lady who used to work there?"

I'd chosen to ask the question just before Bill executed his approach shot to the tricky green. He ignored me and promptly shanked his Titleist out of bounds.

"Would you please just shut the fuck up when I'm getting ready to hit? Goddamn."

"Gee whiz, really sorry, buddy. Had no idea you were that sensitive. Um, you do know that's gonna cost you, at least on this hole."

He dropped a new ball and managed to scrape it onto the green.

"Anyway, do you remember our conversation?"

"Of course I do. Don't tell me, though, let me guess. You went down there, found out stuff about shit that's none of your business. Then you ran with that shit, found out more stuff, and managed to either get someone killed or, at the very least, you got another enforcement agency involved. And now, now you want some help from me.

"Am I close? I told Shelly if we gave you that info about the vanadium suppliers, it would come back to bite me in the ass. So, how about it? Tell me how much shit you've stirred up."

"Sheesh, you make it sound as if I'm a troublemaker."

"You are."

"Now I'm not so sure I want to let you know what's going on." I felt terrible baiting the hook this way. Sure I did.

"Just tell me, asshole."

I proceeded to fill my pal in on everything that had happened since we last spoke. To his credit, the only interruption was to tell me to shut the fuck up while he three-putted for a triple bogey.

I completed the story just before hitting our tee shots on the fifth. When he landed safely on the fairway, he gave me a look I'd seen before, one that said, *Why do I even get involved with you? Only two things can happen: it'll get much worse before it gets better, or it'll be absolutely fucking awful, and it won't ever get better.*

He finally engaged his vocal cords. "Where is this Balducci now?"

"I'm guessing in jail somewhere."

"Great. You said the deputy was sure this was going to the FBI?"

"It's what he told us. Do you think Matt Steele might know something?"

Matt and Bill had been in the middle of a terrorist attack several years before and had handled the situation masterfully; of course, my help in the caper proved indispensable.

"I'll check with him when we're finished; maybe he'll know something. Now can we please play golf? I've got some ground to make up."

Bill was my best friend and the most dependable guy I'd ever known. The gruff front he liked to display was a precursor to solid detective work and a bulldog-like tenacity. His approach was to constantly under-promise and always, over-deliver. I was confident if any information were available, he would find it.

NINETEEN

When Nikki Baker heard that the Rothwell team had been unsuccessful in halting the vanadium research, she was furious. She had fronted forty grand to the Fuscos when they had guaranteed they would put a stop to it.

Because of her connections in the industry, it was easy to find out about the shipments to Northport. She had investigated the technology initially before discarding it and still knew some of the players at Oswego.

Baker was a single woman with no desire to get married. Still, in her late forties, she was an attractive woman who had clawed her way past most of the men in her field. As director of research and development for MDV, she oversaw only a dozen scientists. Where she earned her keep was in negotiating the purchase of the two Chilean mines.

At five-seven, with dark hair, startling green eyes, and an athletic frame, she was a willing target for testosterone-fueled corporate officers. Or had been at her previous postings, one of which was a short stint at the Pacific Northwest National Laboratory.

Since joining MDV shortly before their IPO, she had gained the trust of both the chairman and the CEO, the only people in the company her seniors. They had sent her to Chile on a whim to see if the mines were worth a look. Several well-known outfits were also there but could not compete with her charms.

The purchase was completed in three days, and Nikki was well on her way to riches beyond her wildest dreams. That was unless this stupid fucking vanadium thing destroyed the market.

She presently held 20 percent of the outstanding shares of MDV, which, at the current price, were worth north of ten million. With the existing SEC laws, she was forbidden to liquidate for a specified "blackout" period, and then only in regulated quantities.

All of this was fine with her unless the stock tanked, which, of course, it would if there was a significant shift to vanadium technology. It was why it was so important to ensure that this Robbins shmuck was forced to end his meddling.

Baker tried to keep tabs on the news from Northport, but it was such a tiny town that it proved difficult. After a bit of research, she found that the *Okanogan Valley Gazette* posted local news. There she found a small blurb mentioning an armed intruder at a rented ranch home on the outskirts of Northport.

The intruder sustained injuries from a dog attack, and no one else was harmed. There was no mention of any other names. That the FBI might get involved was indicated.

"You promised you'd take care of this, Eddie, when you were more than happy to take my forty grand." Nikki was pissed. She had Eddie Fusco on the line, and she damn well was going to hold his feet to the fire.

"I'm sorry, Nikki. Our on-site contractor fucked up. I've got another one I'm sending in to do the job."

"Let me see. You said it was handled months ago, and you were wrong. Then I told you there were some research notes some old lady had on some goddamn island, and you weren't able to get them. Then I find out where Robbins is, let you know, and you fuck that up a second time. I'm beginning to think you're not very good. Am I mistaken?"

"Nikki, Nikki, no. I mean, yes, you are mistaken. That place is so remote we had to use whoever we could get up there. The woman we sent searched the old lady's house and couldn't find anything there."

"So am I to believe there were no notes? That's not what my Richland contact told me, and I believe him. That old lady was working with Robbins, and my contact said she always kept notes of her work. I want them."

Nikki could hear Eddie's breathing over the phone.

"I promise we will put an end to this. I'll get someone to go back and search the island house again, and I'll send one of my best men to take care of Robbins. I've told you this before, but if we have to eliminate the threat, then it's gonna cost another fifty or sixty K."

Nikki had the money; she just wanted to make sure her millions in stock and options kept their value. "Just get it taken care of, Eddie; I'll get you paid. I don't want any more excuses."

Rothwell and Associates, in this case, Eddie, was not used to complaints from their clients. Their cadre of ex-cons was generally dependable, at least when it came to simple threats and, if necessary, robbery or physical harm.

The Baker woman was higher on the food chain than Rothwell's everyday client. If she was unhappy, other clients might get wind of it. Eddie couldn't have that.

"That woman at MDV is pissed off. The doofus we had on the Robbins thing dropped the ball again. Let's get Stanley on the line." When problems arose, Eddie always went to Bobbie. She had a good head for cutting through the bullshit and often finding straightforward solutions to what, at least to Eddie, seemed like complex issues.

The two of them were sitting in their home office with a speakerphone set up on the conference table.

"This is Johnston."

Bobbie took the lead, "Stanley, it's Eddie and me. Tell me why this Robbins fiasco has become a major clusterfuck."

"Ah, shit. Sorry about this, Bobbie. It's just that the only person who would even go up there was Balducci. Some dog tore up his arm, or it would have gone smoothly. Now he's back in jail. I've already put some feelers out for a new recruit."

"Who did you have toss the old lady's place on that island?"

"I used Lisa, the one who planted the stolen goods on the state senator who our client ran against. You remember her?"

"Well, Lisa also botched things. According to our client, who has someone inside at PNNL, the old woman always took notes. And it looks like those notes are very important. We need to get them to ensure nobody else can develop the technology. Got it?"

After thirty seconds went by, Eddie lost patience. "Stan, you there?"

"I'm here, I'm here, Eddie. I'm just trying to come up with someone to put a stop to this once and for all. Can we spend a little more?"

Bobbie gave a quizzical glance to her husband. "Why do you ask, Stanley?"

"If we can double the pot, I think I can get someone to take care of both sides of the deal. He's been out for a few years now, and he's perfect for this."

"And who is this special fellow?" Bobbie sounded doubtful.

"He doesn't want anyone to know. It's how he's been able to keep such a low profile. He never wants to see the inside of a cell again. Besides, you're better off not knowing. Right?"

They nodded at each other even though Stanley couldn't see it.

"Okay, Stan, go get your specialist. We'll pony up the money. Just make damn sure we button it up this time."

After they disconnected, Eddie turned to Bobbie. "What do you think, hon?"

"I think Stanley better come through this time. That Baker broad smells like trouble if we fuck this up again."

Eddie nodded in agreement. "I agree. She's already giving me an ulcer."

Twenty

Randall "Randy" Rhodes was simply an average joe.

He wasn't tall at five-ten. He was neither old nor young, having been on this earth for forty-eight years. He was of average weight for his height—170 pounds.

Questioning brown eyes, an unremarkable nose, and thinnish lips adorned a vaguely Northern European canvas. His dark, shortish hair sported flecks of gray, which were rarely seen due to the omnipresent Kraken ball cap. He'd recently ditched the Mariners cap for the expansion hockey team in the hopes that *they* could possibly make the playoffs. He'd given up on the M's.

Rhodes had been back on the street for 876 days. Of this, he was sure. His dislike for incarceration encouraged him to savor every day on the outside. He was never going back, ever. The twenty years behind bars were plenty for a lifetime.

Raised as an only child by strict, god-fearing parents, Rhodes had an IQ of almost Mensa material, which was why his dreadful life choices were so disappointing.

After a dismal academic freshman year of mostly partying and cutting classes, he promised his folks, who were paying for his transgressions, he would clean up his act. In his second year at Washington State, his grades improved dramatically.

They did so not because of discipline and dedication to study but because of his uncanny knack for convincing others and paying them to allow him to benefit from *their* hard work.

At the beginning of the year, he placed a small ad for a woman's fragrance in the regional edition of a national publication. This magical elixir promised sexual prowess through pheromone manipulation. The advertisement stated the going price for a few ounces of the stuff was a hundred dollars. The only way to purchase was through an authorized representative, however.

Rhodes was the self-appointed and the only authorized representative. His MO was to take the magazine with him, show the product's legitimacy to a prospective sucker, and offer a 50 percent discount.

Word spread, and a steady supply of hormone-driven undergrads beat a path to his dorm room. Fortunately, his caches of perfume bottles, colored water, and a gallon jug of British Sterling for women were kept in a U-Haul offsite storage locker.

When many of his disappointed clients showed up to complain, Randy agreed, said the company had gone out of business. Still, the impressive amount of cash was enough to fund his cheating and related activities.

Because his test scores had improved so much, he was asked to meet with his guidance counselor to be congratulated. Unfortunately, several of his conspirators, victims of the perfume ruse, got to the counselor first and exposed his reprehensible ways. Instead of congrats, Randy was issued his walking papers. He was told to never show up again on campus.

With his experience in the perfume business fresh in his mind, Randy tried similar scams on the general public. The customers in his hometown of Tacoma were either more intelligent or poorer than his captive college marks because nothing he tried worked.

His entrepreneurial skills finally led him to the illicit drug trade. He started on the street, then swiftly moved up the supply chain. It wasn't long before he had his own territory.

In addition to his "average" everything, Rhodes was never a violent person. He preferred negotiation to bloodshed. The problem was that his associates and competition felt otherwise. Rather than indulge in such vicious activity, he simply avoided it and moved on to easier marks, where simple threats of bodily harm were often all that was needed.

As often happened in his chosen line of work, one of his collectors was caught beating the shit out of some poor addict who wouldn't pay what he owed. Nowhere near Mensa caliber, the associate proceeded to spill his guts on the entire Rhodes enterprise.

The drug-related activities and several beatings performed by his underlings were mentioned. Randy was headed for the big house for dealing at a time when penalties were stiff and justice was sidestepped.

Ever since his release, he had kept his nose clean. Stanley Johnston, an acquaintance from the Washington State Penitentiary in Walla Walla, had contacted him several times about potential employment, but the services required were not worth the risk. The money he had stashed away from his drug days would have to last him a little longer.

When his phone buzzed, he saw the call was again from Johnston. Against his better judgment, he answered. "What is it, Stan?"

"I think I've got something for you."

"I've told you before; it's not worth it. I'm not taking the risk."

"Would fifty grand make it worth your time?"

Randy paused for a minute. Fifty K was some serious dough, and he was running low. "What do you have?"

Johnston told Rhodes the whole story. All of it, including Balducci's spectacular failures and the unsuccessful raid on the Waffle house.

"Who's the client?"

"I can't tell you."

"Then forget it."

"No, wait. I'll tell you. It's a highly placed executive at MDV."

"When does it need to be done, and are there any rules of engagement?"

"No rules, Randy. Do it however you want, but remember, nothing comes back to us. It needs to be done yesterday."

"Okay. As soon as I get the initial twenty-five grand, I'll get started. Hopefully, you won't hear from me until after I've taken care of it."

TWENTY-ONE

After the O'Malleys had returned to their home, Alice continued to work with Seth in Northport. Their relationship had quickly progressed from professional to personal.

Spending every waking hour with someone was a new experience for the language professor. She was seriously falling for the man. She had abandoned her room in the main house and was now bunking with Seth.

The daylight increased by over two minutes every twenty-four hours at this time of the year, but it was still almost 8:30 before there was any appreciable visibility. After an extended stay in the makeshift lab the previous day, the two had slept in.

"I hate to bring this up, Seth, but I'm going to have to go back to school before they eliminate my job."

He rolled to his side, facing her. "That sounds terrible. I've gotten used to having you around." He threw his arm across her and feigned sobbing.

"Knock it off, buddy, or I'll toss your notes into the fireplace." She was utterly blindsided at how easy this man was to be with. He appreciated her intelligence and adored her irreverence. That she would find love in an itty bitty town in the middle of nowhere was beyond belief. She'd hate to leave.

"I have an idea." He rolled back and propped himself up on an elbow. "Listen before you say no, okay?"

Alice wasn't sure where this was going, but she was a tiny bit apprehensive.

Now she turned to face him. "Go ahead."

"You know how we've made excellent progress since we've incorporated Sharon's notes with my research?"

"Yes."

"And you know how I feel that something's still missing. The notes you brought with you skip ahead a bit, almost as if there is a process or formula or something that was missed or lost."

"Agreed."

"So, what if I drove back to the Seattle area with you. Jenne said she wasn't sure what she would do with Sharon's house. Maybe I could rent it for a while. I could look through it with a fine-tooth comb, maybe see if there's more there, something that was overlooked. I should be safe there, too, now that they've put that Balducci away.

"Also, there's the added benefit of us being closer geographically. If you don't already know this, I'm growing attached to you." He delivered this with a sincere look.

"Well, you know what I think, Seth? I think that's a fabulous idea." She gave him a playful hug that somehow developed into a much longer one.

It took them most of the day to pack up all of his gear. The camper top on the long bed of the old pickup allowed ample space for the prototypes and Seth's and Alice's items. Rather than spend one more night, they took off and made it to Wenatchee before calling it quits.

"Now that we have decent cell service, how about we call Jenne? It's her place, after all."

"You're way ahead of me, Alice. Let me go check in here, and we can do it from the room."

They entered their serviceable if not luxurious room at the Wenatchee La Quinta Inn and collapsed on the bed. "This isn't the biggest town in the world, but it's nice to be back in civilization. It's been a while for me."

Alice nodded her agreement. "Yup, I know what you mean. Let's call the O'Malleys."

"Alice, great to hear from you. You still in Northport?" Jenne sounded genuinely happy to hear from her.

"Nope. I'm in Wenatchee."

"Huh? How come?"

"First of all, you forget the cell service in Northport, remember? We wouldn't be talking if we were there."

"We?"

"Yep, the scientist is here with me." She squeezed his hand.

"What's going on?"

Alice went through their thinking and finished by asking if Jenne would like a tenant for her property.

"As long as he doesn't mind roughing it. This wouldn't have anything to do with you too, would it?"

Seth listened the whole time and leaned over to put his two cents in. "Of course it would. Why do you think I suggested it?"

The three of them laughed. Then Jenne turned serious. "One thing, Seth. The place is off the grid, but I'm pretty sure there's power available; I'll look into getting it hooked up. Sharon preferred her independence from the energy companies. I'll see what I can do."

"I forgot to ask about the rent, Jenne."

"Let's just keep it where it is right now. Zero. You pay the utilities and clean up the place, and we'll call it good."

Twenty-two

Rhodes visited Northport, not expecting any success. It was the last place his target was seen, though, and he needed to start somewhere.

He made it to the ranch where Balducci was arrested, having gotten the address from the police blotter in the local paper. Other than obvious signs of recent meals, there wasn't much from which to deduce. He continued to the smaller building to the rear of the house and found more evidence of recent occupants.

Here, though, were also signs of scientific activity. Crumpled notes with formulas beyond his understanding were strewn about the place. Scraps of metal were present, and the smell of chemicals permeated the air. It was apparent, too, that more than one person had slept in the bed.

Keeping some of the discarded notes with him, he left the small town and finally managed to call Johnston an hour later when there was adequate cell service.

"Robbins is no longer in Northport. It looked like he was bunking with someone while he was there too. I may have another loose end here. Any idea where he went?"

"No. Let me get back to the client. She seems to have some inside knowledge about things. I'll get back to you."

Having no leads to follow up, Rhodes figured he might as well head over to Seattle to see what he could find at the old woman's house.

Still living in Tacoma, Randy was mildly pissed off. He'd traveled over the pass in shitty weather to get to Northport and now had to return to the Puget Sound area. Again, in shitty weather and with nothing to show for his efforts. He'd make damn sure to bill Johnston for his expenses.

After the rain had abated for a time the following day, he made the trip to Mukilteo and took the ferry over to Whidbey Island. With the address supplied by Johnston already plugged into his nav system, he headed to Langley. The property he was looking for was about five miles north of the quaint town, and he was in no hurry.

Even though he was a native to the Northwest, it was his first time on the island, and he was enjoying the scenery. He frequently saw soaring eagles and views of the snowcapped Cascades and Olympic mountains as he headed north in unusually clear weather.

He'd seen the signs for deer crossing often but, of course, disregarded them. After coming over a rise, he was forced to brake quickly to avoid a fawn and its mother strolling across the road; in the future, he made a greater effort to be aware. Hitting a two-hundred-pound animal at any speed could be lethal, and it appeared there were plenty of them on Whidbey.

Just off Saratoga Road, he reached the address and slowly drove by. The homes were scattered about in this area, interspersed with large parcels of pasture and wooded forests. Although he couldn't see the house from the road, he could see an old pickup slowly traveling up the drive to where he assumed it to be.

Johnston's information was that the house was empty since its former occupant was deceased. It always pissed him off when his intel was faulty. That's when mistakes happened and when people went to jail. It wasn't going to happen to *him*.

Rhodes pulled into what looked like a small lot for a trailhead and made the call.

Without even a hello, he tore into Stanley. "I thought you said the house was empty."

"It is, I mean was. It's supposed to be."

"Well, it doesn't look like it is. There was an old truck headed into the place when I drove by. The damn thing is stuck back in the fucking trees. I couldn't see anything from the road."

"Okay, well, it either is or isn't occupied. Just do your job and let me know when you're done. It's why you're getting the big bucks, Randy."

After twenty years of guards telling him what to do and where to go, Rhodes felt his hair bristle on the back of his neck when he was ordered around.

"Hey, Stan?"

"Yeah?"

"Watch your fucking mouth. You came to me, remember? I'll handle my end of it, but I'm not taking shit from you or anyone. Got it?"

Stanley was quiet a moment. Rhodes was positive he couldn't get anyone else to do the job, at least anyone with his talents.

He was right. "Okay, sorry, Randy. It's just that the Fuscos are on my ass, and this client is turning out to be a real bitch. What kind of truck was it? I'll talk to Lisa and Balducci, if they'll let him use the phone, and see if I can come up with something."

"I don't know the year, but I think it was an old Chevy. It was sort of a shit brown and beat up pretty good."

"I'll get back to you, but it might not be until tomorrow."

With no alternative but to wait for more information, spending the night on the island made sense. Rhodes assumed there'd be little trouble finding a room since it was off-season.

He'd passed a cute New England-style inn on his way to the house formerly occupied by Sharon Waffle. Rather than call them, he simply stopped in to see about lodging for the night. The Saratoga Inn proved to be a charming little place overlooking the Saratoga Passage.

He managed to take the only vacancy available of the sixteen rooms on the property. Rhodes was surprised that the hotel was as full as it was, given the time of year. He correctly attributed it to weekend retreats by traffic-weary Seattleites. The inn was only an hour away, including the twenty-minute ferry trip.

The room rate wasn't particularly cheap, but he saw no reason not to splurge when away from home after spending two decades in a six-by-eight cell. He relaxed on the luxuriously made bed and considered his situation.

The fifty grand would indeed come in handy. The funds he managed to stash away before his incarceration were being depleted at an alarming rate. Unfortunately, his job shutting down a solitary researcher had blossomed into a much more complex operation.

Initially, turning the house upside down looked to be easy-peasy. Now that someone was staying there, if indeed that were true, there'd be additional risk involved. From what he saw at the Northport location, at least one other person in addition to Robbins needed to be addressed. The 50K was starting to look like small change.

While considering all that needed to be done, Rhodes became oblivious to his surroundings. He suddenly realized the outside sky had darkened, and the only sound he could discern was the click of the second hand on the clock at his bedside. The brochure at the front desk had mentioned something about "peaceful," but it had barely registered at the time. Compared to the constant sounds and yells bouncing off the hard surfaces at The Penn, this was pure bliss.

As he switched the bedside lamp on, a plan began to develop. First, he needed another body to help out. It would cost him, but he would pass that along to Rothwell. Rhodes figured once the job was done, he'd have a big hammer to hold over his employer's head. The last thing they needed was someone going to the Feds and ratting them out. Before he was done with them, he figured he'd be able to double his fee.

Before his time behind bars, Rhodes had employed a half-dozen or so support staff. The services provided included collections, enforcement, and a bit of rough stuff on the infrequent occasion. Two of the team turned state's evidence and squealed on Rhodes and the others. Only one managed to skate.

Still lying on top of the down comforter, he made one call and received another. Then he made one more.

"Smitty, it's Rhodes."

Silence.

"Smitty, you there?"

"Randy?"

"Of course, who the fuck did you think it was? How's it shaking?"

"Last time I talked to you was ten years ago when I stopped by The Penn in Walla Walla."

"I know, and don't think I didn't appreciate the visit. I wanted to thank you again for not joining the other assholes who stabbed me in the back."

"I felt bad about splitting, but when the shit started to roll downhill, I thought it best if I just disappeared."

"You were right to do what you did."

"Where'd you get the number?" There was concern in Chauncy "Smitty" Smith's voice.

"You knew my folks died when I was off the street, right?"

"I did. Sorry."

"I have an uncle, my dad's brother. We were close. He even wrote to me while I was inside."

"Okay, and…"

"He's done some things that were a little on the fringes of the law, but he's managed to avoid any time. He's retired now, but his last job was with Verizon, and he still has some connections there. I asked him to see if he could find you. He did."

"I never give my number out."

"Yeah, but you have to pay your bill, don't you?"

"Sheesh, talk about no secrets."

"No worries, bro, no one else is gonna get it. How would you like to earn some cash?"

"How much?"

"Not sure, maybe twenty or thirty K."

"What do I have to do?"

"At this stage, it looks like one subject needs to rearrange his priorities, maybe two. Then a little B&E, possibly some other stuff. I'll make it worth your while."

"Sound interesting. I'm not doing anything here that can't be put on the back burner. Still collections and shit. I'm kinda getting tired of it."

"Well, at least you'll get a change of scenery. Meet me at the Saratoga Inn tomorrow morning. It's on Whidbey Island."

"Did you say island?"

"Yup."

"How will I find it?"

"Go to Mukilteo and get on the next boat you see; they run every half hour. When you get off the boat, head to Langley. You'll see the sign. When you get to the town, you'll see the inn. It's a tiny town; you won't get lost."

"Huh, an island. Go figure. See you tomorrow."

TWENTY-THREE

With Alice's help, Seth moved into the Waffle House—we still called it that. Jenne and I spent the entire day cleaning up and ensuring the electricity was working correctly. Sharon had simply turned the main breaker to the panel off.

I wished I had known the woman while she was alive. That she was passionate about the planet was obvious. From what I had learned over the past few weeks, it was also clear she was a genius. Even well into her eighties, she continued to develop an energy storage solution that would make a serious dent in fossil fuel emissions.

We found ourselves in the smaller building behind the main house where we had collected Sharon's research notes, but it was still disheveled. While Seth and Alice continued to move in, Jenne and I thought we could clear away some of the mess.

"Maybe we're better off letting Seth do this," I said. "There may still be information that could help him. I'd hate to toss it and find out later that it was important."

"Are you just saying that to get out of a little work?"

"I'm hurt that you'd think that of me." I'll admit I'd used that excuse before for that very reason, but I was being sincere this time.

"Maybe *this* time you make some sense. Let's not touch anything."

"Works for me, hon. Maybe we should leave them alone. I'll bet this won't be the last time we see Alice up here."

"They seem very happy. It'll be nice to have Seth for a neighbor."

A blue, late model Audi slowly drove by as we left the house. At the time, I didn't think much of it.

TWENTY-FOUR

While Robbins was settling into his new digs, Nikki Baker wrapped up another negotiation at MDV.

When word of the company's purchase of the Chilean mines became public, their stock price doubled, and the clamoring for the subsequent issue of shares was frenzied. The company was currently traded over the counter and had gotten the attention of several suitors.

Both Coupetek and Encel had expressed an interest in acquiring MDV since owning two lithium mines would go a long way in vertically integrating their companies. After back and forth meetings and correspondence, Encel became the last one standing.

Because of her success with the mine acquisitions, Baker was chosen to head up the negotiations with Encel. With visions of vast riches constantly grabbing her attention, she had to remind herself to focus. Once the merger was approved, she would be a very wealthy woman. Somewhere, deeply tucked in the corner of her mind, the vanadium issue persisted. She knew it was out there. Still alive and percolating.

Both parties approved the merger, and the closing date was set six months ahead. Since it was a U.S. company acquiring a Canadian one, there were several hurdles to cross. Nikki would have been happy if the damn thing closed tomorrow, but she was at the mercy of the SEC and the Investment Canada Act. Now all she had to do was make certain Seth Robbins' research never saw the light of day. She needed to get personally involved, it appeared.

Baker's portfolio would increase by 30 percent when the merger went through. Nothing was going to risk that.

Despite Eddie Fusco's assurances, Nikki Baker was still not convinced her concerns about the threat from the vanadium technology would be resolved.

She placed another call to Eddie. "I want to know who you've got working on my problem."

"I'm sorry, Nikki, you know I can't do that. The only way we're able to stay in business is with cutouts. The less we know about who's taking care of our clients' issues, the better. It's how we stay ahead of the law."

"I don't care. I've already forked over a lot of cash, and this means a great deal to me. If you don't tell me who the players are, then I'll be forced to take action."

"And what does that mean? I'm not sure I like where you're going with this."

"I don't care what you like. This is important to me, Eddie."

She thought he'd hung up on her until he offered a compromise.

"I'll give you the name of the manager who's in charge of your case. It's the best I can do. If he wants to give you any more information, then it's on him. His name is Stanley Johnston; here's his contact info."

Nikki was on the phone with Johnston immediately. "Eddie gave me your number. I want to know who's handling my case."

"We don't give out that information."

"Do you know how I got your number, Stanley?"

"Nope."

"Eddie gave it to me because I threatened him. I can do the same to you, but I'd much rather you took the easy way out and just give me what I want."

"You know if you are in contact with the person we've hired to resolve your situation, then you'll be at risk if things don't go according to plan."

"I'm aware of that. It's why I'm getting involved here. I'll make certain it doesn't go sideways. Now, I'd like that information. Please."

TWENTY-FIVE

"Yes, hello?"

"Is this Randy?"

"It is."

"My name is Nikki Baker. I'm..."

"I know who you are. Why are you calling me? There was supposed to be no contact between us." He didn't know the woman, and he was already annoyed.

"Stan Johnston gave me your name. Eddie gave me his."

"I don't know Eddie, just Johnston, and I know how to handle my job."

"Yes, I'm sure you do, but I'm calling the shots now. My money is funding this, and I'm sort of a hands-on manager. Know what I mean?"

Rhodes did not like this woman, goddamn bossy smart-ass.

"What do you want?"

"A meeting. I want to sit down with you and develop a solid plan to handle the situation."

"I've already got one."

"Yes, I'm sure you do. I'll consider it when we get together."

"Fuck this; we're not getting together."

"Oh, Randy?"

"What?"

"Here's the way this is gonna work. First, we *are* going to meet. Secondly, you will do what I say when I say it. Got it?"

"No fuh..."

"Randy!" a shout. "Shut up and listen. You are doing this for the money, correct?"

"Yes."

"*I'm* the one with the money. I've paid Eddie some already. He's the owner, by the way. I don't give a shit how much or how little he pays you, but what I *can* do is pay you directly. And I'm betting it'll be lots more than you would otherwise get. Ya think?"

Rhodes still hated this bitch, but he now *was* listening. "Okay, but if I don't like the plan, I quit." He needed to assert himself in some way, at least.

"Um, yes, I'm sure you feel that way. Now, where are you? I'm coming to the States tomorrow."

This nasty woman had a way of making him feel inferior; maybe when the dust settled, he could have Smitty slap her around a little. After he got paid, that is.

He told her where and when to meet him.

The woman had changed the dynamics of the situation. Instead of Smitty and he taking care of it their way, now they had to take orders from some skirt. Rhodes called his associate to make sure he got to the inn before the wicked bitch from the north arrived.

"Goddamn cold on that boat, Randy." Chauncy Smith was still rubbing his huge hands together as he walked into the hotel room.

Smith was a former left tackle for Washington State University. Even with the paltry class load that many college jocks carried, he flunked out after his first year. He never went to class, was a legendary partier, and cared little for academic achievement. He was also not a very good football player. But that was twenty-five years ago.

Today he tipped the scales at 360. Whatever he retained as muscle took a back seat to the layers of avoirdupois that served to disguise it. A prominent brow, hooded eyes squeezed from below by puffy cheeks, and a smallish pug-nose were complemented by a permanent wide grin displaying a perfect set of choppers.

At six-five, he towered over Rhodes. "I told you to stay in the car, Smitty; it's only a short ferry trip."

"Yeah, I know, I just never was on one of those. I had to go up on the deck to take a look. Nearly froze my ass off." That all this was spoken with such a broad smile could have been disturbing to those unfamiliar with this man.

"So what's the scoop? We gotta take orders from some broad?"

"Her name is Nikki Baker, and she's a big shot with an outfit called MDV based up in B.C. They're some kind of mining company, and for some reason, she's got a hard-on for this guy Robbins and the research he's been up to.

"Anyway, she's the money behind this operation, and she wants to run the show. She's offering to pay me directly and skip over Rothwell, which means they don't get a cut. They'll most likely be pissed off, but who cares? I'll probably never work with them again. Besides, she said she would pay more, whatever that means. I'll make sure we have an agreement before we commit to doing anything, don't worry.

"Just to be upfront with you, Smitty, you'll get thirty percent. Is that cool?"

"That's great, Randy, thanks. Appreciate the hell out of it."

With twenty-five thou of Rothwell's already in his pocket, Rhodes stood to make a killing on this job. Stanley and Eddie could go fuck themselves for all he cared.

"I told her to be here around noon. How about we go to the lobby for scones and coffee?"

"Now you're talking." It was clear Chauncy never missed an opportunity to fuel his full-figured physique. "Nice place you got here, Randy." The smile was still firmly in place.

It was 11:30 by the time they returned to the room, Smitty having devoured every last scone offered by the inn. Randy figured they were reconsidering their complimentary breakfast offering after seeing the damage one person could inflict.

The phone rang as soon as they walked through the door. "This is Nikki; where should we meet?"

The room was not fitting, and the lobby was not private enough. "There's a café down the street, next to the Star Store. Let's meet there."

"What's a Star Store?"

"You'll see, just go there." It was small, but Randy felt just a tiny bit better after ordering the woman to do something.

The Star Store was the center of commerce in Langley and had been so for over a hundred years. They offered everything from groceries to apparel to fine wines. When someone asked what it was, it was a certainty they had never been on the island. Randy felt another lift to his slightly misogynistic ego.

The two men approached the only table with a single woman seated. And she was a looker, even if she was a shade on the older side.

"Nikki?"

"Yes. Please have a seat." There it was again, that snotty, superiority thing.

Rhodes threw a snarky look at his companion as they both grabbed a chair. Smitty, of course, continued to grin.

Nikki looked directly at the large man. "Is there something funny?"

Rhodes jumped in to excuse his friend's peculiarity. "Don't mind Chauncy, Nikki. He's always smiling. I guess he was told that if he smiled all the time, the world would seem a happier place. Isn't that right, Smitty?"

"Yup. My momma always taught us kids, the only thing we could control was ourselves. She said smiling always made things better, so I always do."

Baker looked like she wasn't buying the explanation, but she brushed it aside.

"Let me explain something to you before we get started. What I'm going to tell you is privileged information, not that it'll make any difference to you since you're not an investor."

She proceeded to tell them about the company merger and that it meant a great deal of money to her. She explained that MDV was a mining development company that based its entire existence on the continued reliance on lithium-ion battery technology. If the industry were to move to vanadium-ion technology suddenly, well, then everything would rapidly turn to shit.

Rhodes nodded attentively, understanding the gist of her situation. Smitty just grinned and played with his coffee and two straws.

After tiring of hearing her talk, Randy interrupted. "I think I understand the situation. What we need to do is just make sure whatever Robbins is working on doesn't see daylight, right?"

"Correct. At least until the merger goes through; then I couldn't care less. What did you have in mind?"

Randy's plan consisted of trashing the house or burning it, then threatening Robbins and whoever was with him. In rethinking it, though, it seemed too unsophisticated for this client.

He chose another approach. "After listening to the situation, it seems our original plan won't apply. What were you thinking?"

"I don't know, exactly, but I would prefer that whatever we do doesn't attract undue attention. If anyone found out what we were doing, then I'd be fucked, and so, by the way, would you."

"Agreed."

"We only have to buy six months, so maybe no one needs to be eliminated. Maybe we just need to find some way to mess up the research."

The always grinning Smitty looked up from his braided straw construction. "How about we torch the place? It might take him a long time to redo his stuff if we burn things up. Maybe even longer than six months, huh?"

Baker looked surprised at the enormous man straining to fit into the café chair. "That's an interesting idea, Chauncy. We find out where Robbins is and set fire to everything."

Rhodes needed to assert himself before Smitty took center stage. He was pleased the talk of murder was off the table; that was never his style. "How do we find out where he went after he left Northport?"

"My contact at the PNNL doesn't know. All he told me was that he was conferring with this old lady who lived here on Whidbey. That's why I had her house searched. Of course, the moron who Johnston used for the job didn't turn up anything."

"The place you're talking about isn't empty. I saw an old truck there yesterday."

"What kind of truck?" Baker seemed suddenly keenly interested.

"I think it was an old Chevy. It was ratty-looking, sort of a dirty-brownish color."

"My contact at the lab told me that when Robbins left there, he took off in some limited edition pickup. He said it looked like a piece of shit but ran as it had just come off the lot. Said it was great in the snow.

"At the time, I wasn't sure why he went on and on about it, but then I remembered. One night, while we were together, he told me he fantasized about restoring a 1953 F100. I should have known right then he was a bozo. What the hell was I thinking."

At this revelation of Baker's indiscretion, Rhodes joined Smitty with a grin. "So you and this guy were an item, eh?"

She even blushed at this a little. "A big mistake, but hey, at least the guy's good for something. It's where I get a lot of my intel. He's been a big help, a huge help."

Randy steered the conversation back on track. "So you're saying you think the truck belongs to Robbins? He's who's at the old woman's house?"

"It seems that way. You'll need to observe the house to make sure, but I'd bet on it. If it's the truck I think it is, there are not many of them around."

"Before we start on this, we need to know what this is worth to you." Randy thought it best to lay his cards on the table.

"Eddie was going to get a hundred K from me. He's already got forty. If you can take care of this problem, I'll give you the sixty thousand Eddie was going to get."

"We want the hundred. I can't help it if Eddie took forty from you. That's your problem. Besides, when your merger deal goes through, you'll be stinking rich. What's another forty K? And we want a third up front."

Baker grimaced but then grudgingly agreed. Randy wasn't sure how much he'd left on the table, but at least he'd bumped it up to a hundred. After giving Smitty thirty, he'd still clear ninety-five with his deposit from Johnston.

"There's not much you can do here now. We plan to confirm Robbins is here, and then if he is, we burn the place. Right?"

"I agree. You two should be able to take care of this on your own. Just make damn sure that you burn his notes, any prototypes, and anything else. Got it? And don't do anything that might get the cops interested."

"What about firemen—okay to get them involved?" Smitty, still grinning, apparently had developed a sense of humor.

This, in turn, elicited a snort from Baker. "Yes, Chauncy, it's fine to get the firemen involved."

She made arrangements to have the deposit sent to the account specified by Rhodes.

TWENTY-SIX

We had invited Seth and Alice to dinner after spending the day moving equipment and personal effects into the Waffle House and had just toasted his new home.

"So, did you get everything squared away down there?" I asked.

"Mostly." Seth answered, " The main house is still a mess, but we're in good shape in the back studio. It's bigger than it looks, and Sharon had it set up nicely."

"I'm still trying to figure out where the property lines are. According to the tax records, there are about twelve acres. It looks like the buildings are smack in the middle, so you should have plenty of privacy."

I was glad Jenne was on top of everything because I sure wasn't.

"Will you be spending the night there? I mean, do you have what you need for tonight? Let us know if we can help."

It sounded like Jenne's mothering instincts were rising to the surface.

"You've done plenty already. We're in good shape. I'm surprised at how rural it is here; I can see why you like it. Alice has to go back to school in the morning, so it looks like I'll be able to focus on the work for the rest of the week." This drew a snarky look from the language professor.

"She's been a real pain in the ass, huh?" I couldn't resist piling on.

"Yeah, I'd probably have solved the world's problems had it not been for her."

Alice shoved her chair back and stood up. "That's it; I'm leaving!"

Seth looked petrified as if he'd pushed it too far. I was concerned as well.

"I'm leaving the table to get up and do this." She reached over to Seth's water glass and promptly poured it over his head. "Now, Kevin, did you want to continue being a clown, or are we done here?"

She said this with a stern look and then burst out laughing. Jenne was the first to join her while Seth and I just looked at each other, knowing we'd been had, and finally joined in with the laughs.

It was rewarding as hell to see how well the two of them got along.

"My classes are on Tuesdays and Thursdays, so I'll be able to get an afternoon boat on Thursday and then return to Seattle on Monday afternoon. Without Seth bugging me, I'll be able to catch up." A glance at her companion brought a nod and a toast from him.

Jenne finally got serious. "Seth, how close are you to finding a solution to reducing the size of the battery?"

"I'm confident the electrode composition is where it needs to be," he said. "It's the solid-state material that still needs adjusting. When we went through Sharon's notes, I could see where she was headed and what she was trying to do. It'll just be trial and error with multiple compounds until we find the optimum one.

"We think some pages are missing because she always dated them, and there were several days without any postings. I suppose she could have just taken time off, but that would be unusual for her. She was very dedicated."

"Would it help if you located them?"

"Maybe...probably. It would have been toward the end. The last page before the unaccounted ones used 'opgewonden' several times."

I spread my arms and turned my hands up in complete confusion. "Neato. Alice, I'm assuming that's Dutch for...?"

"Excited. She was excited about the compound she had formulated. She said the trials would begin the next day, and that's where the notes stopped. There weren't anymore after that."

"Yikes, it sounds like those are important," Jenne said. "Have you looked everywhere?"

"We have, Jenne, but that doesn't mean they're not there. The studio is stacked with books and bottles and chemicals, not to mention mounds of laboratory equipment, so we'll continue searching. For now, though, I'll just pick up where her notes left off and see what I can do with them.

Seth continued, "I don't know. If we found the missing notes, it could be a month or two. If not, it might take over a year or more. We just keep on pushing; we'll get there eventually."

"Is it really a game-changer?" I was having trouble seeing the research in practical terms.

"Unbelievably so. Just eliminating the need for mining lithium is huge. The amount of water they use for that is off the charts. Imagine the savings in electricity generation if all cars were electric and a single charge would go a thousand miles. The batteries would be incredibly safe as well. None of that bursting into flames stuff."

"If it's that important, why aren't the big battery companies working on this?"

"A few are, but not aggressively. They have so much capital tied up in mines and infrastructure for lithium products that it would be years before they'd recoup the cost of new investment. My goal is to get over this final hurdle and present the findings to the scientific community at large. The people in the world who are genuinely concerned about the planet will demand companies get behind the new technology, you'll see. It'll happen."

I never doubted Seth's commitment and dedication, but the intensity in his voice was impressive. I was sure if anybody could resolve the situation, it would be him.

We moved along to lighter topics and spent the evening enjoying each other's company.

TWENTY-SEVEN

Nikki Baker took the Deception Pass Bridge leaving Whidbey Island. She was headed back to B.C., and while the two-lane bridge was not without its challenges, it was much shorter than the southern route via ferry.

She was reasonably confident that Rhodes and his odd helper could resolve her concerns. She felt much better now that she'd eliminated the need for dealing with Eddie Fusco or Stanley Johnston. She'd always been of the mind that if you wanted something done right, you'd have to do it yourself. At least that's what her mother told her.

Sure, the 40K she'd given Eddie was toast, but she had plenty of money. She'd have plenty more, too, when the merger went through. The only threat now was Robbins, but it was likely his research was soon to be going up in flames. Literally.

The two men she reported to trusted her explicitly. They were family men and never showed any interest in straying, which turned out to be a blessing. During her past positions, her approach was to target the person who could advance her career the fastest and ply him with her feminine wiles. And it was *always* a man. And *almost* always, it worked.

When neither the chairman nor the CEO was attracted to her, she simply did her job. When it came to the mine negotiations, *then* she busted out the charms. And that's how she beat out the others. She couldn't vouch for all Chileans, she thought, but the ones she met were great in the sack.

The only guy she regretted sleeping with was that dipstick from the lab. He was no fun, a terrible performer, and had awful breath. She had regrets, yes, but Slattery was at least good for something. Information.

Without him, she could never have found the location of Robbins, nor would she have known about the Waffle connection. Now, because the dickwad enjoyed fantasies about old trucks, she had found Robbins again. She thought. But it had to be. It made sense. Unless she heard from Rhodes, she'd assume it to be so.

The line at the border was short, and she made it back to Vancouver in a little over two hours. She'd spend the time until the merger closed doing all she could to speed up the process. Hopefully, none of Robbins' research would ever see the light of day.

TWENTY-EIGHT

"Hi, Bill, I've been gone for a week, and I wasn't able to return your call right away. So far, this Balducci they've got over in Spokane is singing like a bird. Unfortunately, he doesn't know all that much."

Matt Steele had returned Bill Owens's call his first day back. The two law officers were good friends, even if they were sometimes on opposite sides regarding jurisdictional issues. Almost always, the FBI took precedence, but because Owens had made Steele look like a hero in the terrorist case, there was no friction between the two.

"Believe it or not, Matt, O'Malley is in the middle of things again. I honestly have no idea how he manages to go from one shitstorm to another."

The agent laughed loudly. "Hey, he's your pal. Maybe you can understand it."

"Yeah, if only. So can you tell me what you've learned?"

"We know the name of the outfit, Rothwell and Associates."

"Who's Rothwell?"

"Nobody. It's just some name they came up with. Eddie and Bobbie Fusco are the real owners, a husband and wife team. Seems they put this together half a dozen years ago, and they've stayed off the radar until now.

"We've got a couple of teams digging everything up they can find on these two. Balducci gave us a Stanley Johnston too. We're trying to find out his priors as well. As soon as we hear more, I'll get back to you, and you can consult with your amateur Sherlock."

"Please don't remind me; he's enough trouble as it is. Strangely enough, though, sometimes he helps."

"I remember. Without him, we'd have had dozens of dead golfers a few years ago. I guess that counts for something."

"Heh, yeah, I guess it's why I keep him around. Talk soon."

TWENTY-NINE

My phone buzzed, displaying the number of one Bill Owens. I knew he'd be thrilled to talk to me about recent events.

"Hey, Bill, nice of you to call."

"Yeah, I'm sure. Just be quiet and listen. Matt was out of town, but he finally got back to me with what he's learned. The information you got from Balducci was accurate. This Rothwell is a husband and wife team out of Vegas. It looks like they're a clearinghouse for contract extortion, among other things. The Vegas office has known about them for a while, but they've never been able to trace anything back to them. They use cutouts and hire ex-cons, and they never disclose their clients, so it's usually a dead end. The Nevada team is trying to get someone on the inside, but it won't happen overnight. They know about Johnston, but they're not going to move on him until they're ready. He's the key. Once they get him, he'll likely turn on the Fuscos."

"So this is a big deal, huh?" I asked.

"Yes, a huge deal. Do me a favor and stay away from it. You'll only screw it up."

"That hurts, Bill, it really hurts. But suppose trouble finds *me*? What do I do then?"

"Then you call your good friend. That would be me."

More mundane topics took over the conversation after he gave me the report. I promised to get back to him if anything out of the ordinary happened.

THIRTY

Due to a cancellation, the room next to Rhodes became available. He told Smitty he would expense it, meaning he'd make sure to nick Baker for the charges.

They found themselves in the lobby for scones and coffee the next morning. Smitty was on his fourth.

"Do we know what this Robbins looks like?" Smitty asked.

"We know he has an old Chevy pickup. While you were off visiting the head, Baker told me Robbins was Black, and her source says he's a handsome man, whatever that means."

It was obvious Rhodes wanted no case of mistaken identity on his watch. He was mildly surprised that Smitty thought to ask.

"So you're saying if a good-looking Black guy is driving a shitty old pickup, then he's our man."

"Very well said, Chauncy. There's hope for you yet." Smitty's smile was even wider at this point. "Grab your coat, and let's take a drive. Let's use your rig."

Rhodes had to use the running board to step up into the driver's seat while Smitty simply turned his fat butt around and rolled into the shotgun position. The truck was a 2015 2500 HD Ram, with all the bells and whistles.

"Where'd you get this ride, Smitty?" Rhodes had to slide the seat forward to reach the pedals.

"One of the users I was collecting from didn't have the cash, so I told him he had to fork over the pickup. The dealer let me have it for a song; he said he admired my creative thinking." He looked proud of himself as he took in the island scenery. "Where to?"

"We're gonna take a drive past the old lady's house. You can't see anything from the road, so I thought if we used your truck, we could just take the driveway right up to the house. If someone's there, we say we took a wrong turn and ended up at the wrong place."

They took Saratoga north from Langley and arrived at the narrow driveway they were searching for five miles later. The 2500 was so wide that blackberry thorns and ironwood branches clawed at the sides. Smitty's grin had dimmed ever so slightly at the damage being done.

Turning into the clearing, they saw the old Chevy parked in front of a small yellow cottage. Off to the side was a twenty-year-old Toyota Corolla that looked like it hadn't been started for months. Before either occupant could say anything, a man came out of the house. He was Black.

Rhodes turned to Smitty. "I'll handle this."

He jumped down from the truck and turned to the man. "Hi. I think we've got the wrong address here. We're looking for the Dawson residence."

Seth looked concerned. "There's no Dawson here. Maybe you should try down the road. What did you say the address was?"

Not knowing anything about the numbering on the road, Rhodes punted. "They told us it was about five miles from town. I didn't write the number down."

Seth paused a moment before he spoke. When he did, it was firmly. "I don't know anyone by that name. Why don't you call whoever gave you the directions and find out the house number? Doesn't that make sense?"

Randy figured it was time to leave. "You're right, sir. That's what I'll do. Sorry to bother you." He climbed back up to the cab, executed a "Y" turn, and drove away. The additional scratches helped to reinforce the previous ones.

"You think he suspected anything?" Smitty asked.

"I don't know. He looked like he might have, but who cares? He doesn't know who we are or who this truck belongs to. When we come back, we'll make sure nobody's home. *Then* we'll torch the place."

"Do we have to take my truck next time?"

"No, Smitty. I think we'll rent a car for that trip. Just in case."

"How will we know when he's gone?"

"Let me think on that. Maybe good old Nikki can help us out." They continued to the ferry terminal in Clinton where Rhodes was able to reach Baker on his cell. "Nikki, Robbins is at the same house where the old lady lived."

"You sure?"

"I'm sure—Black guy with a shitty brown pickup. Couldn't be a coincidence; no way, not on this island." He hated it when she questioned him.

"Well, okay then. Do what you need to do, and I'll be happy to send you the balance."

"Um, we need you to do something."

"What's that?"

"Because of where this place is, it's tough to guess when Robbins is gone. Is there something you can do to get him out of there at a specific time?"

There was a pause on the other end. Presumably, she was thinking.

"Maybe."

"Maybe?"

"Let me make a call to my buddy who fantasizes about old pickups. He might be interested in a rendezvous."

Rhodes and Smith had just walked into the Saratoga Inn lobby when a phone buzzed. It was Rhodes's.

"Yeah?"

"It's Baker. You better take care of this properly, or I'm going to be pissed. I had to promise to get together with Slattery tomorrow night in Seattle. Ugh!"

"How does that help us?"

"It helps because what I get in return for jumping in the sack with this clown is him guaranteeing to get Robbins away from that house. He'll call him, tell him he will be in Seattle for a meeting, and ask him to meet and bring him up to speed on his research. I told him I wanted to have somebody peek at his notes to help me at work. I'll let you know what time."

"How does Slattery know where he is?"

"They're still paying him. Robbins agreed to touch base from time to time, and since he's still working, they still send him his monthly check. They need to know where to send it."

Rhodes was impressed. "Well, shit, ain't that just perfect. When do you think it will be?"

"I'll have to confirm, but he said he'd try for Thursday morning."

"That means we'll be stuck on this island for two more days."

"Yes, yes, it does," Baker said. "Maybe you and your buddy will be able to share some quality time sightseeing or whatever they do on that bloody island. Good luck: I'll confirm the time as soon as I hear back."

Rhodes looked over at Smitty as he ended the call. "Guess what, pal?"

"We're gonna be here longer?"

"Yup. Look at it this way; we get to screw off for a couple of days before we have to do anything. Then we make a trip up the road, set the house on fire, and hop a ferry back home. Easy peasy."

"Yeah, easy peasy." The full-faced grin was now firmly in place.

THIRTY-ONE

Seth spent the following days trying to duplicate Sharon Waffle's work, but he knew of no better way than trial and error. *If only I could come up with the missing notes.*

He had gone to the main house for coffee when the huge pickup drove in and had just walked out the door when they stopped, looking for an address. Supposedly.

Except for the incident in Northport, he might have just ignored them. He knew the lowlife who had attacked them was now incarcerated, but, he supposed, that was no guarantee whoever sent him wouldn't send someone else. Or maybe he imagined things.

When he went back to the studio to pick up where he'd left off, he saw a missed call from his former boss. He returned it.

"Hey, Mike, what's up?"

"Hi, Seth. All good?"

"Making headway, but it's slower than I'd like. The notes from Sharon helped a lot, but there are a few missing pages that could really help."

"The progress sounds good. Do you think we can meet the day after tomorrow? I'll be in Seattle for a team meeting, and I'd like to see how far along you are."

"Of course. When's a good time?"

"Let's do late morning; then we can grab a bite after. How are things on Whidbey, by the way?"

"Weather sucks, but you know that. It's beautiful here; I like it. I can see why everyone wants to keep it a secret."

"Good to hear. I'm glad it works for you. See you Thursday."

Seth thought the call from his boss was somewhat out of character, but hey, they were still paying him. Since he would be there Thursday anyway, he thought it made sense to visit Alice on her turf for a change. Seth gave her a call right after he finished with Slattery.

"Alice, I have to be in Seattle Thursday. Can we get together for dinner?"

"That sounds great. I was going to take the late ferry to come up Thursday afternoon, but now we can spend the night here and go to Whidbey Friday morning. How come you'll be in town?"

"Got a call from my boss. He needed to be in Seattle for a meeting and wanted to meet so he can review my progress."

"Huh, when's the last time you saw him?"

"That was the day I left Richland. We've talked on the phone a couple of times, but that's about it. I guess, since they're still sending me checks, they'd like to know what I'm doing."

"I guess. Still, it seems sort of out of the blue."

"That's what I thought too, but it's no big deal. I'll tell him where I am in the development, which should be enough. I'm sure he has budgets and folks to report to as well."

"Yeah, enough about that," she said. "There's a new restaurant over in Ballard that I'd love to try. I'll make a reservation. Can't wait to see you."

"Me too. It seems like weeks since I saw you."

"Um, yes. It's been a whole day, but I agree; it does."

"I forgot to tell you. Some yahoos came up the drive today looking for someone named Dawson. I thought it was a little weird, especially after the thing with Balducci."

"Did they look like thugs?"

"One looked like an accountant or something, and the other was huge. He kept grinning at me."

"That sounds ominous."

"The vibe I got was off-putting. I'll let Jenne and Kevin know I'm going to be gone for the night, and they can run by when they are out and about."

"Sounds good. See you at my place around four. If you get there first, just make yourself at home. You still have the key I gave you?"

"You mean the one you gave me yesterday?"

"That one."

"Geez, I dunno. I think I've misplaced it."

"If you're gonna be a dick, then maybe I made a mistake in giving it to you."

Seth loved it when she threw shit right back at him. "Okay, okay, I think I know where it is."

"Good thing, smart-ass. Can't wait to see you. Bye."

The following morning Seth pulled his notes together while in the main house and wrote a quick summary of his findings to date. The synopsis would be enough for the meeting with Slattery. Next, he returned to the studio and took several pictures of his prototypes. Then, he locked up, jumped in the Timberliner, and headed for the eight o'clock ferry.

He was still a little concerned.

THIRTY-TWO

Baker let Rhodes know that Robbins would be away on Thursday by 9 a.m.

With national car rental agencies on South Whidbey Island nonexistent, the best Rhodes and Smitty could come up with was a gas station in Clinton that had a half-dozen five-year-old sedans parked on the side. The good news was, with cash up front, the kid managing the enterprise wasn't all that fussy about credit cards or other documentation. A brief flash of Rhodes's license was sufficient.

After parking Smitty's rig in a vacant lot down the street, they walked to the station and picked up their ride.

At 9:30, they stopped at Sebo's Hardware to pick up needed supplies. Two five-gallon gas cans, a box of construction rags, a mason jar, and several butane lighters did the trick.

They filled the cans at the next station they passed and headed down Saratoga to the Robbins house. Smitty's wide grin narrowed slightly.

"Suppose he's there?"

"He won't be."

"But just suppose he is?"

"Then we're fucked. Don't worry, Smitty; he won't be." Although Rhodes had worked with his large accomplice before, he'd forgotten how childlike he could be.

Without a moment's hesitation, they pulled into the Waffle House drive at ten on the dot. Both occupants exited the dented Camry and strode directly to the small front porch.

"Be my guest, Smitty." Rhodes waved his hand as if he were a maître d' leading guests to their table.

The big man lifted his size sixteen right foot and smashed through the inexpensive QuickLoc deadbolt. The six-panel, solid wood, fir door crashed open. Splinters and metal pieces were thrown everywhere.

"Excellent, partner. Lovely job. Let's look around first."

"It's so neat, it doesn't look like anyone lives here."

"I agree. Look in the bedroom, Smitty; maybe there will be something there."

Rhodes pulled a few books off shelves just for the hell of it. Wandering into the compact kitchen, he saw several stacks of paper on the table and flipped through them.

"Come in here, Smitty."

Upon Smitty's arrival, Rhodes reported on the bedroom. "His bed's not made, so I guess he was here. Other than that, there's nothing there."

"Look at these," said Smitty. They each grabbed a few pages, but neither man could make any sense of them. "These are in some other language, and these other ones are in English, but there are all sorts of symbols and charts and stuff. I have no fucking idea what they say."

Rhodes was quiet, considering what he was looking at. "I guess this is what Baker was all worried about, but I thought there'd be more."

"How about we just take these and not burn everything?"

"Maybe he's got more notes hidden away in here. We can't be sure. Anyway, we told her we would burn everything, so let's get to it."

"Should we take the papers?"

"Nah, leave them. They'll burn up with everything else."

They returned to the car, and each took a five-gallon can of regular back to the house.

"Smitty, look through those kitchen drawers. Find a knife or a screwdriver or something."

They proceeded to douse everything to the point where the fumes made it impossible to stay inside. After filling the mason jar with gas, they threw the cans back into the house and cleaned themselves up with the construction rags.

Rhodes took one of the rags, drenched it from the jar, poked a hole in the tin top with a steak knife, and stuffed the wet rag through the opening.

"You do the honors, Smitty. Light me up."

His huge associate took one of the lighters and ignited the Molotov cocktail with a flourish. He quickly threw it through the destroyed doorway, crashing against the brick surround. With a WHUMP, it seemed the entire structure burst into flame at once. Such was the combustion that the two arsonists even felt the oxygen being sucked from where they stood.

"Get in the car, Smitty. Let's get the fuck out of here before someone comes."

They tore down the driveway, away from the inferno, leaving the studio, several hundred yards in the woods, the only building standing.

Thirty-three

"Are you going off-island today?"

"I thought I'd get the noon boat and make a Costco run. Anything you need from there?"

I thought there were lots of things I'd like from there, but very little I needed. "Don't think so, dear, but if they have that gallon jar of shelled pistachios, you can pick one of those up."

I wasn't sure if my wife enjoyed the Costco experience or if she was a trooper. The crowded aisles, massive shopping carts, and constant hawking of samples were overwhelming. My online suggestions to the company to install traffic lights at the aisle intersections were either overlooked or cast aside. Sure it would be expensive, but at least a semblance of order could be established.

At any rate, the monthly visit to round up paper towels, toilet paper, and snacks was her domain. Thank God.

"Sure thing, Kev. See you when I get back."

I couldn't be sure if that meant I was in for the pistachios or not, so I let it go and said goodbye.

Only minutes after her car left the driveway, my phone buzzed.

"Hey, Jenne, what did you forget?"

"Kevin, I just called 911. The Waffle House is burning!"

"Where are you?"

"In the drive. It's awful."

"Okay, I'll be there in a minute. Best you park on the side of the road so the fire trucks can get in there. See you in a sec."

I left Emma at home and rushed down the road. As soon as I rounded the curve, I could see black smoke mushrooming into the air.

Jenne's Outback was parked a hundred feet west of the entrance. She was standing to the side of it, and two other gawkers had pulled their vehicles over. I parked on the shoulder and jogged over to my wife.

"Did they say how long?" I asked.

"No, but from what I could see, the whole house was engulfed."

"I can hear the sirens now."

We just stood there watching the smoke while the firefighters did their thing. I was always impressed by their discipline and training. Every movement was done quickly and efficiently, with no hesitation, no wasted hurrying, and minimal conversation.

After about an hour, the flames had subsided, and the diminishing smoke had turned white. The looky-loos were gone, and the fire crew appeared to be wrapping up. The woman who seemed to be in charge ambled over to us.

"Did you call this in?"

"I did, yes. It's my property. My tenant left for Seattle earlier today. I was heading for the ferry when I saw the smoke. How could this have happened?"

Standing there with a soot-covered yellow slicker and trousers of the same ilk, she looked at us and grimaced. "It happened because someone poured gasoline all over the house and set fire to it."

"Are you sure?" Jenne's eyes opened wide.

"I'm no investigator, but I've seen a lot of house fires. The smell of gasoline is unmistakable. Come on up and see for yourselves. My name is Jamie, by the way."

We introduced ourselves and walked up the driveway. She was correct; the place reeked of gas.

"What about the other building?" I was acutely aware of Seth's work and what might have happened to it.

"What other building?"

"There's a studio in the back where our tenant does his work." Jenne, too, was now anxious.

Jamie looked at us, somewhat surprised. "Let's take a look."

We trudged through the brush and found the studio unharmed.

"Looks like whoever did this either didn't know this was here or didn't care about it."

I had déjà vu, flashing back to when we found the Waffle House ransacked and the studio untouched as well. "Someone is not giving up on whatever Seth is into."

"Who's Seth?" Jamie asked.

"Our tenant. He does research for the PNNL."

"We'll be taking off soon, and I'll refer this to our arson investigator. You can go into this back building, but don't touch anything in the burned-out one until he's finished. He'll get here this afternoon or in the morning. In the meantime, *you* need to talk to the cops."

"We know an officer named Willkie."

"Roger's good people. I'll call him on the way back; then you can talk to him when he gets here. He'll want to see this."

Willkie showed up a half-hour later. I guessed the crime wave on Whidbey was restricted to just the Waffle House.

"This place again?"

"Yeah, but this time they didn't bother trashing it; they just burned it to the ground."

The only thing left was the cast-iron woodstove. We stood far enough away to avoid the acrid stench of scorched wood and gasoline.

"Any ideas?" Roger asked.

Jenne told him what we were both thinking. "Sharon was working on the same project that Seth Robbins is researching. It's got to be that; there's nothing else. When we were in Northport recently, we were attacked at Seth's place. If it hadn't been for Emma, things might have turned out differently."

"Who is this Seth?"

I jumped in. "He is the person who was renting this house. After the run-in east of the mountains, he thought it best to come here. He's working with a translator from UDub."

"He's working here at the house?"

"Mostly in the studio out back. He told us he had a meeting in Seattle today. We were supposed to check the place out while he was gone. He told us about a strange truck and a case of mistaken address a couple of days ago."

"Tell me more."

"That's all we know. Jenne, have you called Seth yet?"

"No, I'll do it now."

While she made the call, I gave Willkie the complete version of our travels during the past week. He agreed that attributing the attacks on both Robbins and Waffle to mere coincidence could be discarded. Someone was behind both the Northport and Whidbey incidents. I told him about the FBI involvement and the Rothwell involvement. I could see his head spinning when I was through.

Meanwhile, Jenne returned. "I had to leave a message; he must be in his meeting. I just said to call me as soon as he could."

I turned back to Willkie. "If the same person orchestrated both attacks, how did they manage the second one when Balducci had been arrested?"

"If the FBI is right about Rothwell, then I guess it's just next man up."

"What will you do now?"

"We'll get some deputies to canvass the area to see if anyone saw anything, but I doubt if we'll get anywhere. Most folks are inside this time of year, and there just aren't that many houses in the area.

"I'll alert the DOT to have their ferry employees keep an eye out for anybody suspicious, but that's a long shot too. I'll make sure to get Agent Steele on it right away. I'm certain they'll want to take the lead on this. We'll handle the local stuff. After the arson team gets here, we'll check to see if they've come up with something.

"Anything we can do?" I asked.

"Just be available. I'm sure we will need to talk again. When Robbins returns, have him call me. Expect a call from the FBI after I tell them what happened here."

Thirty-four

Seth was a little surprised at the brevity of his meeting with Slattery and even more surprised at his lack of enthusiasm for the progress being made.

There was a text from Jenne and a missed call, but they would have to wait until after lunch with the boss. The lunch consisted of tacos from a food truck, a freezing outdoor table, and a brief discussion about old friends and team members at the lab. Seth was relieved when they said goodbye.

Because his ancient truck wasn't equipped with Bluetooth, he sat in the parking lot with the heater running while he made the call.

"Seth, thank god you called."

"What is it, Jenne? Is something wrong? Alice?"

"No, Seth, I'm sure Alice is fine, but your house, well, my house, was set on fire. Everything is burned to the ground."

"All of it? The studio too?"

"No, the studio wasn't touched. I don't think they knew it was back there."

Seth was quiet, seemingly gathering his thoughts. "I left most of Sharon's notes, and mine, in the house. So they're gone."

"I'm sorry, Seth."

"But they didn't get to any of the prototypes, and those formulae are still in the studio. We had pretty much exhausted everything we could accomplish with the notes that burned anyway. I mean, it would have been better if we still had them, but I think I'll be okay. I'm sorry about your house."

Jenne was relieved that things weren't as bad as she initially feared. "The house isn't a big deal, Seth. It can be rebuilt. We're just glad your research can continue. Do you still want to use the studio?"

"If you'll let me. I'll need to find a place to stay, though, on the island, that is."

"Let me think about it. In a pinch, you can use the sofa here, but I wouldn't recommend it long-term for your back. I'll make some calls."

"Are the cops involved?"

"Yes, and the FBI too. They have some leads, according to Kevin. They think that things will abate, at least now that they feel they've burned up your research. But be careful just the same."

"I will, and thanks for everything, Jenne. I'll spend at least tonight at Alice's, maybe tomorrow too. Call me if you come up with anything."

THIRTY-FIVE

I spent thirty minutes on the phone with Matt Steele. We covered everything from our visit and the subsequent attack in Northport up to the fire at the Waffle house. We discussed a little of Seth's research and the high probability that the orchestrator of the mayhem was a person or persons who stood to benefit substantially.

I told him Seth would continue in the studio and that he would be staying on the island. He promised to keep us informed.

"Do you think they'll try again?" Jenne was still unnerved by everything that had happened.

"As long as they don't know that Seth is still making progress, he should be safe. The problem is they always seem one step ahead. We need to chat with Seth and Alice when they get here today. Maybe we can come up with something. It was nice of those folks at the Saratoga Inn to allow him to stay there until that rental you found is ready."

"We were lucky the couple who owns the beach house are out of the country for a few months. Even luckier that Tim, next door, is the woman's father."

With the university on semester break, Alice planned to spend the week on the island. She was shocked at the fire and worried about Seth until we told her that it was unlikely they would attempt something in the short term.

After a week at the Saratoga, their rental at Bells Beach became available. The twelve-hundred-square-foot cabin overlooked beautiful Saratoga Passage, and during the winter months, most of the homeowners were elsewhere. Privacy would not be a concern.

"Look at it this way, Seth: you're only five minutes from the studio, you get to live on the beach, and you still have us as neighbors. Nice, huh?"

Alice and Seth had us down to the new digs a few days after he'd moved in. "I love this view. Earlier today, there was a huge gray out there with a calf. She put on a show for us. I could easily get used to this," Seth said.

"Between the screeching of the eagles and the owls, at night, it's impossible to get any sleep here." Alice's sarcasm was becoming legendary. It seemed the more complicated their situation, the closer she and Seth became.

The fire at the Waffle House had allowed us to let down our guards, if only by a few degrees.

"So, what's the plan going forward, Seth?" Jenne quizzed.

"I still have two prototypes that need to be excluded. I haven't had a chance to try those yet. I feel like I'm getting close, but either the efficiency isn't there, or the recharge rate is too slow. I should be able to do that tomorrow. If both are failures, I expect it's off in a new direction. I sure wish those last few pages of Sharon's notes would turn up."

"How long will you be here, Alice?"

"School starts up again tomorrow, so it's back to my place until Thursday afternoons, and then I come back here for four-day weekends."

"It's a good thing, too. I can barely get any work done." Seth had to quickly dodge a dinner roll that sailed close to his ear.

He regrouped and asked where things stood on the investigation.

"My buddy, Bill, the detective who's in touch with the FBI, caught me up this morning," I said. "The feds know who ordered the attacks and the fire. As you know, they have Balducci in custody. They don't yet, however, have a line on the arsonist. There's an outfit out of Las Vegas that uses ex-cons to do their dirty work. They've been on the FBI's radar for a while but haven't been able to get enough hard evidence yet to prosecute.

"They also know about someone named Stanley Johnston, who works for Rothwell. That's the Vegas connection. He seems to be the individual who hires the ex-cons, and they think he's the key. The couple who own Rothwell and Associates always keep their hands clean. They never know who does the dirty work. If the agents can turn Johnston against his bosses, they'll be successful. What they want is the people who pay Rothwell to do the extortion; they're the big fish."

"What about the local cops?" Seth asked.

"Roger Willkie told me he has no leads as of yet. The investigators confirmed what we suspected, that the fire was arson. No one saw anything suspicious; again, not surprising. He told me to let the feds handle things, and he felt we would be okay, at least in the short term."

"Well, hell, that works for me," said Alice. "Now, if I could just have a little more vino, I'll be able to sleep through that racket out there. Good thing I'll be back at school tomorrow, and my man here will be able to focus on his work. Really, Seth, you can do better than that."

Thirty- six

After reading about the fire in the *Whidbey News-Times*, Nikki Baker felt much better. She wasn't particularly fond of Rhodes or his odd companion, but at least they were competent. She'd already forwarded the balance of the money they'd agreed upon and hoped never to require their services again.

Going direct had been the right move instead of dealing with those idiots, the Fuscos. All those assholes did was take a slice of the pie. At least Johnston knew where to find the talent, but tough shit for him too.

In three or four months, she'd be rich beyond her dreams. All she had to do between now and then was keep the train on the tracks until the merger was complete. Thank God the vanadium research was on permanent hold. She told Slattery to let her know if he heard anything about any other study or progress. He was repulsive, definitely, but he *was* useful.

Thirty-seven

Mike Slattery was a career middle-manager. Finding a job at the highly regarded PNNL was thought by the entirety of his college professors to be beyond his reach. It would have been, too, had it not been for his wife's brother, Jeremy.

With a Harvard degree in mathematics and post-graduate work at MIT in physics, Jeremy Whitely was a local boy from Kennewick. As he had been on their radar since high school, the PNNL made him an offer he couldn't refuse. His first job was as a team leader over the energy group. He rose swiftly through the ranks and, after twenty-five years, was now second in command of the entire Richland operation.

Slattery knew Whitely loved his sister dearly and took advantage of the familial ties. He had been hired as a team leader, and after fifteen years, he was *still* a team leader.

It was okay with him. All he had to do was watch over and report on seven researchers. Slattery suspected his brother-in-law knew of his dalliances, but he would never say anything to hurt his sister.

Slattery had little interest in any research done at the lab, even if it meant saving the planet. Seth Robbins had reported to him for only a year before the scientist was threatened in his lab. At the time, he thought it odd, as did the cops he reported it to. He couldn't have cared less where Robbins did his work, and if it made him feel better to continue off-site, it was okay with him. One less person to worry about.

The recent hook-up with Nikki Baker left him with mixed feelings. He was intelligent enough to know she wasn't sleeping with him because of his money or looks. Still, it helped his ego to think that he could even score with such a fine-looking woman.

It had started over a year ago when they met at an industry function in Seattle. That he was even there was an oddity since, typically, it was only for senior team leaders. He chalked it up to a favor from his brother-in-law.

Baker was making herself known to the higher-ups at an evening cocktail reception when he managed to stumble into her. "Sorry, really sorry. Let me get you another drink."

With only a perfunctory smile, she nodded that he should. Upon his return, he introduced himself as a senior manager at the lab. She looked disinterested at first, but then appeared to have second thoughts.

"What are your people working on presently?" she asked.

When his standard security disclaimers landed with a thud, he immediately recovered. "I shouldn't say anything, but we're making incredible headway with alternate energy storage solutions."

This perked her interest up instantly. "In what direction?"

"We're looking at miniaturizing vanadium as a solid-state energy source."

It was as if he were suddenly transformed into Brad Pitt.

"It's Mike, isn't it?" she said with a now dazzling smile.

"Y-yes, it is."

"It's boring in here. How about we go someplace quieter where we can sit and have a real drink and talk."

Since their initial tryst, they had been together several more times. They texted often and occasionally chatted on the phone. In the beginning, it was dangerous and fun, and he didn't mind being used. Now though, he had misgivings.

When O'Malley had visited the lab months ago, Slattery had delivered the company line concerning secrecy. The man seemed sincere, and when told of Sharon Waffle's death, Slattery felt genuine sadness. She had been a kind woman.

He knew of Baker's elevated position at MDV and assumed that she was using the information he was providing to her advantage. He just didn't know precisely how.

Reports of the Northport attack on one of his scientists never reached him. Robbins had always seemed a private sort, and if he wanted to move to some island, then fine. Slattery's only inconvenience was ensuring that HR was kept current on the employee's address.

Baker's keen interest in the lab's research into energy storage systems he wrote off to corporate spying. He was positive she was angling for MDV to be first in line if and when Robbins was successful.

He was wrong.

THIRTY-EIGHT

We watched as the contractor we hired cleared off the blackened shell of a structure that used to be the Waffle House. It was crunched up and carted off in less than three hours. The only hint of Sharon's house that remained was a small concrete slab that had been under the single bedroom. Even the cement blocks used to form the crawlspace were disposed of.

"It makes me sad, Kev. We never knew her, and now her house is gone forever."

"Yes, and she left it to you because you were kind to her." I put my arms around Jenne and hugged her. "Sorry, babe, you two would have been good friends." We stood like that for a few minutes until we heard Seth's Timberliner make the turn into the driveway.

Rolling down his window, he pulled alongside. "Hey Kevin, Jenne, is everything all right?"

"We're good, Seth. We were thinking about Sharon after they removed what remained from the fire."

"I felt as if I knew her. I'm just sorry I never got to meet her in person; she was a brilliant scientist."

The three of us were quiet for a moment; the only sounds were birds chattering.

"How did you make out with those two prototypes you tested?" Jenne asked.

"Unfortunately, the results were similar to all the others," Seth replied. "One showed a minor improvement in the recharging speed but was nowhere near enough to pursue. I thought once I determined the most effective alloy for the electrode, I'd be home free, but no. Trying to formulate the electrolyte composition without any signposts is frustratingly difficult. The compounds and percentages of each are infinite. I sure could use Sharon right now."

I could sense his sense of futility. "So, what, just keep going using trial and error?"

"That's what I've been doing. The most I've accomplished is in being able to eliminate the makeup of the failed prototypes."

"How's the beach house working for you?" I thought a change of subject might lighten his mood.

"Oh, it's great. Alice loves it. She hates going back to Wallingford on Monday afternoons."

"You really like her, don't you?" Leave it to my wife to hit a guy between the eyes.

With misty eyes and a downward glance, he paused slightly, then looked up at Jenne. "Yes, I do; very much so. I was married for a couple of years. It ended mutually about five years ago. She was a researcher as well and a talented scientist. I met her at the lab, and we shared a comfort level, but that was it. When an opportunity arose for her to take a job on the East Coast, she jumped at it. Didn't even ask me about it. I took that as a clue, and we parted amicably.

"Looking back now, I feel I should thank her. I was so immersed in this project that I hadn't given any thought to having a relationship. Then Alice and I stumbled into each other, literally. I love everything about her; the spontaneity, the irreverence, and sarcasm, even the mouth on her. I'm as happy as I've ever been. Thanks to you two."

"We just happened to be there, and we've enjoyed the hell out of seeing you together. Both of us wish you the best." Jenne reached out for his arm resting on the door and squeezed it.

"Is the studio still working for you?"

"It's perfect. It's quiet and private, and it's so far from the road, no one knows it's there. Good thing too, eh?"

I had to agree. "If whoever set the fire knew where it was, you'd be starting from scratch."

"I know, I can't imagine. Okay, I'm going to work. See you later?"

"Stop by on your way home. We'll have a glass."

"Will do."

THIRTY-NINE

"Hey, Kevin? KEV?"

"YEAH?" I was in the basement putting the finishing touches on a small table for the kitchen area. Jenne had mentioned more times than I cared to remember that we absolutely needed one.

I could hear her footsteps as she walked to the top of the stairs. "When you're done down there, how about hauling those wood scraps and all that sawdust out to the shed. We can put it out for the trash pickup in the morning."

"Got it." I guess she thought I'd be leaving shit all over the place and not cleaning up. I couldn't imagine where she'd ever come up with an idea like that.

I tightened the last screw on the leg and began the cleanup. It was easier to pick the scraps of wood from the table saw up first and then sweep up the sawdust. And that's what I did. The last time I put the sawdust in the trash can with the wood pieces, I got a nasty note from the driver telling me to put it in a separate bag so it wouldn't blow all over his face when he dumped the can. I had never considered the hazards that vocation had to face before, but now I did, so I dutifully swept the fine grains of wood into a smaller bag.

While putting a twist tie on the bag, I noticed a scrap of paper had also been swept into it. I thought it a bit odd since I hadn't been working from any plans. I pulled the torn two-inch-by-three-inch piece out and saw the writing on it. It was in another language—Dutch. I ran up the stairs.

"Jenne, where did you put Sharon's notes while they were here?"

"I put them in that closet in your shop down there. Why?"

"And when you brought them up for our trip to Northport, did you drop anything?"

She looked up to the ceiling trying to recall. "I don't think so…no, wait. I grabbed the banker's box by the holes on the side, and when I turned, I bumped my elbow on that goddamn stack of clamps you had in there. One of the holes ripped, and some of the notes spilled out. I put them back, and that was it."

I thought it best not to point out that just because my clamps were in the closet didn't mean it was my fault. "Let's go down there and take a look."

"Why?"

"You know how dark it is in there. I think it's possible we missed a page or two."

The closet was a little cubby under the stairs with a pull string for a bare bulb light. We stored wine in there, among other things, and rarely turned the light on because our hands were usually occupied when we stooped over to go in there. The spillover from the lights in the shop was mostly sufficient.

"I've swept that out a few times since that box of Sharon's was in there, you know," Jenne said.

"Yeah, but still, it's hard to see in there. Let's look."

I reached in and pulled the string. The forty-watt bulb was barely bright enough for the small area. I went out to the shop and grabbed my battery-powered LED light. After sliding several boxes of five-year-old tax records aside, I aimed the powerful lamp inside where the stairs had lowered the height to three feet.

"Look there, Jenne. I think some papers have slid under the wall's bottom plate. When you were sweeping, they must have been shoved under. You wouldn't have known without any light. I swept up a piece from this side. It must have torn off."

My knees scraped the concrete as I bent down and shuffled over to where I could grab them. The floor was uneven enough at this point to where the plate was not tight to the concrete, and the papers slid right out. I backed out, we both moved into the shop, and we straightened out the pages. They were in Dutch.

FORTY

Rather than call Seth, we rushed down to the studio. He was hunched over his worktable, deeply engrossed in something. Startled, he looked up as we entered. "Damn! You guys scared the shit out of me. I know everyone thinks I'm safe for now, but I'm still a little on edge."

"Sorry, Seth, but we thought this was important. Take a look."

Jenne handed over the four pages we had found.

Seth looked at them like they were the holy grail. "Are these what I think they are?"

"We don't know for sure. We're convinced they fell out of the box when we retrieved it from the basement. They were stuck under the bottom plate of the wall in Kevin's workshop."

"Yeah, that's why there's dust and dirt all over them."

Jenne's look was enough for me to realize I was an idiot for announcing the obvious.

Going for a quick recovery, I asked a legitimate question. "Are these going to help?"

"Well, they *are* in a language I don't understand. But they definitely could be the missing notes we suspected existed."

"We need Alice, don't we?"

Seth concurred. "Yes, we do. But she's in Seattle until the day after tomorrow. I think I'd like to get on this right away, though. I'm going to catch the next boat and head down there. I'll call her on the way."

"Anything we can do here?"

"Not unless you have some ideas about transforming a vanadium redox battery from a nine-cubic-foot liquid state to a solid-state version that's the size of a standard D cell."

"Um. That would be a no. We'll stay and make sure to check on security here."

"Thanks. I'll text you and let you know what we find out. Great job coming up with these."

"It was nothing. All I had to do was clean up my shop at the behest of my wife." Judging from the looks I received from both of them, I had finally scored.

It wasn't until the following morning that we heard from Seth. The pages that we discovered proved to be the last notes from Sharon. And, if he could duplicate her theories, there was a good chance it would solve the electrolyte problem.

I reported to Jenne about the text I'd received. "He says he'll stay there until Thursday and return when Alice joins him. I guess the reagents and chemicals he needs are available at the supply houses in town. When he gets back, he thinks he'll be ready to put a prototype together."

"How can he be so sure it'll work?"

"Don't know. Maybe things clicked into place after he saw what Sharon was working on. If it does, though, we could be witnessing a giant leap in technology for the world. Just think, we wouldn't even be here if you hadn't stopped to chat with her on your walk that day."

"Yeah, seems like a long time ago."

FORTY-ONE

Seth was excited to show Alice the notes. He was confident that, if not the precise formula, it was close enough to where he could tweak it successfully.

As soon as she walked through the door, he hugged her and presented the pages handwritten in Dutch. "These are the notes that were missing. Can you take a look?"

"Nice to see you too." The significance of the discovery hadn't seemed to register yet. "Oh, you mean..."

"Yeah...I mean..."

"Seth, wow! Will they be helpful?"

"I hope so. Can we, *you*, look them over right away?"

"Give them to me."

They retreated to the kitchen table, where Alice grabbed a pen and a legal pad and began writing. She handed the translation to Seth one page at a time, and with each new revelation, he could barely control himself.

"Of course, how could I have missed this...and this...and this."

"I wish I understood some of it, but the words don't mean anything to me."

"What she was doing was altering the pH of the electrolyte by using a combination of sulfuric and hydrochloric acid. The ratios are critical, especially when using such thin membranes."

"Oh, of course, how could I have missed that."

"Sorry. Basically, it's the same stuff I was working with, but the percentages are almost opposite of what I was using."

"Okay..."

"Now I see why she went in this direction. I need to get back to work, but first, I need to get some supplies."

"Can you stay until Thursday, and we can go up together?"

In his excitement over the discovery, Seth was only focused on the steps he needed to take to resolve the issues he'd been stymied by for so long. Then he looked into Alice's hopeful eyes, and he melted. As impactful as his life's work might be, she had allowed him to feel loved again. He'd never take her for granted.

"That's a great idea, Alice. I'll spend tomorrow getting what I need around town; we can have dinner and go back to Whidbey right after your classes on Thursday. I may have to get a few things overnighted anyway."

Her misty eyes confirmed Seth's appropriate response. "What about dinner tonight?"

"How hungry are you?"

"Why?"

"I thought we could celebrate."

"How…oh…that way…well, hell yes! Food can wait."

FORTY-TWO

Alice and Seth went directly to the studio as soon as they got to the island.

"How long will it take to pull the components together?" Alice asked.

Seth was already clearing chemicals and jars off the lab table. "Some of these reagents require twenty-four hours to cure fully. I'll put those together first, then work on assembling the case. For this first one, I'm using a standard car battery case. If it works like I think it will, it'll be a simple thing to either reduce its size or scale it up. By tomorrow at this time, the assembly should be complete. Then I want to do a slow charge overnight, just to be on the safe side.

"If everything is still good, we'll check the discharge rate, bring it all the way down, and try a rapid charge for an hour."

"An hour?"

"If this works like I hope it will, an electric car using a battery like this will be able to charge in less than an hour and have a thousand-mile range."

"You're kidding..."

"Nope. It's not hyperbole, it's true. *If* it works."

"When will you let the folks at PNNL know?"

Seth considered for a moment before he spoke. "I'm not saying anything until I'm sure it works. Even then, I'll be careful. There will be a feeding frenzy by the big companies if word gets out. The battery makers, the oil companies, the automakers, the mining concerns—this technology can literally alter the direction of the planet. It's much too important for any one organization to control. I would think Uncle Sam will have a say in things as well."

"It's that big, huh?"

"Yup, and you're the reason we've made it this far. Fingers crossed for the next thirty-six hours."

With Alice's help, Seth worked well into the night. The reagents were formulated, finally, by meticulously following Sharon's specifications. After confirming there was no more to accomplish, they returned to the beach house and fell into bed, exhausted.

The next morning produced a rarity for early February in the Pacific Northwest. An actual sunrise. They slept in and awakened just as the sun rose over Mt. Pilchuck, bathing the morning sky in crimson.

"Incredible, Seth. I could live here."

"I'd like that too. When this chapter is over, maybe we can find a way to do it."

"Do you think we'll get sick of each other?"

"I suppose anything's possible. Like if I found out you were a serial killer or something."

"Well, what if you didn't find out?"

"I guess if you were quiet about it and I never found out, then no, I don't think I'd get sick of you."

"Whew, that's a relief. I'll be sure to keep my past a secret."

"Enough of this nonsense; let's get over to the studio and put the finishing touches on the battery case."

They assembled the battery's internal components by dinner, and by 8 p.m., it was on the charger.

FORTY-THREE

Seth texted us that he and Alice would be working odd hours in an effort to incorporate Sharon's formulas into his work as soon as possible. We checked on the studio early Friday morning and found everything in order. There had been considerable activity inside.

I called Seth just to touch base. "Looks like you're making headway in there."

"I think we're on the right track. We'll be back early afternoon to keep going and should be able to start charging this evening."

"Yikes, that's great news. Anything we can do?"

"You've been great, but I think it's up to me to get this over the finish line."

"We're here if you need anything; maybe we'll be by to say hi."

After making a half-dozen sandwiches, we took a six-pack from the fridge and headed to the studio at seven. We guessed correctly that Seth and Alice would still be there.

"Still at it, eh? We thought you'd like some refreshments."

"You're a lifesaver, Jenne," said Alice. "We're almost finished here, but I'm famished. And thirsty. Pass a Mirror Pond this way."

Seth was just finished turning on the charger. "I'll take one too, please. When we check on this in the morning, we'll have a good idea if it's going to perform."

The haphazard appearance of the prototype looked a little rudimentary, so I asked about it. "How come it looks like something I put together?"

After I got three looks of disapproval, Seth answered. "Kevin, it's not a real battery. It's a model, a one of a kind. In a real-world application, the cells would be closed, and you wouldn't see any of the electrodes or the electrolyte medium."

"Oh...yeah, that's what I thought. So we'll know tomorrow?"

"Probably. There are still lots of hoops to jump through, but we'll know if the charge holds, we'll know the discharge rate, and later in the day we'll know how well a rapid charge will perform."

We were almost as anxious as Seth was about the results of the initial charging, so we met him and Alice at the studio just after eight.

They had already connected a multimeter to the battery and measured the voltage. "Right now, with the overnight charge, it's measuring 4.2 volts," Seth explained.

"Is that good or bad?" I had no idea what any of the numbers meant.

"It's good. It's charged to its maximum voltage, so at least we know that part works."

"Now what?" Jenne had her elbows on the table, squinting to make out the tiny numbers on the measuring device. Alice was looking over her shoulder, trying to do the same.

"Now we use that discharger over there to see how rapidly the voltage will degrade."

He reached for something that looked like another battery, but it had clamps attached, like those on jumper cables.

"We'll set this to discharge at twice the voltage of the battery. Any more than that might damage the components. An existing lithium-ion battery will degrade to fifty percent capacity in four hours at the same rate. This should tell us a lot."

"So, what now, more waiting?" I felt more ownership in this experiment than I should have.

"We'll check in four hours. At least by then, we'll have some idea of what we have."

"I guess we'll head back home and take the dog for a walk," I said. "Do you two have plans? You're welcome to join us."

Alice glanced over at Seth and said, "We thought we'd take a drive. There are a couple of houses that just came on the market that we'd like to look at."

"You're looking? On the island?" The thought of new neighbors, especially ones Jenne was fond of, was too much to hope for.

"We're not entirely committed to it yet, but we thought we'd look around to see what's out there. If we did, there are lots of logistical issues to deal with, but we think looking is a good place to start." Seth, too, seemed intrigued by the idea.

"It's a bit of a seller's market now, but you never know; it's Whidbey after all." Memories of our difficulty in finding a home two years ago were still fresh in my mind.

"It's the first glance; we'll see what's out there. Will we see you here around two?"

"Wouldn't miss it."

After a walk on the beach and a bite to eat, we made our way back to the former Waffle property. The house hunters pulled in just ahead of us. We couldn't wait to see the results.

"Well, what's the verdict?" I waited only until Seth hooked up the multimeter to pop the question. He ignored me and continued to check the connections and tap the needle on the meter.

Finally, he answered. "According to this, only twenty percent of the charge has been depleted. That's incredible! Even the most advanced lithium batteries would be completely discharged over this period."

"That's good, right?"

"It's unbelievable. But we still have to take it down to at least ten percent. At this rate, it won't be until tomorrow morning."

"So, more waiting?" I asked.

"Yup. Nothing can be done until this baby is discharged. How about Alice and I take you to dinner tonight."

"You don't have to ask twice. Where and when?"

It was clear they had discussed the event earlier. Alice replied, "Our place. We were going to celebrate, but I think it's too early yet for that. Let's just call it a thank you for all you've done for us. We can talk about what we saw today too."

"What can we bring?" Jenne was always two steps ahead of me.

"Nothing, just the two of you."

Her reply left no room for discussion, and we agreed to see them in the evening.

By the time six o'clock rolled around, darkness was complete. The clear skies of the previous day had surrendered to the relentless drizzle and low fog that was too familiar this time of year.

We turned off Saratoga Road, went down the hill on Center Street, and hooked a left on Bells Beach Road. The quaint, shingle-style house was the last one, almost another half mile down the single-lane street.

Since most residents of this beach community were either in warmer climes or on the mainland working, the only lights were those peeking from the windows of the beach bungalow.

Getting out of the car after we pulled behind Seth's truck, we were struck by the extraordinary stillness the island offered. "This house reminds me of that painting by Russell Chatham, the one from the Northwest Suite," Jenne whispered, not wanting to spoil the moment.

I knew the one. It had been my favorite of all the artist's works. I whispered back, "Exactly." Then I kissed her on the forehead. "Let's see what the kids are up to."

The house was vintage Whidbey. Wide plank fir floors anchored white shiplap walls and ceilings. A bluestone fireplace dominated the eastern wall, flanked by double doors on each side; each would provide panoramic views of Saratoga Passage during daylight hours. Well-located lamps supplied warm, low-level lighting throughout, while a simple pine picnic table, illuminated with a dozen tealight candles, earned our attention.

Alice showed us to a welcoming loveseat, upholstered with khaki-colored canvas material. "Please have a seat and let me get you something to drink."

"Geez, Alice," I said, "how come we're being treated like royalty?"

"Things have been so hectic the last six weeks, we haven't taken the time to thank you properly. This is us doing that."

"We love helping out. There's no need for you to do this."

Seth walked in and handed us each a glass of wine. "We disagree. You have gone above and beyond what good friends do. Without you two, I guarantee I wouldn't be this far along with my research, and, more importantly, I never would have met this woman. Please accept our sincere thanks. We hope you'll always be in our lives."

Jenne spoke for both of us. "That's enough. You keep this shit up and I'll start leaking. But thank you. You mean a lot to us."

We toasted each other, then got down to the business of eating, drinking, and enjoying each other's company.

FORTY-FOUR

Jenne and I were up early the following day. The halibut piccata from the previous night was a fond, delectable memory. Alice and Seth were more than capable in the kitchen, and by the end of the evening, the more unsavory events of the recent past were forgotten.

During a lighter moment in the evening, we were anointed formal members of the research team, complete with a secret handshake, which we now implemented at the door to the studio.

"C'mon, Seth, get this door opened so we can see what we've got." I was as anxious as everyone else.

"We're down to ten percent; unbelievable that it took that long. Kevin, will you wheel that dolly with the charger on it over here? Now we see how fast we can get it up to fully charged. If we're lucky, we'll be able to do it in less than two hours."

We put the clamps on the battery, set the charge level, and sat down with the lattes that Alice was kind enough to bring.

"How will we know when we're fully charged?" I asked.

"There's a sensor that shuts the charger off when the battery's full so that it won't get damaged. It'll sound a buzzer when it shuts down."

We passed the time sharing stories of the early years with only occasional glances across the room at what might be a keystone in the fight against climate change. Alice entertained us with tales of her less than willing student-athletes and their struggles with the German language.

She was in the middle of a sentence when the buzzer sounded. All four of us were startled.

"How much time?" Seth was immediately in scientist mode.

I looked at my watch. "About forty-seven minutes."

"You're shitting me."

"No, I've got the same," said Jenne.

"Give me a second. Let me confirm with the multimeter." Seth went through the exercise of removing the rapid charger clamps, replacing them with the alligator clips of the meter.

"A hundred percent! In less than an hour. This is incredible."

"Does this mean it's a complete success?"

"I've got to do one more thing. We will use the discharger at the same rate we used after slow-charging the battery. Hopefully, the time to get to ten percent will be close to what we got from the overnight charge."

We set things up and agreed to meet at 8 p.m.

Back in the studio, after dark, was beginning to be a habit. After the same time on the discharger, the battery showed about 12 percent. Seth was ecstatic.

"We did it; we did it!" He grabbed Alice and hugged her tightly.

We were happy just to have witnessed the birth of what could be an entire industrial movement. Energy storage challenges in third-world countries could be resolved, and fossil fuels could finally take a back seat. The discovery was monumental.

"Congratulations, Seth," I said. "It's an unbelievable achievement."

"Thank Sharon. It's her work that made this possible."

"Where do you go from here?"

"I need to let the lab know what's happened. Then I'll build another model, a more polished version of this, suitable for presentation. While I'm putting that together, I'll collate all the notes and formulae and document the technical specifications. They'll need to be in a format that can be disseminated to the scientific community at large. The PNNL will take care of all the publicity and the timing of their announcement."

"This is a big deal, huh?" An understatement, but all I had in me at the moment.

Seth turned to me, deadly serious. "Kevin, this will change everything."

FORTY-FIVE

"Mike, we did it!"

It was Monday morning, precisely nine o'clock. Slattery had seen it was Seth Robbins calling, so he picked up.

"Did what?"

"The solid-state vanadium storage battery. It exceeds everything I thought was even possible. In six months, lithium-ion units will be an afterthought."

Slattery was a pencil pusher and rarely got excited about anything, but Seth's enthusiasm was infectious. "Seriously? You're sure?"

"Yes and yes. I've run it through all the tests. The only thing I can't do is test the efficacy over an extended period. But knowing the durability of the metals and the electrolyte makeup, I'm a hundred percent the unit will outlast conventional products by a factor of ten."

"Holy shit, you are serious."

"I am."

"Seth, this is fucking big."

"I know."

"Let me run this up to the top. The big dogs will shit themselves."

"I'm working on a more polished version to present to them. I should be ready with it and the documentation in ten days."

"That's fabulous." Slattery didn't know much about energy storage, but he had heard rumblings about vanadium alternatives and their possibilities. He couldn't wait to tell his brother-in-law.

"Let me get back to you after I talk to Whitely. This is gonna be good."

"Sure thing. I'm going back to work now. Thanks, Mike."

Slattery called Whitely's administrative assistant immediately after hanging up on Robbins. "Robin, it's Mike Slattery. Tell Jeremy I'm on my way up to see him."

"He's meeting with some industry reps right now, Mike. How about in an hour?"

"This can't wait. Interrupt him and tell him he'll want this news right away. I'll see you in a sec." Without waiting, he took the stairs two at a time on his way to the senior executive level.

Whitely offered apologies and ushered a man and two women from his office when Slattery arrived.

His face simmering with annoyance, he turned to his brother-in-law. "This better be good, Mike. Those people contribute a great deal to our funding efforts."

"It is, Jeremy, I promise."

After closing the door to his spacious workplace, Whitely crossed his arms and faced the twerp married to his sister. "Tell me what's so important that you had to interrupt."

"Robbins did it."

"What?" Whitely's confused look revealed that he hadn't the slightest idea what was coming next.

"He discovered a way to miniaturize a solid-state vanadium alloy storage battery. He already has a prototype."

Whitely, a highly educated scientist, was no dummy. Although his hands-on research years were in the rearview mirror, he still kept current on recent discoveries and hints of the same. He recalled one of Slattery's people was working on energy storage solutions and even remembered the vanadium angle.

"You're telling me it works?"

"Yes. He's run it through trickle and fast charges with equal discharge rates. He says the efficiency is off the charts. It's a game-changer." Even Slattery was caught up in the moment.

When his boss was quiet for a minute, Slattery wasn't exactly sure what was coming next. Whitely suddenly looked directly at him. "Mike, if this is true, it will dwarf anything we've ever done here. We'll need to vet this in every way possible to be certain. This cannot get into the public domain until we're confident it's reproducible. Right now, we're the only two people besides Robbins who know, correct?"

"As far as I know."

"Good. We need to keep it that way. I'll contact him myself regarding the next steps. Leave his contact information with Robin. And Mike?"

"Yeah?"

"Nice work on this. I know it hasn't always been roses between us, but good job. I mean it."

Slattery was shocked. Even Whitely was being nice to him. "Thanks, Jeremy, it means a lot."

After returning to his workstation, he considered what he should do to celebrate his newly elevated standing at the lab. It was either take his wife to dinner or try for a roll in the hay with Baker. It was not a difficult choice. He picked up the phone.

"Hi Nikki, you gonna be in the States anytime soon?" The compliment from his boss had supplied a generous boost to Slattery's ego.

"I don't think so, Mike."

"Oh, too bad. Some interesting developments going on here at the lab."

"And what would they be?"

"I can't say over the phone, but it's something that will likely change the world in many ways. It's big."

"Why will it interest me?"

"It has before, and I'll bet it will again."

"Maybe I can make it to Seattle tomorrow. Can you get up there?"

"No problem. I'll just tell the wife we have a meeting."

"Where should we meet?"

"Let's do the Four Seasons. We can have dinner and then see where that leads."

"Seems a bit over the top, doesn't it?"

"For some reason, I feel like splurging, and I've always wanted to try that place."

"It's your dime. See you there."

Like hell it was going to be his dime. Before he gave her the goods on the battery, he'd make her promise to pick up the tab. If word ever got out that a senior MDV executive staff member was using privileged information to advance her company, she'd be toast. He convinced himself that he held the high cards in this relationship.

FORTY-SIX

Nikki despised the little weasel, and she had a bad feeling about their meeting. He was almost giddy with her on the phone, something she hadn't seen before. She'd be pissed if he made her come to Seattle for nothing. But it *was* the Four Seasons.

They met in the lobby at six and headed straight for their table at the Goldfinch Tavern. The Ethan Stowell gem had been open for six years and had won every available culinary award. And it was expensive.

"To what do I owe the pleasure of dining here, Mike?"

"I thought it would be nice to celebrate."

"Celebrate what?"

"Well...I'm not supposed to say anything, but we've had a breakthrough achievement at the lab, and I think the information should help your company."

"What is it?"

"I think I'd rather wait until, you know...after."

Right now, she felt like throttling the little fucker, but whatever it was could wait a little longer. No sense in pissing him off if he had information she could use.

They finished a sumptuous dinner, complete with two bottles of magnificent Sea Smoke pinot noir from Santa Rita Hills, and proceeded to the two-room suite Slattery had reserved.

Slattery had drunk the lion's share of the pinot and appeared somewhat tipsy while negotiating the corridor. Nikki had been careful not to over imbibe.

She waited until they made themselves comfortable in the suite's modern yet comfortable loveseat before she got down to business. "Mike, tell me what you got me here for before we, you know, go in the bedroom."

Slattery sat there with a shit-eating grin on his face, looking like the cat who ate the canary. "You're gonna like it."

"What? Stop jerking my chain and tell me."

"Okay…okay. You remember that guy who was working on the vanadium thingy?"

"What about him?"

"Well…he did it."

"Did what?"

"He figured out how to make the goddamn battery. He fucking did it, and it works. It works really fucking good, too."

Nikki was having trouble breathing. It couldn't be. Those goons burned his place down with all the notes.

She caught him by the shoulders and turned him to face her. "How is this possible?"

"Dunno. He's smart. He did it. I thought you'd be happy; your company could use the info to be first in line for it."

Before she completely lost it, she needed more information. "Is it public yet?"

"Nah, gotta wait a couple weeks before they announce. Need to get another model made, pull the publicity together, yadda, yadda…"

"Is he back in Richland?"

"Nope. Same island he was on…"

"What island?" *How could he still be on Whidbey after they burned his house?*

"Hibdeydoo, same one."

"Whidbey?"

"Yup, that's it. How do you know?"

She ignored him and tried to figure out what to do, where to turn. One thing was sure; she'd have to contact Rhodes again. If the fucker had taken her money without taking care of business, then heads would roll.

Slattery said she had a week, maybe longer, to make something happen. It was going to be close.

"I'm leaving. I need to get back." She stood and went for her bag.

"No, no, wait…you can't. We have to go to the next room, you know, to celebrate."

"You go to the next room. I'm leaving."

"Well...you gotta pay for things on the way out."

"You're dreaming, asshole. You pay."

"If you don't, I'll tell people we were screwing around, and you'll get in trouble."

"Listen to me." She grabbed his shirt under his neck and shook him mercilessly, his head resembling a vintage Ichiro bobblehead.

"I have a pile of shit to deal with, and, no, this great news of yours does me absolutely no good. It's terrible. If you so much as hint at trying to blackmail me, I will tell the fucking world that you've revealed privileged information. You'll be in jail in a New York minute.

"Now get your scrawny little ferret-like ass downstairs and pay for this shit. I'm never seeing you again. If you even think of calling me, I will personally show up and bury your balls so deep, you'll be choking on them. Got it?"

"Um...yes. Sorry..."

"You're fucking disgusting."

With this final declaration, Nikki Baker slammed the door on the beautiful Four Seasons executive suite. She had arrangements to make.

Forty-seven

As soon as Baker left the hotel, she headed north on I5. It was at least three hours until she got back to Vancouver, and she was damn well going to kick some ass between now and then. If news of the vanadium success got out, her shares would be worth pennies on the dollar.

That stupid little ass-wipe thought he was doing her a favor with the news. On top of it all, he thought he could blackmail her into paying for everything. If she never saw the prick again, it would be too soon. *God-damn,* she thought, *I can't believe I let the slimebag even touch me. Yeech!*

She called the number for Rhodes immediately after the traffic started thinning out, just on the north side of Everett.

"Yeah?"

"This Rhodes?"

"Who wants to know?"

"I do, you inept motherfucker. You told me you took care of that issue on Whidbey Island, and now I find out that the son of a bitch has finished his work and is going public with it in a week. Talk to me."

"You can check the news; we burned the place to the ground. We even saw all his papers in there."

"You missed something. He's still around, and unless we find a way to stop the announcement, I'm screwed."

"We?"

"Yes, we, you asshat. I paid you for a job, and it's not finished. Get your little buddy and get your ass back to that island to finish what you were supposed to do. And do it yesterday; there's not much time."

"We did what you told us to do. I disagree that it's my fault it didn't work. You'll need to pay us again."

Nikki was livid. She'd already forked over 100K, and still, this Robbins was making her life miserable. Now her hired goons were bending her over. She bit her lip, not wanting to run off her only dog in the show. "What do you have in mind?"

"Exactly what do you want us to do?"

"Get rid of Robbins. Get rid of him and his stupid invention and every last scrap of paper he has. Is that clear enough?"

"Yup, and it's gonna cost you a hundred grand, half up front. There's a lot of risk involved."

She couldn't believe she'd have to do this again. "Here's my offer; I'll give you forty immediately and the balance when the job is complete. We're both at risk here, and if I stiff you, you can always turn me in." She figured this way, if they weren't successful, she'd at least save sixty grand.

Rhodes seemed to be considering the arrangement. "How do you want us to do it?"

"Any way you want. An accident is best, but I'll take a complete disappearance too. Just get it done."

"You've still got my bank info?"

"Yes. It'll be done by tomorrow morning. I'll get this handled."

She disconnected. Part of her wished she could short her position with the stock she owned, but the securities regulators frowned upon the practice for obvious reasons. Her only option now was to make sure Robbins and his work never saw the light of day.

FORTY-EIGHT

"Smitty, guess what?" Rhodes was on the phone to his cohort as soon as Baker was off the line.

"What is it?"

"That Baker broad wants to give us more money. How would you like another thirty grand?"

"What do we gotta do?"

"I guess the fire didn't do the job. Now she wants us to get rid of the guy along with his work."

"We gotta *kill* him?"

"That's what she said, but I think we can convince him by threatening bodily harm instead."

"That's good, Randy, I can handle that, but my momma frowned upon taking another's life."

Rhodes was shocked by his accomplice's admission and too embarrassed to admit the same.

"That's good to know, Smitty."

"Where is he now?"

"I'm not sure, but she says he's still on the island somewhere."

"How do we find him?"

"Good question. I'll meet you in the long-term parking in Mukilteo, and we can hop right on the boat. We'll come up with a plan on the way. Let's take your rig over; it fits in better."

FORTY-NINE

Without much to do but hang around the house, I grew antsy. Although Northwest golfers pride themselves on playing in rain and cold temperatures, the weather was colder than usual, and playing on frozen greens wasn't an option for me.

I called my good friend and tormenter, Bill, to cancel our date to play. I also wanted to hear what he'd learned from Agent Steele. "Hey, Bill, too cold today, right?"

"Yup. I've got a pile of paperwork here to get through, too, so let's bag it."

"Good with me. Hear anything from Matt?"

"I knew you'd go there. Can't seem to keep your grubby little hands off the case, can you?"

"Um, no, I guess not. What have you heard?"

"They picked up this Johnston in Las Vegas. Balducci told them where he was. They think with the information they're getting from him, they'll have enough to close down the Fuscos, the couple who own the outfit."

"How big is it?"

"Big. They have another guy in Texas and one on the West Coast. Johnston did more business than the other two, but the Fibbies have also picked them up. This thing is unbelievable."

"Does that mean that Robbins is safe?"

"I'm not sure. Johnston says he hired someone to handle it, but he lost track of him. He thinks the client may have gone directly to the operator."

"Do we know who the client is?"

"It's someone from MDV out of Vancouver, B.C."

"Huh, why?"

"They haven't gotten that far yet. They've alerted the RCMP to the situation, so they're aware."

"Did they get the name of the fellow Johnston hired after Balducci?"

"They did. The name is Randy Rhodes. He's been on the street for over two years now, and, as far as we know, he's kept his nose clean. Last known address is in Tacoma. They're gonna try to find him tomorrow and ask him some questions."

"Sheesh, this thing has tentacles all over the country."

"Well, most of it."

"Do we think Rhodes is the one who burned the house?"

"It makes sense, but there's no way to prove anything. Our best bet is to get the client to tell us what's going on or, somehow, catch Rhodes before he does anything."

"How did Rhodes know where Robbins was?"

Owens was quiet for a moment. "I don't know. I hadn't thought about it."

"Whoever is pulling the strings knows where Robbins is. They knew he was in Northport; they knew about Sharon's house and what progress Robbins was making. How is that possible?"

"It pisses me off when you start to make sense. I'll get back to Matt. Someone has been feeding the locations to Johnston."

"If the goal is to put a stop to the research that Robbins is doing and they know where he is, then they'll know he's succeeded."

"What? What do you mean?"

"I'm sworn to secrecy, Bill. But Seth has come up with an energy storage unit that is going to revolutionize the industrial world."

"Come on, that's bullshit. There's nothing that can do that."

"I'm being serious, Bill. This thing is bigger than the internal combustion engine. I wish I could share, but I can't. The breakthrough came a few days ago, and it will be announced soon after the PNNL gives its blessing."

"If it's as big as you say, it doesn't surprise me that people who are happy with the status quo would try to stop it. I'd tell Seth to be very careful until we can find Rhodes or, maybe more importantly, find out where the intel is coming from."

"Let me know if Matt hears anything more, will you?"

Fifty

After I chatted with Owens, Jenne and I stopped by the studio to see how Seth was progressing and, more importantly, fill him in on the investigations. Alice was back in school until Thursday.

"Looks like the new, improved model is shaping up." I offered.

"That was the easy part," said Seth. "All I had to do was duplicate the first one and put a cover over the cells. It's essentially the same as the prototype with a better paint job and a plastic cover on the top."

"So, are you ready to go public on this?" Jenne couldn't wait to see the reaction when the discovery was announced.

"Not yet. I still need to go over all the documentation and calculations. That stuff has to be buttoned down tighter than a gnat's ass. Jeremy Whitely, who oversees every project, called me after talking to Slattery.

"He wanted to emphasize that when the community at large begins reviewing it, if just one comma is out of line, they'll pounce on it. That period can be brutal at times, but it's necessary. Unless the data can withstand the scrutiny, it'll be considered a failure. Nobody wants a process or product that can't be duplicated. Those were his exact words."

"But you've already done that, right?" Jenne asked.

"Yes, and that's why I'm not overly concerned. Still, the reports need to be perfect to avoid even token questioning of the results."

"Got it. We'll get out of your hair, but Bill is still concerned that whoever is behind the attacks may not give up. I'll touch base with Willkie and ask him to check in with you from time to time. I'm certain Matt Steele has kept him in the loop."

"That's a little disconcerting, but thanks for talking to Roger. Alice will be back the day after tomorrow, and with her help, I should be able to wrap things up by Sunday night or Monday."

"That's terrific. I think the sooner this is public, the safer you'll be."

Seth saw us out to my truck. Jenne got in the passenger side, and as I turned to get in, Emma stuck her moist snout in my face. *Shit, why not?*

"Hey, Seth, how would you like to take care of Emma for a few days?"

"I don't know, Kev; I'm pretty busy." He looked at me, confusion on his face as well as Jenne's.

"Let me say it another way. Hey, Seth, how would you like Emma to take care of *you* for a few days?"

As soon as it dawned on Jenne, she was all in. "Yes, absolutely. You two get along great, and she'll know if anyone even gets near the place."

"Well, I planned on sleeping here the next two nights, and having her around will be reassuring. Sure, if it's okay with you, I'd love it."

I opened the rear door. "Emma, out. Girl, out." She dutifully hopped down from the truck and walked over to Seth. "You'll need to keep her inside until we're gone so she won't run after us."

"I'll come back with her bed and food. When she knows we haven't abandoned her, she'll feel more secure." Jenne always looked out for her girl.

"Thanks, guys; I appreciate it."

FIFTY-ONE

Rhodes and his extra-large sidekick arrived late the next morning at the Clinton ferry dock, still without a plan. Now that they were to intimidate the man physically, the element of surprise was hardly necessary. First, though, they had to determine where Robbins was.

Smitty, with his ever-present grin intact, suggested the obvious. "Let's drive by where we burned the house down."

"Great idea, Smitty, let's." Rhodes had nothing, so what the hell.

They headed north on Saratoga for five miles. As they approached the drive that led to the house they had burned, a black Honda Ridgeline emerged from the tree line.

"Keep going, Smitty. Don't slow down."

"Who was that?"

"I don't know, but a better question is what were they doing, and why even go in there when there's no house? Turn around, Smitty. We need to go somewhere and develop a plan."

"How about that donut place?"

"What place is that?"

"The one everyone at the hotel talked about last time we were here."

"You remember *that*?"

"They're supposed to be really, really good donuts, Randy."

"Sure, what the fuck? It's as good as anyplace."

They drove to Bayview, less a town than an intersection on South Whidbey. A dilapidated two-story structure, sitting on the corner of Bayview Road and Marshview Avenue, is the home of Whidbey Donuts, known far and wide for their delectable, deep-fried dough. It is also a local gathering place for neighborhood gossip.

The eclectic mix of homemade furniture and antique accents scattered about several smaller rooms gave the shop a 1960s hippie ambiance. Smitty ordered a half dozen of the scrumptious delights, each one a different flavor, and immediately started putting them away.

"How can you eat like that, Smitty?"

"Like what?"

"Like it's your last meal on the planet."

"These things are incredible, Randy. You should have one too."

Rather than humor his large companion, he pulled out his Galaxy Note 8 and went to work.

He went to the Island County website and immediately pulled up the interactive map tab. The satellite imagery on the maps was uncannily accurate and showed the individual tax parcels on the island.

After zeroing in on the property just off Saratoga Road, he enlarged the image to see the land parcel boundaries of the house they had destroyed.

"Take a look at this, Smitty. The property is a lot bigger than I thought. And look here, way in the back, there's a small building that we didn't even know was there."

"So you think maybe we burned the wrong building, and that's where he's doing his work?"

"Yeah, that's what I think."

"How do you wanna do this?"

"I say we wait until after dark, and then we visit Robbins. Since we need to have some face-time, we don't care if he hears us. We only care if the other people in the neighborhood can see us."

"What are we gonna do for the rest of the day?"

"Well, we could sit here all day feeding your face, or we could go back to that little town and see what's going on."

Smitty looked mildly depressed, as if the former choice was the better of the two; the stern look from his partner, however, encouraged him to check out the local scene.

They spent the remainder of the day wandering around the tiny hamlet of Langley, somehow managing to blend in with the surprisingly large crowd of tourists.

At just before 5:00 p.m., when the sun had dipped below the western horizon, the two felons made their way back to the former Waffle property. As they turned onto the narrow gravel driveway, they could see a very faint light shining through the trees, far beyond the remaining scars of the burned cottage.

Rhodes, doing the driving, switched the lights off and proceeded deliberately but with caution. When they arrived at the charred concrete pad, he switched off the ignition.

"I don't see any other way back there but to walk, Smitty. Are you packing?"

"Are you kidding?"

"Okay, just checking."

They managed to get about fifty feet beyond the clearing when Smitty made the unfortunate mistake of placing his right foot squarely on top of a two-inch fir limb that had fallen from a nearby tree. The thunderous snap of the branch echoed through the stillness of the night. And then the shit hit the fan.

FIFTY-TWO

Emma was curled up on her bed while Seth pored over his calculations. She was restless at first, but she calmed down after he fed her, and went to sleep. He hated to admit it, but it felt good having her with him. He remembered growing up with these dogs and had forgotten how devoted they could be. When he and Alice settled down, he was sure that a GSD would find its way to their home.

He was so immersed in his work that he forgot that Jenne told him Emma needed to go out after eating. Knowing that she could be confused because of the unfamiliar location, he put her on a leash.

As soon as he opened the door, Emma went on alert. Her ears perked up, and she held her nose high in the air. Something was not as it should have been. A loud crack penetrated the silence of the heavily wooded property, followed by a faint "Ah fuck."

The two-inch leather leash was strong, but Emma was stronger. Something had to give, and in this instance, it was Seth's grip. The snapping of the fir bough was loud, but the barking and snarling of the German shepherd filled the night air. She bolted toward the sound, crashing through the brush without feeling a thing; it was her job, after all.

FIFTY-THREE

"Ah fuck."

Rhodes cringed at the sound. Gone was any hope of concealment.

The next sound they heard was either a pack of wolves or an unbelievably angry German shepherd. Smitty may have been a big strong football player with a perpetual grin, but now it was missing. When he was a child, he had been nipped by one of the neighborhood dogs, and he had never forgotten it. He was afraid of them, didn't like them, and was especially terrified of police dogs. He couldn't be sure what specific creature this was, but there was no fucking way he was hanging around to find out. He turned and bolted.

"Smitty, get your fat ass back here."

"No way, no way. I'm not gonna let that dog bite me."

"Come on, you big pussy. It's just a dog. We can shoot it."

"You shoot it. I'm going back to the truck."

"Ah shit." *So much for a clean operation.*

With no other choice, Rhodes turned and ran back to the truck as well. Smitty was already behind the wheel with the engine running. As soon as the passenger door slammed, he spun the tires and sped down the driveway. The big guy was doing fifty by the time he reached Saratoga Road.

"Slow down, Smitty; the last thing we need is to have one of the local cops pick us up."

"I'm not a dog person, Randy."

"Really?"

"They scare me."

"You don't say?"

"I mean it."

"Yes, I gathered that, Smitty. It looks as though we are going to have to come up with another plan." Rhodes busied himself by glaring out the window, mulling over what to do next and where to spend the night.

Fifty-four

Emma made it to the end of the driveway before she stopped, and Seth finally caught up with her. The dust from the big truck had not yet settled, and he could still see the faint red glow of the taillights as it tore down the road.

"Emma, it's okay, girl, come." Still alert but somewhat quieter, she dutifully came to his side. He immediately called the number for Roger Willkie to report the incident and followed that with a phone call to the O'Malley residence.

"I told Roger everything, Kevin, and he said he'd stop by right away. I'm not sure what good it'll do, but at least I'll be able to tell him what I saw."

"Jenne and I will be there in a few, Seth."

While he waited for Kevin and Jenne, he returned to his work. If someone was still after him, then it was more urgent than ever that he get his submittals done quickly. Emma sat by the door, still on watch.

FIFTY-FIVE

It took us five minutes to get to the studio, where Emma was standing vigilant. Her olfactory prowess, honed through tens of thousands of years of evolution, identified us as family before we got to the door. As soon as we opened it, she jumped up and squealed with joy.

"Tell us what happened," I said.

Seth related the brief encounter and Emma's part in chasing off the intruders. "I'm not sure what would have happened if she wasn't here; she's a hero."

Before I could respond, we heard another vehicle pull into the clearing. The strobe lights told us who it was.

"This place is never out of the news for long; what gives, Kevin?"

"Thanks for coming, Roger. It seems Seth had visitors, and Emma ran them off."

"Could it have been something innocent?"

"I don't think so. Even though I couldn't see much, the truck seemed the same size as the one that stopped by the other day looking for a fake address. I heard two doors slam, so there had to be two of them."

"There's not much I can do here. I'll look around outside right now to see if there's anything obvious, and I'll return tomorrow when it's daylight. I doubt they'll be back tonight, but it's probably a good idea to have Emma stay."

We all nodded as the deputy left.

"Are you still spending the night here, Seth?" Jenne's concern was obvious.

"I think it's more important than ever, now. Will it be okay with you if Emma stays?"

"Of course," we said simultaneously.

We started to leave when Willkie walked into the light supplied by the jelly jar sconce to the side of the door. A large section of a cracked limb from a nearby Douglas fir was in his hands.

"Look what I found. It's fresh, and judging by its thickness, whoever stepped on this was a very heavy man. Something to keep in mind."

"One of the men that stopped the other day looked like an offensive lineman. Had a funny smile on his face the whole time. He gave me the creeps."

"That helps. Now we know we're looking for two men who aren't locals, and one of 'em's huge. Do you remember the other one?"

"Not too much; he was average. But he did seem to be the one in charge. The one with the smile was constantly looking at him."

"Okay, one big and one average. Do you think you could come up with a picture if you worked with a sketch artist?"

"I only saw them for a few seconds, so I doubt if I could be of much help."

"No worries. I'll be back tomorrow; in the meantime, if something strikes you, call me."

"Will do, Roger, and thanks."

Fifty-six

The Saratoga Inn was full, so Rhodes and Smitty ended up at a clean but austere motel in Freeland, a half-dozen miles from their quarry.

"Seems like every time we try to put a stop to Robbins, something gets in the way."

"What next?"

"I don't know, Smitty. It's so hard to tail someone on this island. There's no place to hide and so few people that we stick out like a sore thumb."

"Maybe we should ditch the truck and get your car."

Rhodes wondered if a being with moderate intelligence had taken over the body of his partner. "Good idea. We'll take the ferry over in the morning and switch vehicles. At least mine will blend in better."

Arriving back on Whidbey, now driving the Audi, the two miscreants pulled into the Star Store parking lot just before noon.

"Why here, Randy?"

"This seems to be where all the locals shop. If Robbins wants to eat, he has to buy food. They have a big supermarket north of here, but I remember the lady at the Saratoga saying this is where most people who live here come."

"So we just wait?"

"You got any better ideas? At least your big rig won't stick out."

"This car's kinda cramped." The sedan was badly listing to the passenger side, so much so that Rhodes was fearful the shocks might fail. Smitty's prodigious stomach was nearly touching the dash.

"Push your seat back."

"I did; that's as far as it goes."

"This is probably not the right time to bring this up, but have you ever tried to lose weight?"

"Um, no."

"Why?"

"Dunno. Never thought about it."

"Maybe you should think about it; lay off the donuts a little."

"Will that help?"

"Yes, Smitty, it will. When we're finished with this, I'll find you a diet that will help you lose weight."

He looked over at Rhodes with sincere gratitude, his smile even wider. "Geez, thanks, Randy, you're a good friend."

What Rhodes hoped was that they could get Robbins alone, without the damn dog. His extra-large copilot would be useless unless that happened.

Fifty-seven

We slept a little later than usual after the excitement at the studio the previous night, and before we headed down to see Seth and Emma, we managed to scarf down a bowl of oatmeal.

"There's a couple of IPOs I wanted to look at quickly before we go, Kev."

I was sure *Jenne* knew what she was talking about; at least one of us did.

"Sure thing, hon, see you outside in ten."

I scraped away the frost that had coated the windshield from the unseasonably cold night and had the truck warmed up nicely when Jenne climbed in.

"Seems weird without Emma in the back, doesn't it?" Jenne was already missing her pal.

"It does. I'm glad she was there last night, though."

"You think they'll find these two?"

"Maybe. I'd rather they get the one who's calling the shots on this. Somebody tells the bad guys where Seth is and how to get to him. That's the person we need to find."

"How?"

"Maybe Seth knows but doesn't know he knows."

"Huh?"

"Somehow, someone's getting information on his whereabouts. There can't be very many people who know where he is, and my guess is it's coming from his employer."

"The lab?"

"They're the only ones who know where he is. It's gotta be."

We pulled into the clearing and walked the path to the studio. Jenne had thought to bring a thermos of coffee and an egg sandwich.

"Morning, Seth."

The words were barely out of my mouth when our furry friend pounced upon me. It was like we had been gone months, not hours.

"I take it no further activity last night?"

"Correct. I still was tossing all night on the cot, but having Emma here was a comfort. Thanks for breakfast, Jenne."

"No worries. Kevin has a theory,"

Seth looked over at me quizzically. "What, Kev?"

"I've been thinking…who, besides Alice, knows where you are?"

"Well…you two, of course, Willkie and your cop friend and the FBI, and I think that's it."

"Nobody at the PNNL?"

"Well, sure. They send me my paycheck, so HR knows."

"No one else?"

"No one except Mike Slattery; he's who I report to."

Neither I nor Jenne said anything.

"You don't think he's involved, do you?"

"What I know for sure is that we haven't told a soul, and I'll bet neither has your girlfriend. That leaves the local cops, my buddy, and the FBI, and I'll bet a load of money that they haven't leaked anything. That only leaves one other person."

"But why? He looks good if I succeed, as does the entire lab. He's got no reason to leak."

"I'll bet if we look hard enough, we'll find something."

"Alice will be here this afternoon, so I plan on taking this paperwork back to the beach house. Do you think it makes sense for me to store the model somewhere?"

"I do. Let us take it; we can keep it out in the storage shed. We're not as isolated as this place is, and Emma will make sure nobody screws with anything.

In the meantime, I'll pass along our conversation to Bill and the FBI. I'm guessing they have ways to see if your boss has any skeletons in his closet."

Fifty-eight

After we got back to the house, I gave Bill Owens a call. As usual, he was thrilled to hear from me.

"Inspector Clouseau, how nice to hear from you."

"Good one, Bill, you haven't used that one before. Nicely done."

"Thanks, I've been saving it. You sorta, kinda remind me of him, you know, without the charm and the French accent. To what do I owe the pleasure?"

"I've been thinking…"

"No, not that again."

"If you'll stop the sniping for a minute, I'll help you and the FBI crack this case."

"Oh boy, I can't wait."

"Stop it. Now listen for a minute. We had another attempt on Seth last night."

"I know, Willkie filled me in, and I passed it on to Matt."

"Good to hear. We just came from there, and finally, we think we know who is passing Seth's location along."

"And that would be?"

"Mike Slattery. His boss."

"Why would he do that?"

"We can't figure that one out, but he's the only possible leak. No one else knows his location, just law enforcement and us and his girlfriend."

"Do we know that Slattery knows where he is?"

"We do; he does."

"Well shit."

"Yes, exactly."

"You could be right."

"I think we are. Is there some way we can find out why he would?"

"I can't, but I'm pretty sure Matt Steele can. With a proper subpoena, the Feds can search his cell phone records. I'll call Matt and get back to you. And Kevin?"

"Yeah?"

"They picked up the Fuscos and two others. They've closed them down. Johnston's cut a deal and will testify. The only outstanding contract is the one on Robbins. Be careful up there."

"Thanks for your help, Bill, we will."

We headed into Langley to pick up a few groceries and drop off several returns to Amazon. It seemed like we were constantly dropping off returns to Amazon. I wondered, to myself, of course, if it were possible to have more returns than orders. It sure seemed like it.

"Stop, Kevin."

"Why, what's wrong?" Whenever Jenne shouted that way, I thought I was about to hit something.

"Nothing. I thought we should check with Seth, see if he needs anything from town."

Knowing better than to suggest a less startling way of asking me to detour, I made the turn into the drive just as Seth was getting into his truck.

"Seth, where are you headed?"

"Since Alice is coming later today, I need to stop by the Star Store to pick up stuff for dinner."

"Great minds. Jenne ordered me to stop to see if you needed us to pick up anything."

"Thanks for thinking of me. I need to resupply the beach house, though, so I guess I'll just see you there. Say, I hate to ask, but would you mind picking up the new model and bringing it with you? I'd feel better keeping it at the Bells Beach house. I'll be working there over the next several days, and I may need it for reference, maybe some pictures for the report."

"Sure, no problem. See you in town."

We retraced our route back to the house and put the twelve-inch cube in the back of the truck. The thought of transporting an item capable of transforming human civilization in my truck, on a country road, on an island, in the middle of Puget Sound injected a dose of reality into my musings. "Jenne, this thing we're carrying is going to change everything. Can you imagine?"

"I've been thinking about that. And about the selfishness of whoever is trying to stop this thing. What would it take for a person to deprive the world of this technology?"

"I don't know, but I think people and companies and governments have had selfish motives in the past and will continue to do so. Even though our contribution has been small, I'm glad we got to help. Now, all we need to do is to get this over the finish line."

We pulled into the back lot of the Star Store and took the space adjacent to Seth's truck. "I guess he's inside. We'll make the exchange when we're both finished."

Neither of us noticed the blue Audi parked on the side of the road. Had we, we would have thought it peculiar to see such a large man stuffed into the bucket seat of the mid-sized sedan.

Fifty-nine

"Is that the truck, Randy?"

Rhodes had nodded off, the steeply angled rays of the winter sun finally warming the car's interior.

"It is. Where's Robbins?"

"He went inside while you were dozing."

"It was just a catnap, Smitty. Why didn't you wake me?"

"I thought you needed sleep. If he started to leave, I would have."

Rhodes let it drop. The thought of Smitty being considerate was another marvel.

"How long has he been in the store?"

"About ten minutes. The truck next to them just got there too. A couple."

"Let's just worry about Robbins, okay?"

Nothing was said for the next twenty minutes when they saw the scientist exit the store carrying several bags. He loaded them on the passenger side of the vehicle, then went to the rear, lowered his tailgate, and sat on it.

"What's he doing?"

"Looks like he's waiting for something."

"What?"

"Smitty, I don't know. Let's just watch."

After only a few minutes, the couple returned to their truck, each carrying a grocery bag. Robbins greeted them and held the bag for the man, who turned to open the tailgate of the Ridgeline.

"They know each other, Randy."

"Yes, they do."

Robbins reached into the bed of the Ridgeline and lifted what appeared to be a heavy plastic box. He placed it into the Chevy pickup, raised the tailgate, and began chatting with the couple as they put their groceries inside the Honda.

"Fuck me."

"What is it, Randy?"

"We've got a problem. It seems as though Robbins isn't the only one we've got to worry about."

"Huh?"

"This other couple, they're in on it too. I think they were holding the battery for Robbins. Remember Baker telling us something about vanadium and batteries?"

"Um, sure, I guess so."

"Maybe Baker doesn't even know about them. This job's gotten much more complicated."

"What do we do?"

"I don't know. It's not like we can commit mass murder. We never signed up for that. A little arson, maybe some threats and robbery here and there, but no fucking way we're doing the rough stuff."

Smitty was bobbing his head ferociously. "Yes, for sure. My momma would kill me if I did."

Ignoring the inconsistency in his partner's statement, Rhodes continued. "We need to get more information. Robbins lives in the little building in the woods; we know that. These other people, though, they're unknowns. Let's follow them and see what we need to do. I think Baker isn't aware of how big a shitshow this is."

When Robbins took off first, they let him go. They knew where to find him. The black Ridgeline pulled out within minutes, the Audi a hundred yards or so behind.

"It looks like they're going back the same way to Robbins's house, Randy."

"There are not that many roads here, Smitty, and the island is narrow. Everybody goes the same way. After a while, they'll branch off, you'll see."

Ten minutes later, they drove by the entrance to the property where the killer dog lived. "Randy, it's the same place."

"No, they're still going."

After another mile, the pickup took a right on Little Dirt Road, a narrow, gravel-packed two-track that looked like something from rural Ireland. Rhodes drove by and stopped after several hundred yards.

"You're not gonna follow?"

"Not now; if they're the only house on the road, they'll make us. Let's go back to the donut shop."

Smitty's face lit up, then dimmed a degree. "I thought they were bad for me, Randy."

"Too many are. You can have one and some coffee. We need to see what's down that road and who those people are."

Mid-afternoon in February, during the week, at Whidbey Donuts was a slow time. With only two of the booths filled, Rhodes thought it best to get their order to go and sit in the ample parking area while availing themselves of the establishment's Wi-Fi.

Again using the county's website, he located Little Dirt Road.

"It's a funny name, huh, Randy?"

"That it is, but it's a funny little island too. Take a look at what's here."

"There are only three places there."

"Correct, and if we click on this little thingy here, we can see who pays taxes on the place. Looks like the name is O'Malley."

"Hey, Randy, who pays taxes on the place where the dog chased us?"

Rhodes hadn't thought about that since all they cared about was where Robbins was. He humored his buddy by checking.

"Holy shit. It's O'Malley. They own that property as well. Maybe they're running the show."

"Um, Randy?"

"Yes?"

"I'm getting a headache trying to figure this out. There are too many pieces to this."

Rhodes had to smile; he felt the same way. "Let's do this, Smitty. We'll go back to the motel, spend the night, and see if we can come up with a plan. If we don't, we say fuck it, keep what we've got already, and let Baker handle this shit on her own. I hate the bitch, anyway."

Smitty popped what was left of a glazed confection into his ginormous pie-hole and washed it down with coffee before answering. "Can we go back to the fancy place?"

"If the Saratoga Inn has a vacancy, yes, we can."

Sixty

" Kev, while you were talking to him in the store, did Seth say how much more he had to do on the report?"

"He thought he'd have it wrapped up by Monday."

"That's a relief. Maybe when that's done, things will settle down."

"I'm sure they will. We only have to get through the weekend."

I was cleaning up the outdoor grill when my cell phone buzzed. The phone ID let me know it was my friend and confidant, Bill Owens. I could choose to continue scraping the grease and grime from the grates or answer the phone. Easy choice.

"Hey, buddy, what's new?"

"Don't be an asshole with all the friendly shit," Owens said.

"You don't miss me?"

"Shut up and listen. As much as it pains me to say, you were right about Robbins's boss. The guy's been screwing some woman from MDV in Vancouver. We don't know everything, but Matt Steele's got enough from the phone records to bring the doofus in for questioning."

"Great, when is that going to happen?"

"It should be happening as we speak. The one teeny problem is that she's a Canadian citizen, and if the FBI wants to move on her, they need the blessings of the authorities in British Columbia."

"So, is that a problem?"

"Not normally. Unfortunately, last September, an agent from Spokane attempted to apprehend a suspect up in Kelowna without contacting the RCMP. They're still pissed about it, and they could be dicks about Matt going to Vancouver."

"Where does that leave us?"

"Even though Feebs can't waltz up there and bring her to the States for trial, the Mounties will make a note of it and will keep tabs on the woman."

"That means whoever is after Robbins is still on the job, right?"

"It seems so. Be alert up there and don't do anything stupid, although I'm confident you'll step in it once again. Later."

Jenne had taken over the grill scrubbing while I was on the phone, so I pretended to sit there thinking about important issues. Cleaning the grill was a messy job, and it was one of the few household chores I was allowed to do. Apparently, my vacuuming, dusting, and tile-cleaning skills were subpar, and I intended to keep it that way.

"Do you think if you sit there with your hands over your face, I'll think you are doing something important?"

"Oh, I uh…I was trying to figure something out."

"Yes, I'm sure you were. How about getting your ass over here and finishing what you started?"

Almost nine years into our wedded bliss, and I still hadn't learned how to pull one over on her. But it wasn't for lack of trying. "Sure thing, hon, you can go back to what you were doing. I'll finish up here." Her pursed lips and smart-ass eyeroll did wonders to lighten my spirits.

I finished by polishing up the stainless steel hood on the grill and then stood back to admire my work. If that didn't deserve a nice cold Bodhizafa, then nothing did. On my way to the fridge, my phone buzzed. It was my sensei once again.

"Well, hi, Detective Owens. Twice in one day, my, my…"

"Please stop being annoying. I know it's difficult for you, maybe even impossible, but just this once, give it an honest try."

"Sheesh, touchy, touchy lawman. Okay, this is me trying. Hi Bill, to what do I owe the pleasure?"

"God, you're insufferable."

"Yes, thanks. Now, what's up?"

"After further questioning of Johnston, they think whoever is after Robbins is dealing directly with the MDV woman."

"Do we have any idea why this woman, if it *is* her, has a hard-on for Robbins? I mean, what's her beef with the guy?"

"Based upon what we've learned from the attacks, she cares less about Robbins than she does about whatever he's working on. She seriously wants it to end, and if getting rid of him is what it takes, Steele thinks she will."

"And so far, we don't know why."

"Correct."

"Slattery doesn't know why she's after Robbins?"

"He was shocked when we told him she was the one going after his research. The dipshit thought she was using the information so her company could be in front of the new technology. He knew nothing about the contract on Robbins."

"So, he's just a throwaway as far as she's concerned."

"Also correct. Unfortunately for him, he's an unwitting accomplice who everybody now knows cheated on his wife. Also, the wife is the sister of the VP of the lab. If she hasn't already filed for the big 'D,' I'm sure it's around the corner. The guy's fucked."

"Well, yes, that sucks for him, but he deserves it. Any other tidbits?"

"That's it for now, Kemosabe. I'll continue to assist in any way possible."

"Thanks, pal, I owe you."

"I know. Bye."

SIXTY-ONE

Luckily, the Saratoga had two adjoining rooms available. Smitty was happy as a clam, the corners of his mouth threatening to reach the corners of his eyes. Rhodes was delighted for his partner and was surprised that he found pleasure in it. He'd used Smitty for a few collections in his former life but hadn't gotten to know him.

Rather than be seen by any of the locals, they opted for takeout from the deli at the Star Store. Rhodes made the two-block journey from the inn, while Smitty played with the remote for the fifty-five-inch TV in his room. He finally found the menu screen, which displayed the cornhole world championship replaying on some cable station.

Smitty, himself an excellent player of the pseudo-sport, sunk his massive frame into the down comforter and watched with the delight of a four-year-old seeing his first cartoon.

"I got us a variety of things, Smitty. Some of them are gonna be new for you, but I thought it would be a good idea to try new foods, you know, if you want to lose a little weight. For your health." Rhodes had knocked on his door just as the team Smitty had aligned himself with was taking the lead.

"Sure, that's fine, thanks." Though Smitty had managed to escape from the comforter to answer the door, his eyes were still glued to the action.

"Cornhole?"

"We used to play this all the time when I was growing up. I'm very good at it."

"They have a world championship?"

"Oh yeah. The guys from the South almost always win, but I'm rooting for the two from California. They're the first gay team to ever get to the finals."

"And why are you rooting for them?"

Smitty tore his eyes from the screen and looked at his companion, a pink hue rising up his face, his grin dimming ever so slightly. "I'm gay, Randy; I thought you knew."

"Um…no, no, I actually did not know." Rhodes was shocked, not so much by the revelation of his accomplice's sexual orientation, but by the fact that he hadn't even considered the subject. Sure, he had never seen the man with a woman, but he attributed that to his physical presence, which possibly some might feel off-putting.

Rhodes had been conflicted sexually since his high school days. While not a big fan of team sports growing up, he made a name for himself, albeit only among those fans of the activity, as the school record holder for the cross-country team.

He dated Kathy Graveline, the captain of the girls' team, off and on his junior year, mostly because she liked him, and everyone else seemed to be pairing up. When she attempted something more than heavy petting after the junior prom, he found it not to his liking. From that moment on, he became more of a loner.

He declined when asked if he would like to captain the team during his senior year. Further, he told the coach he was done running. Something had surfaced after the junior prom, and he was confused by it. Shortly after, he found himself involved in activities on the edge of skirting the law.

With intelligence in the upper one percentile, he found he had a knack for getting others to do things for him. First, it was cigarettes, then came weed. Before graduation, he had a cadre of freshman ne'er-do-wells purveying his illegal merchandise to the entire high school student body.

Although there were occasional threats and warnings, he was cunning enough to avoid serious disciplinary actions. That the faculty, en masse, was relieved upon his graduation was clear. It was whispered in the halls that under one year in college was the surer bet.

His two decades in the cages at Walla Walla did nothing to clarify his sexual bias. Much of the population was engaged in homosexual activity, but that was less a sexual orientation than a matter of convenience. Although he was never a participant, the frequent activity was more annoying than anything; his preference was to be left alone.

Smitty's admission left him feeling slightly envious. He wondered what it would be like to put those questions to rest finally.

"Randy?"

"Sorry, I was just thinking,"

"Does me being gay bother you?"

He felt terrible that his friend had come to that conclusion. "Of course not, Smitty. I couldn't care less who you're attracted to. I'm glad that you're out and proud of who you are. I was back in the slammer there for a minute, just thinking about things."

"That must've been shitty, huh?"

"Yes, shitty it was. Now, let's see what's for dinner."

Rhodes set the containers on the coffee table and opened things while Smitty looked on with concern. "What is that stuff?"

"Let's see. This one is quinoa with roasted veggies, and that one is pickled fava beans. I've got a rotisserie chicken, and there's some smoked salmon paté here too. You can use those gluten-free crackers to dip with."

It was the tiniest smile he'd ever seen on Smitty's face.

"Hey, c'mon, try some of this. If you hate everything, I can go get something else."

"I dunno, Randy. This stuff looks weird."

"Try it."

The big man gently stuck a toothpick into one of the fava beans and carefully placed it in his large mouth. Very slowly, he chewed, and suddenly his eyes brightened. "Yikes, Randy, this is pretty good."

"Told ya. Now try this other stuff; it's good for you."

They took turns sharing the food containers, each new taste eliciting a gasp of surprise and pleasure from Smitty.

"I knew the chicken would be good, but all this other stuff is amazing. Is it all good for me?"

"It's way better than the crap you usually eat. When we're done with this island, I'll put a menu together for you so you can get in shape."

"Thanks, Randy, you've been great."

"No worries. Now let's figure out how we're gonna do this tomorrow."

With only crumbs and napkins left of the feast, they spent an hour discussing the best way to accomplish their assignment and do it in a nonlethal manner.

"The problem is the addition of these O'Malleys. Where do they fit in? Even if we're successful in stopping Robbins, can they do something to screw us up?"

"I don't know." Smitty was doing his best to focus after experiencing such gastronomic delights.

"What if we pay them a visit tomorrow?"

"And do what?"

"Tell them about Baker."

"Huh? Why, what for?"

"Here's the way I see it. This thing has gone off the rails; there are just way too many pieces on the board. The only way we could stop this battery thing is by some kind of mass murder. Fuck that."

"Yeah, fuck that." Now Smitty was paying attention. "So why do we tell them about Baker?"

It had been bothering Rhodes ever since yesterday. CNN reported that the FBI had shut down an extortion for hire organization out of Vegas, and he knew that's who Johnston worked for. He also knew that the man was a weasel who'd roll over on his mother if he thought it would benefit him.

If the couple who ran the criminal enterprise gave up Johnston, it was only a matter of time before Rhodes and Smitty would hear from the feds. It was time to cut bait.

"We tell them about Baker because I think the FBI will be calling soon, and I'd like to find a way to avoid going back to jail. If we tell them what's going on, they can go to the feds and say we helped and maybe get us off the hook. So far, all we've done is burn that crappy house down."

"Do you think that will work?"

"I don't know, but right now, I think that's our only hope."

Sixty-two

Nikki Baker often met informally with her two superiors; today was different, however. She received notice of the 9 a.m. meeting the previous evening via email. This, in itself, was unusual since normally a phone call would have sufficed, and along with her other worries, the contribution to her reflux was unavoidable.

Entering the small conference room ten minutes early, she was surprised to see both Jerry Duffy and Kenji Nakamura already seated. They spoke in hushed tones and immediately halted their conversation when they saw her.

The fifty-four-inch round, lightweight concrete conference table often sat five or six people, but only three Aeron chairs were present today.

"Good morning, Nikki; please have a seat. Coffee and scones are over on the side table if you wish." Jerry, the CEO of MDV, was in his early sixties and easily looked the part of the successful executive. At six-three, he had a prominent jaw and brilliant green eyes, and his salt-and-pepper hair was always perfectly coiffed. The permanent tan, established by frequent trips to the desert, was supplemented by the occasional blast from a cancer-producing sunbed. The deep, former smoker-enhanced articulation lent gravitas to the most mundane utterance.

Duffy, a previous shaker and mover in several high-profile investment groups in the Vancouver area, was credited with assembling a dozen of his closest, filthy-rich buddies to fund the initial start-up capital. His brief stint as president of a small mining development company led him to believe there would be untold riches coming his way if the lithium battery industry continued its steep incline.

Of course, for that to happen, MDV would need to acquire the highest producing mines with the highest reserves. And they had. Nikki Baker had seen to that.

Kenji was hand-picked by Duffy just after MDV was incorporated. The Japanese auto industry and its mammoth electronics industries were prime markets for the go-to element required for the leading-edge batteries currently and in the foreseeable future.

Initially, Nakamura was simply a nod to marketing, but his savvy instincts and, at times, ruthless management style dictated his ascension to COO of the company. He had suggested Baker be sent to Chile to negotiate the mine purchase. As he rose quickly to become the hands-on manager of the firm, he was awarded generous stock options as bonuses.

Despite his fifty years, his diminutive stature and boyish face often led employees and adversaries to underestimate the steel resolve he summoned when facing a difficult or complex challenge. His decisions were swift, final, and often merciless. People in the industry—peers, adversaries, and even employees—referred to him and Duffy as "Mutt and Jeff," but never to their faces.

When Baker joined the company, both of them could see her usefulness. While her charm assault proved fruitless on the two executives, they were correct in assuming it would prove worthwhile when negotiating future business opportunities.

"Thanks, Jerry, but I think I'll pass today. Too much junk food while I was traveling." Nikki thought she sounded okay, that her voice hadn't betrayed the nervousness she was feeling. "What's up?"

"We've noticed you've been gone a lot lately. What are you working on?" Kenji's voice, consistently low and velvety, seemed to have a bit of accusation in it.

"Just some loose ends on an issue that came up. I think we're in good shape now, though."

"Could you elaborate? Both Kenji and I appreciate all you've done for MDV, and we give you a great deal of autonomy, but we feel better when we know everything that's happening."

Baker was hoping that all this vanadium bullshit would be toast before any of it came to light. These two would fucking come unglued when they found out what had happened. She hated that everything in her world depended on a pain-in-the-ass ex-con and his gigantic goofball associate. Right now, though, she could see no other way but to tell her superiors what was going on. The consequences of them finding out some other way were terrifying.

"Sure. Do you remember when someone came to us with that vanadium mine?"

"I think so. Didn't we take a look at it, Jerry? And, Nikki, didn't you say you did some work and found that the market was stagnant? That stuff is used in some kind of metallurgy, right?"

"Yes, it is, and yes, the market for use in alloys is flat. What I did not know is that someone from the States, from the Pacific Northwest National Laboratory, the PNNL, was doing some research. Vanadium is already used in redox flow batteries, which are very large and not necessarily portable. This is a growing market, but nothing like the lithium-ion battery market."

"Okay, and that's why we bought the lithium mines, correct?"

"Correct." She wished terribly that she could stop here, but she had to continue. "Well, some scientist at the lab was trying to see if he could find a way to use vanadium in a solid-state battery. If that were possible, then it could be used in everything—cars, computers, everything."

"So what, it's just a different battery, nothing special, right?" Duffy was paying attention but didn't seem overly concerned. Nakamura's poker face gave nothing away.

"Well…not exactly."

"What are you saying?" Kenji no longer sported a poker face. It was as if he expected the other shoe to drop.

After a deep breath, Baker continued, this time with a quiet, timid delivery. "Um, vanadium batteries would be *very* different."

"Like how? More expensive?"

"Uh, no, they would probably be a little cheaper."

"Yeah, but they couldn't measure up with chargeability, right?"

She finally gave up on holding anything back. "Here's the deal. If it became possible to produce a solid-state vanadium battery that even came close to the redox flow batteries, the world, as we know it, would change dramatically. Third-world countries could store energy without limits. Electric cars could go a thousand miles on a single charge. Generators would be obsolete. A single battery could last through twenty years of recharging with no loss in power. There would be no danger of spontaneous combustion. Vanadium is cheaper and cleaner to mine, and the reserves are unlimited. *That's* the deal!"

Both executives looked stunned, and neither could find his voice.

Duffy, always forward-looking, finally spoke. "So, what were you doing on your travels?"

"I found out about the research from some lightweight at the PNNL." She knew if she confessed to hiring someone to thwart the project, she would be admitting to breaking the law. Alternatively, if she did not, she faced the wrath of her bosses. "I hired somebody to put a stop to the project. They were to get rid of the research notes and any samples or prototypes."

Nakamura grabbed her wrist. "Were they successful?"

"They almost were. They got rid of much of the study documents, but the scientist, his name is Robbins, is still working on it." She pulled her hand away with a glare.

"How far away is this scientist from producing an actual prototype?"

"Unfortunately, he's already done it. It just happened, so everything is still under wraps. Supposedly there will be no announcement until later next week."

The conference room was completely quiet. Baker was considering her next moves while she assumed her bosses were mulling over their astronomic asset depreciation and the very probable extinction of their company.

"Is there anything we can do to avoid this going public until the merger?" Duffy's pale complexion betrayed his fears.

"Short of getting rid of the scientist, along with all his notes and working model, I don't think so."

Kenji immediately went into mitigation mode. "What about whoever you hired? Are they still there, and who is it?"

"They are, and I got their name from an outfit in Vegas. They're working directly for me now, though."

"How confident are you that they'll take care of things?"

"On a scale of one to ten, I'd give it a five or six. They already fucked up once. It's two guys—one's a bit of an asshole, and the other is just odd."

"So the future of our entire company—along with Jerry's and my future and financial well-being, not to mention yours—is riding on the shoulders of two buffoons who may or may not do the job. Is that about right?"

"It sounds bad when you put it that way." Nikki hated herself when the smart-ass in her reared its ugly head.

"It fucking *is* bad." Nakamura's voice was higher than she'd ever heard it. "Get your things together. *We* are going to pay this Robbins a visit. If he doesn't listen to huge sums of money, then we will make absolutely certain this vanadium thing never sees the light of day. Where are we going?"

"Uh, that would be Whidbey Island."

"What? What island?"

"Whidbey."

"We'd be? What the fuck kind of name is that?"

"It's Whidbey, w-h-i-d-b-e-y, named after some old captain."

"Fucking great," said Kenji. "Get your shit; we'll take my Discovery. I'll pick you up in thirty minutes. Jerry, don't worry, I've got this. I'll call when things are squared away."

Baker expected decisive action from Nakamura. What she didn't expect was the anxiety, concern, and downright fear in Jerry Duffy's face.

Sixty-three

Rhodes slept fitfully. Off and on, visions of being back in his cell scared him. When he was sentenced, anything to do with drugs received the maximum penalty. In the current climate, people were beginning to realize that filling the nation's prisons with drug users and non-violent offenders was a waste of taxpayers' money and a recipe for recidivism.

Still, as a prior offender, he'd be looking at a long stretch. During a particularly vivid dream, he shouted, waking himself. Sitting up, he was drenched in sweat. He made a trip to the bathroom, changed his T-shirt, and tried to go back to sleep. He reflected back to Smitty telling him he was gay and wondered how he could not have known.

Twenty-two years ago, Smitty had managed to escape prosecution. Rhodes thought it exceedingly fortunate that his buddy had avoided a stint in The Penn, which would have resulted in permanent scarring of his psyche. Now, after spending many hours with him, he saw his friend in a different light. With only a high school diploma and very little ambition, at least at the time, his turning to collecting debts for drug dealers was the path of least resistance.

Their interaction back then had been brief. Smitty collected the debt, turned the money in, and was paid with a small percentage of the collection. Because of his size and peculiar facial expression, he only had to show up to get paid. No user, regardless of their impairment, even thought about refusing. If the customer was short of funds, Smitty said he'd return at a specific time, and they'd better have it. No one was willing to test the consequences.

With Rhodes' parents long dead, the only person to have visited while he was incarcerated was the fellow in the other room. That counted for something. If they managed to get out of this mess, he would make sure Smitty was taken care of. Somehow.

He thought ahead to tomorrow and confronting the O'Malleys. He knew nothing about them except they had been keeping the prototype for Robbins. He thought about going to Robbins first, but then he would still need to address burning the house, apparently owned by O'Malley. No, he thought, O'Malley first, then on to Robbins.

The Baker woman popped into his mind. He chuckled at how seldom he thought of her anymore. If he could find any way to turn her in as a tradeoff for him and Smitty, he would do it. She was offering to pay them to kill someone. A person who had invented something that would hurt her if the news got out. It was also, supposedly, a really big deal. He made a mental note to look into precisely what this battery thing was when he had the time.

Try as he might, sleep would not come. Finally, at five-thirty, he got dressed, made some coffee with the excellent Nespresso machine in the room, and propped himself up on the bed pillows to do a little research on vanadium.

At 8 a.m., he heard a gentle knock on the adjoining door and a small voice. "Randy, you up?"

He went to the door and let Smitty in the room.

"How did you sleep?" Smitty asked.

"Not great; had some shitty dreams. You?"

"Great. These beds are comfortable; maybe I'll get one when we're done with all this."

"Yeah, I was up early and started looking into this vanadium stuff. From the little I've read, if this Robbins has found a way to make a solid-state battery that's small, it's not just a big deal, it's a huge fucking deal."

"How do you mean?"

"It's big enough to change industries the world over. It's limitless."

"Why does Baker want to stop it then?"

"Simple, more money for her."

"But what about everyone else?"

"She doesn't care. I feel even better about turning on her now. I had no idea this thing was so big. Smitty, we could be at a turning point in history."

"Cool. Can we stop at the donut shop on the way to O'Malley's house?"

Randy smiled; it was back to the present. "Of course; let's hit the road."

Sixty-four

It was typical weather for mid-February. In most of the country, a storm arrives, dumps its moisture, and leaves. In the Northwest, if an organized storm shows up during the winter months, the rain is heavy, and the winds are strong. In the absence of storms, the Pacific Ocean supplies a comforting marine layer that blocks the sun while providing a constant drizzle. It was one of those days.

I was on my way into town to pick up groceries and planned on stopping by Seth's on the return trip to check on his progress. Jenne planned on taking Emma for a walk before stopping at Useless Bay Golf Club for a session in the gym.

Had I known a few things before taking off, I'm sure I would have done things differently.

Jenne did take Emma for a walk. Instead of the usual two-mile route, she shortened it to just one. She was going to the gym, after all.

She got back home, made sure Emma was settled and had plenty of water, and walked back outside to her car. After brushing some fir needles from the hood, she climbed into the driver's seat, put her phone on the console, and started the engine. As she put it in reverse, she felt a list to the right rear, the car fighting to turn. After shutting off the ignition, she swung the door wide, with probably more force than necessary, and walked to the back of the vehicle, sure to be pissed off at what she expected to find.

She was correct—a flat tire. It was the exact tire that had been the problem two months ago. "Goddammit, the same fucking tire. Argh."

Jenne was independent, occasionally to a fault. Having grown up with two siblings, both boys, she was better equipped than most women—and, for that matter, most men I knew—to deal with any mechanical issue or household chore that required tools. Changing a flat in the drizzle at forty degrees may have been a more significant challenge than necessary for a fifty-five-year-old woman, albeit in excellent physical condition.

She opened the hatchback and lifted the cover, exposing the spare, along with a scissor jack and lug wrench. There was also a laminated card with pictures and diagrams showing the proper placement for the jack.

Feeling underneath the rear quarter panel, she located the contact point for the jack. Because the courtyard was gravel, she made sure to brush away any loose stones that could cause the tool's base to sit unevenly.

She followed the instructions and loosened the lug nuts before engaging the gear on the scissor portion of the jack. After thirty or so cranks, the tire was lifted sufficiently to be removed, which she accomplished with little effort. She next grabbed the spare and attempted to mount it to the wheel, but the clearance from the gravel wasn't enough.

Had she thought it through, she might have realized the flat was smaller by several inches. She continued to raise the vehicle when she noticed the jack begin to list, perhaps due to a missed stone or two. Immediately she reversed her cranking direction, only to find the damn thing was stuck, possibly because of its current uneven position.

After consulting the instruction card once again, she noticed a caution box that said in no uncertain terms that it was essential the jack be placed on a smooth, even surface.

If I had been home, this is where I would have thrown in the towel and called in the pros. But not my wife; no siree.

She turned back to the recalcitrant tool and did what any self-respecting man would have done. She sat in front of the jack, reared back with a sneakered right foot, and kicked the shit out of it.

Whatever small stones had been underneath the device's base chose this moment to dislodge. The auto teetered off the jack before Jenne could retract her foot, and the 2019 Subaru Outback landed squarely on her ankle.

In most civilized places, a scream as loud as my wife's would have been met with all manner of rescue attempts. However, we lived in a quiet rural setting with only two neighbors, and both were now in Palm

Springs. Emma could have been of some help, at least some consolation, but she was in the house.

Her cell phone, of course, was comfortably nestled on the passenger seat.

These events occurred just as I entered the Star Store. By the time I was finished shopping, then on to Seth's for a cup of coffee and a visit, I figured Jenne would be back from the gym. I was sadly mistaken.

SIXTY-FIVE

"Do you know how to get there, Randy?"

"Yes, Smitty, we saw it on the satellite map, remember?"

They had just left the donut shop, Smitty carrying a brown bag containing three of the jellied version of the yummy donuts, just in case the car broke down and they were stranded.

"I told you those things are fattening."

"I know. It's just that I get hungry when I'm nervous, and I'm nervous."

"We'll be fine. We're not breaking any laws, at least not right now. We're just going to meet with O'Malley and have a conversation."

They took their time going up Lone Lake Road and then to Saratoga. After another mile, they came to Little Dirt Road.

"I still think it's a funny name, Randy."

"Yes, Smitty, it still is. Let's go face the music."

They turned onto the narrow lane and drove slowly, naked blackberry stems occasionally brushing the car if they got too close to the side.

"Is that it?"

"Nope. It's just those two neighbors, but it looks like nobody's home at either place."

They went around a gentle curve, and a weathered, shingled Dutch colonial appeared. Rhodes stopped before turning in and rolled down the window to take a breath and prepare. As he did, he heard a woman's voice, half shouting, half screaming.

"Randy, what's that? We need to leave."

"No, wait. I think someone's hurt. We're pulling in."

As soon as they cleared the vegetation lining the driveway, they saw a woman sprawled on her back, her leg buried under a car.

Chauncy Smith and Randy Rhodes were not pillars of the community, but in the grand scheme of things, they weren't terribly evil either.

Smitty, amazingly, was first out with Rhodes close behind.

"Please help me. I'm stuck; the goddamn jack slipped."

"Okay, ma'am, okay; we've got this. Randy, get some water for her."

If Rhodes was surprised at his partner taking charge, he didn't let on.

Smitty was crouched over when he returned, speaking quietly to the woman. Taking the water bottle, he handed it to her.

"How do you want to do this, Smitty?"

"You take her under the arms and pull when I tell you to."

Both Jenne's and Rhodes' eyes widened at what was being proposed.

"No, wait."

"It's all right, ma'am, I've got this. Randy, grab her and get ready; on three."

Smitty straddled Jenne's legs, bent over, and grabbed the edge of the Outback. Rhodes, squatting, already held her under the arms.

"Okay, ready, one…two…THREE! On three, the soft-spoken, grinning behemoth of a man easily lifted enough of the vehicle to provide clearance from her ankle. Randy Rhodes quickly snatched her away from any further danger.

"Clear, Smitty, clear!"

The improbable rescuer dropped the car with a whump, its rear wheel now resting on the gravel, the uncooperative jack somewhere underneath.

Something about these two was vaguely familiar, but Jenne couldn't put her finger on it. Right now, she was so relieved to be out from under the car she didn't care. She had no idea why they were here but was thankful they were.

"Let's take a look at your ankle there."

The one who had lifted the car—she still wasn't sure if she'd seen that or imagined it—was gently lifting her leg. She looked down at it and wished she hadn't. There was a fair amount of blood, and something white was sticking through the skin. Then it was lights out.

When she came to, she was half sitting, half lying in the back seat of someone's car. Pillows from her sofa were under her leg, and several towels were wrapped around it, blood seeping through them.

"Who, hey, where are we? What happened?"

The smaller guy who was driving answered. "You passed out. We thought your ankle looked pretty bad, so we're taking you to the hospital. According to our search, the closest is in Coupeville."

She remembered that she'd left Emma in the house and wondered how the sofa pillow ended up here in the car with her. She was also worried about Kevin, where he was, and what he knew.

"How did you get the pillows and the towels?"

"Well, that was a bit of a challenge. We got the keys from inside your car and your phone too. We have it here, by the way. We went to unlock the house door when your dog seemed to take exception to our entry. As an aside, I think we've almost met it before, right, Smitty?"

"I'm pretty sure it's the one."

"Anyway, neither one of us wanted to go in there."

"Especially me," said Smitty.

"It's a she. Emma is her name."

"Smitty doesn't like dogs. So, he went down to the lower level and banged on the window. Your guard dog, I mean Emma, ran down the stairs and started barking and jumping at the window while I went quietly inside and took some supplies."

"That dog even scares me when it's locked inside."

As solid and robust as her rescuer was, Jenne understood that an angry German shepherd was still a significant deterrent. Now that she was slightly more conscious, she asked, "How did you guys show up at our house?"

"We came there to have a conversation about some things that have been going on."

A tiny seed of recognition began sprouting in her consciousness. "What things?"

Smitty chose to answer. "The Robbins guy, the fire, those things."

She suddenly felt vulnerable. One guy was big, the other average. Where had she heard that? Willkie!

"Don't worry. We aren't going to hurt anybody. If we were, we wouldn't be taking you to the hospital." The driver seemed to sense her unease.

"And we're sorry about the fire too," Smitty chimed in.

"You two set the fire?"

"Yes."

"Why?"

"We were hired to do it."

"Again, why?"

"It's a very long story. Would you mind if we waited until we could tell both you and your husband everything? You're safe now, and so is Robbins."

Still unsure of her situation, she asked, "Can you give me my phone so I can call my husband?"

"Sure, of course, here you go."

Taking her phone from the passenger in the front, she proceeded to call Kevin.

Sixty-six

I was seated at the kitchen picnic table, enjoying the coffee and my visit with Seth and Alice.

"You think you'll be done by Monday?" I asked Seth.

"It looks that way, as long as Alice will leave me alone."

"You keep talking like that, and maybe I will."

"Now, now, kids, you sound like an old married couple. Like us." It was heartwarming to see how much these two cared for each other. "You never said anything about your house-hunting escapade."

"Practically nothing on the market, and what there was, was priced off the charts."

Alice chimed in, "I haven't looked at houses for a few years, and I agree, sticker shock."

"You've got your home in Wallingford and this place for a couple more months, so you should be good."

"We're not exactly sure what the living arrangements will be, except that we'll be together." Alice nodded, turning to Seth.

"Glad to hear it. Will the lab make the announcement right away?"

"Jeremy's taking a hands-on approach now that they've fired Slattery, who'll be lucky if they don't prosecute him for breaching his security oath. Whitely wants to make a big splash with this. He'll want the Secretary of Energy there, as well as the national networks and papers. He's thinking at least a week after I get everything to him."

"That's terrific, Seth… I…sorry, my phone." I glanced at the screen. "Hi Jenne, I was just… WHAT?"

"I said there was an accident; I'm on my way to the hospital."

"In Coupeville?"

"Yeah, we're almost there."

"What happened? Are you all right?"

"Not exactly. I think, no, I know I've got a busted ankle."

While I was on the phone, in shock, both Alice and Seth looked on with grave concern.

"How, where, anyone else involved?"

"It wasn't a car accident, well, it *was* a car accident, just not the kind you would think. The details can wait until you get here. No, wait, Emma's at home by herself...hold on a sec..."

I had a million questions, but at least she sounded okay. I held an OK sign up to let my hosts know she would be fine.

"Randy says he'll wait and bring me back."

"I'm sorry, who is Randy?"

"He's one of the guys who set fire to the Waffle house."

"WHAT?"

"Yeah, he and his buddy Smitty, they're nice guys. Smitty lifted the car off me."

"Honey, are you taking any drugs? You sorta sound like it."

"I know, I know, it is all a little strange. You go home and take care of Emma; we're almost at the hospital. I'll call when I know something. Love you, bye."

I sat there looking at the screen on my phone as if it could explain the conversation I'd just had with Jenne.

"Tell us what happened." Seth was still worried.

"I'll tell you what I know, and then you'll be as much in the dark as I am. Jenne has a broken ankle, she says. She told me that two men, evidently the ones who burned down your house, were driving her, and they would bring her back. She also said one of them lifted a car off her."

"Kevin, it sounds like she was under the influence." Alice agreed with me.

"I agree, but she says not. I'm going back to the house to check on Emma. I'll call the hospital from there to see exactly what's going on; then, I'll probably drive up there with the dog."

"Kev, let us help. We can come over and watch Emma."

"Thanks much; maybe I'll take you up on that. I'll call you after I've talked to the hospital. I'm still unclear on the two men she's with, but she doesn't seem concerned. I'll talk to you in a few."

The curving road wasn't designed for the speed I was driving on my way home; I only prayed that none of the local deer population chose to cross my path. From Little Dirt, I took our driveway, negotiated the slight bend, and stood on the brakes when I saw Jenne's car tilted toward the back right, the steel wheel drum resting on the gravel.

Taking a more deliberate approach, I exited the truck and walked a little closer to the scene of the accident. Already I could hear Emma barking up a storm inside the house. Both the spare and the flat that had been removed were lying to the side. It was clear what had happened; it wasn't clear how any human could lift the side of the car, even if only enough to get clearance to pull Jenne away.

Putting that question to the side, I went inside to rescue our shepherd. As always, she squealed and ran in circles, her standard greeting whether I was gone for ten days or ten minutes.

"Emmy, hey girl, what's happened to your mom? Who was here with her? Tell me what happened." As she always did whenever I asked her questions, she looked directly at me and screwed her head sideways, searching for some word besides "mom" that she understood.

She badly needed a stop in the yard, so we headed outside. I planned to pack her in the truck and head to Coupeville. That was until my phone buzzed with a 360 number that I did not recognize.

"Yes?"

"Is this Mr. O'Malley?"

"It is."

"This is Dr. Anya Singh. I'm the ER physician here in Coupeville; please call me Anya."

"How is my wife?"

"Right now, she is quietly sleeping. She has received a dose of pain medication, and we are prepping her for surgery. She has a compound fracture of her right ankle, and we need to repair it as well as treat her for any possible infection due to the break in the skin."

"Will she fully recover?"

"Certainly. She was lucky to have her friends with her. They reduced the bleeding significantly, making our job here much simpler. We may have to put a couple of pins in to immobilize the joint, but again, it is standard procedure."

"How long will she be there?"

"Usually, the surgery would take less than an hour. Because this is more serious, it may take twice as long. She'll be in a splint when she wakes up and will require a cast after a week or two. Only one of the bones is broken, so that's good; it's the infection we need to stay on top of."

"Will she be there overnight?"

"I think she'll be okay to go home after she recovers from surgery. Normally we see significant blood loss with these injuries, but wrapping the wound tightly with clean towels saved us from a riskier situation. She's very lucky."

"I'll be leaving here shortly."

"Take your time. There's nothing you can do right now, and we prefer not to have any more accidents from your family today. You'll be here by the time we're done with surgery; I'll talk to you then."

"Thanks very much, Anya. Oh, are her friends still there?"

"Yes, they are also waiting."

"Could you have one of them call me?"

"Of course. Goodbye for now."

Minutes later, my phone buzzed. The call was from 253 area code, which covered a large geographical area, mainly south of Seattle.

"This is O'Malley."

"Hi, my name is Randy Rhodes. The doctor asked me to call you."

"Thank you, Randy; call me Kevin. The doctor said you and your friend brought my wife in and took care of her along the way."

"Um, yes."

"She also said she would be in much worse shape if you hadn't done that. Jenne, my wife, told me you rescued her from her accident."

"Well, we were just lucky we got there when we did. And we're even luckier that my partner is as strong as an ox."

I thought now that maybe Jenne wasn't on drugs when I spoke with her.

"We were coming to your house to explain what has been going on with Seth Robbins. We thought it was time to clear the air."

"Jenne said something about that. Where will you be later on?"

"Right here. Smitty says he's not leaving until he's sure everything's okay with your wife."

"You don't have to, you know."

"We do. When Smitty decides something, there's not much I can do to change his mind. He's already eaten everything out of the vending machines, so if you don't mind, could you stop at McDonald's or someplace on the way? He's not leaving the hospital."

"I can do that; we can talk when I get there."

We disconnected; I called Seth and Alice to report and ask if they'd mind watching Emma. I'd need the entire back seat for Jenne.

They were happy to help. I fed our dog a handful of her favorite treats, told her I'd be back later with her mom and be good for Seth and Alice, none of which she understood, of course, but I felt better about leaving her.

It took only thirty minutes to get to the hospital, but the McDonald's stop added another twenty. I walked into the ER waiting area to see a slightly built, average-looking man sitting with an enormous individual wearing the widest smile I'd ever seen. Both were wearing jeans and Kraken sweatshirts with matching caps. Despite the smiling man, there was an element of trepidation and tiredness in their eyes.

I walked over to them and handed the giant bag of burgers and two shakes to the large fellow, who hungrily took it. "Thanks. I'm Smitty."

"Sorta guessed that. I'm Kevin, and you must be Randy." We shook hands except for Smitty, who was busy unwrapping Quarter Pounders.

Not knowing exactly where to begin, I opted for, "Has the doc been out yet?"

"Not yet. She said it would take a while." Randy spoke; Smitty ate.

"Look, regardless of what happened before this, I want to thank you. If you hadn't shown up when you did, I'm scared to think what could have happened. Also, the doc said putting compression on the wound saved a lot of blood; that made a big difference too."

"That was Smitty. While I was detained in Walla Walla, he took some nursing classes at Tacoma Community. He still works at other things, but he thinks maybe nursing's in his blood. Right, Smitty?"

"Umm." With his mouth full of Mickey D's finest, it wasn't easy to understand anything Smitty said.

"You know, if you'd like to leave, you can. I can take over."

"We can't for a couple of reasons. We need to have a long talk with you about some issues, and I think we should do it when your wife is present. Also, you're going to need some help getting her home. My buddy, here, will be helpful, trust me."

It was difficult to argue with the latter and, based upon what I now knew, I was taking his word for the former.

Before I could respond, a petite woman, dressed in scrubs, walked through a set of swinging doors directly toward us.

"You must be Kevin. I'm Anya." She spoke with a slight Indian accent.

"Moow mifsh he?" Before I could ask anything, Smitty rose faster than I would have expected.

Anya turned to him, her eyes smiling. "She's going to be just fine, Smitty." Turning back to me, she said, "These two took excellent care of her and have been worried. You're fortunate to have such good friends."

"Yes, yes, we are. Everything worked out okay?"

"Yes. We put three steel pins in to immobilize the bones so they'll mend properly. The wound required a dozen stitches, and she received a dose of IV antibiotics to ward off any infection. She's splinted now, and when the swelling subsides, we'll put her in a cast. She's in recovery and should be waking up shortly. After we take her vitals and give her a chance to know what's going on, she can go home.

"She'll be in a bit of pain after the local wears off, so we'll send you home with some pain meds. She'll need them. You can go back now if you like, but just one at a time."

"Thanks, Anya, you've been great," I said.

"Hey, it's my job. It pleases me very much when the outcome is this good."

As she walked away, a nurse came out to show me the way to the recovery room. I turned to the heroes and said, "I'll be back out in a bit to let you know how she is, okay?" They both nodded, and I went to see my wife.

The recovery area was small, with individual cubbies separated by full-length curtains. The nurse closed Jenne's after I entered. The beep of the monitors, the mounds of medical equipment, and the IV tubes made her look frail and small. My eyes teared as I saw a vision of what might have been, save for the two criminals visiting us. The difference between good outcomes and horrific ones was so random, it was frightening. I said a quick thank you prayer to whoever intervened in this case. Then, with a snort and a gasp, Jenne opened her eyes.

"Howdy there, kiddo." I wiped my eyes quickly, hoping she didn't see.

"Howdy yourself. I'm in the hospital."

"Yes, you are. How do you feel?"

"Great. Nothing hurts. I thought it was gonna be painful, but I guess not."

"Do you know what they did to you?"

"Operated."

"Yes, they did. You've got a few pins in your foot and a big bandage where they stitched you up. Twelve of 'em."

"You know, Kev, when they pulled me out from under the car, I looked at my ankle and fainted. I think I was out for a while."

"Well, I can guarantee if I saw it, I would have fainted too. You're in a splint until the swelling goes down, maybe a week or so; then you get a cast for six weeks. Fun times, baby."

"So, no golf for now?"

"Probably not."

"Where are Randy and Smitty?"

"Believe it or not, they're still out in the waiting area. They said they'd help us get home."

"They were something, Kev; I mean it."

"I can't wait to hear their story. They said it was best if we heard it together."

"Me too. They don't seem to be evil people."

"Judging by their actions, I agree. We'll see when we know the whole saga."

I jumped as the curtains were swung open. "Time to check the vitals. If everything's good, as I expect, I'll help her get dressed, and you can get her home. You can wait with your friends." The nurse sounded like a drill sergeant, but she did it with good humor.

"Got it, ma'am; see you in a minute, honey." I managed a short kiss before I left the room.

I waited with my two new BFFs for another half hour while Jenne was disconnected from the machines and dressed.

The doors swung open, and my injured wife was wheeled out with her foot elevated on the front of the chair. She was still a little loopy from the drugs, but according to Dr. Singh, once they wore off, she'd be hurting.

Rhodes and Smitty immediately went to her side to offer sympathy.

"Why don't you pull your truck over and we'll get her into the back seat." Smitty had evidently eaten everything available, because now his mouth was empty, and he could talk.

I did as he suggested and pulled in front of the building. Before I could get out, Randy had the rear door open and Smitty had carefully lifted Jenne out of the chair and was gently easing her into the back seat. Randy must've put the sofa cushions in the truck while I was in recovery because they were there and neatly arranged so that her leg was elevated.

These guys were starting to make me look bad, *and* they were being kind and gentle. Finally, it was time to head home. Despite all that had happened, I was looking forward to their story.

SIXTY-SEVEN

Jenne and I led the two-vehicle parade back to Little Dirt Road. We arrived at our home in less than thirty minutes since there was little traffic to delay us; it was South Whidbey Island, after all, there was never any traffic.

The unmistakable sounds of a German shepherd announcing visitors greeted us when we arrived. I pulled into the middle of the courtyard to allow plenty of room to get Jenne out. Although the hospital supplied crutches, it would be a little while before she felt comfortable using them.

Both Seth and Alice were on the front porch anxiously awaiting our arrival. As soon as we left the hospital, I called to bring them up to date on events and to let them know we were having guests.

Seth and Alice approached the truck and opened the rear door. "Jenne, damn, you scared us to death."

"Yeah, me too. Last time I change a fucking tire."

"Glad to see you haven't lost your sense of humor."

"If you had the drugs I have in me, you'd be happy too."

"We made up the sofa in the family room so you'd be comfortable."

"Thanks, guys."

"Okay, let me through here so we can get her inside." When the giant with the smile approached, Seth's mouth hung open. "I'm Smitty, and that's Randy over there. You're Seth Robbins, right?"

"Yes, and this is Alice."

"Hi, Seth and Alice, if you could move over a little, I'll get Mrs. O'Malley into the house. But I'm a little afraid of the dog. Could you put her somewhere?"

"Alice, will you put Emma downstairs? And it's Jenne, Smitty, okay?"

"Yes, ma'am. Got it; here we go…"

Randy assisted by opening doors and moving things while the three of us stood by like it was a Broadway play.

"C'mon, you three, let's get this party rolling. As long as I'm feeling like this, you may as well have a drink. Kevin, how 'bout it?"

She was loopy, but that didn't mean she had a bad idea. Once Jenne was comfortable, everyone else found a seat while I took drink orders. The Audi duo chose the Bodhizafa, while the rest of us settled for a chardonnay.

Jenne was drinking water; she was high enough. "I want my girl," she said.

I knew it would only be a matter of time before I'd hear this. The look on Smitty's face was pure panic. It was the first time I'd seen his mouth without the grin.

"Tell you what, Smitty," I said. "You know how you helped Jenne, and you told me to trust that you weren't going to do anything to harm her?"

"Yeah, but…"

"Listen, here's what I'm going to do. I'll put Emma on a leash and bring her up. She will bark very loudly when she comes up, and she'll want to come over to you. You just sit there with your hands in your lap and don't move. Can you do that?"

Sweat started beading on the big man's forehead. "I don't know."

"All she wants to do is sniff you. When she sees you being friendly with us, she'll just sit down and look at you."

"I don't know."

Randy took over. "Smitty, you can do this; I know you can."

I heard, "Okay," in a soft little voice.

After putting the leash on Emma, I brought her up. True to form, she rattled the glasses with her barking. She tugged at the leash, trying to pull a scent off the newcomers, and pulled me over to where Smitty was sitting, his eyes pleading to be left alone. After fifteen seconds, she stopped, sniffed his legs and hands, then did the same to Randy.

Then she ran to her mom and squealed with delight. So did her mom.

"Is it okay now?" Smitty seemed to want to scratch his nose or something.

"Sure, just don't jump up suddenly," I said. "She's never sure if you're going to threaten one of us. I think she's hyper-cautious because she was at the studio when you tried to go after Seth."

"We weren't gonna hurt him."

"If she's guarding and someone sneaks up in the dark, too bad for them."

"She remembers?"

"Hah, she'll remember five years from now."

Although his smile had returned somewhat, Smitty's eyes never left Emma.

"Randy, the floor is yours. Tell us what the hell is going on."

He started at the beginning, from his initial contract with Rothwell via Stanley Johnston to his wasted trip to Northport and his eventual trips to Whidbey. He went through bringing Smitty on board and their meeting with Nikki Baker.

"So, she was the one giving the orders, correct?"

Smitty put his two cents in. "Yes. She seems like she's used to doing that."

"Anyway, we set the fire," said Randy. "We only did the house because we didn't know about the other building. Then Baker called us and told us that Seth was still making progress. I guess she was being fed information by that guy at the research place.

"She told us to get rid of him and whoever else knew anything."

"You mean *kill* me?" Seth exclaimed.

"Um, yes; sorry about that. We didn't want anything to do with any killing. We thought we could sneak into that little building in the woods and threaten you. But then Smitty cracked a branch, and this dog chased us away.

"After that, we waited at the Star Store, and that's where we saw you and Jenne giving something to Seth. After we saw that, we started having second thoughts about everything."

Randy looked around the room before he continued. "Look, I've broken the law and served my time. My friend here collects for some drug dealers in Tacoma, but we're not killers, and neither of us has ever hurt anybody. I took this gig because the money was good, and I needed it, but there was never a plan to hurt people. We're both very sorry for the grief we've caused."

It was quiet for a minute while all of us digested Randy's words. All of us but Jenne; no digesting there. She was zonked, the drugs doing their magic. I started to ask something, but Randy continued.

"There's something else. While we were driving here from the hospital, we got a call from Nikki Baker. She's pulled us off the job. It looks like she's driving here with one of the other corporate dudes. He thinks he can buy you off, Seth, at least for a few months until their merger goes through."

"Well, he can't."

"I thought you'd say that. She seems to think that will work, but she said they would take other measures if it didn't. I think there's really big money involved here."

"Do you know when they plan on getting here?" I didn't like the sound of things.

"They were just crossing the border, but there must be a big backup at the Peace Arch because she was pissed off and swearing that it was taking forever."

"That at least gives us a little time. I can't imagine they'll try anything until morning. Seth, you and Alice will be fine at the beach. Did you know where they were, Randy?"

"No, we thought they, or Seth—we weren't sure about Alice—were in the little studio down the street."

"Good; that means Baker won't know where they are either. What about Jenne and me?"

"We hadn't said anything about you two yet."

"Excellent. Do you and Smitty have a place to stay tonight?"

"We were at the Saratoga last night, and they're full tonight, so I'm not sure."

"Seth, what's in the studio for beds?"

"There's a small sofa and a bed that I used when I spent the night there."

"Would you mind if these two used it?"

"Course not. It's kinda messy in there, but if they don't mind that, they're welcome to it."

"Will they be in any danger?" Alice looked concerned.

"We'll be fine. We have a weapon, just in case. Is there any food there?" Smitty's mind was never far from nourishment.

"Not much, I'm afraid."

Jenne woke up just in time to hear the food question. "We have plenty of food here, Smitty. You got a microwave in there, Seth?"

"Yes."

"Good. Kevin, there's a bunch of stuff all made up in the freezer. Let Smitty take whatever he wants."

I thought maybe there would be nothing but ice cubes left when he was done, but I kept that to myself. "Of course," I replied. "No problem."

"That's very nice of you, but what about tomorrow, when Baker visits Seth?"

"Let me think about that, Randy. Let's get you and Smitty on your way. Then the four of us," I glanced over at my drowsy wife, "three and a half, will come up with something. Will you two help if we need you?"

"Yup, no problem. Now can we see what's in the freezer?"

Randy just shook his head at the predictable response from his partner.

SIXTY-EIGHT

Although only two people had left, it seemed as though the room was empty. Jenne was in and out of consciousness while the rest of us tried to formulate a plan of action for the next day.

"Why don't we call your cop friend or the FBI and have them show up and arrest Baker and whoever she's with?"

"I guess we could, Alice, but then they would want to arrest Randy and Smitty for arson as well."

Alice was on the same page, "Okay, something else then. There's no way Jenne would let that happen. After what they went through to save her, I think they've more than made up for the fire."

"I agree. I'm the one they were after, but after spending some time with them, I think they're harmless, at least to us."

"They're going to try to get to you, Seth, and they most likely think you're at the studio, correct?"

"That makes sense."

"Randy says they're gonna try to buy you off, right?"

"Yes, but this is too big to let that happen."

"I agree, but suppose they offer you a couple hundred thousand, and you *say* you agree."

"They'll want some insurance to be sure I behave."

"You still have all your notes from the failed efforts before we found Sharon's research, don't you?"

"Yes, all that's still in the studio."

"So you let them have that, and you give them one of the old prototypes. They won't know the difference. It's not like they're scientists."

"I guess it could work, but then when it's released in a week or two, they'll know I screwed them over. They could come after me again."

"Right. We need to find a way to have them arrested without endangering Rhodes and Smith."

"You know once that vanadium thingy is made public, MDV will be in the shitter, right?" We were all a little startled to hear from the sleeping beauty on the sofa. "I bet you thought I wasn't listening."

"We did, hon. You looked passed out over there."

"Well, I did hear a few things. Where are my rescuers?"

"They left, remember?"

"Oh yeah, right, they did. Anyway, they own lithium mines, and that stuff will eventually be worthless for use in batteries. That merger isn't going through, and their stock will be worth pennies."

"How do you know this?"

"When I heard Bill talking to you about them, I checked out their company profile and stock prices. Baker is third in shares owned, by the way."

"Do you have any ideas now that you're able to talk?"

"I do have one. Tell my pals to take all the money that they've been paid to a brokerage, deposit it, and short all the MDV stock they can. In two weeks, they'll be able to buy it back for pennies. They'll be able to turn fifty grand into almost a million. I think you could make a case for calling it insider trading, but what the hell? Maybe then they won't need to skirt the law anymore."

We looked at Jenne as if she were speaking in tongues, which, to me, she was. "How do you know all this stuff?"

"I've been studying the markets. Someone in this family needs to know how to invest, dontcha think?"

Rather than take any offense, I *was* glad that someone in the family knew this shit. "Well, great, we've got the boys squared away; now what about the rest of this?"

Seth, after taking it all in, offered a proposal. "How about this. First thing tomorrow I'll go to the studio because that's where they'll expect me to be. I'd like to take Emma with me if you don't mind. I may not be a member of her pack, but she's proven to be a highly effective hedge against any violence. Randy and Smitty can come back here, and you can talk to them about shorting MDV.

"I'll agree to be paid off, and I'll turn over the useless notes and one of the failed models. All the real material is at the beach house anyway, so no problem there. Hopefully, they'll buy it."

"Hopefully, they will. If we can convince the boys that Jenne's scheme makes sense, they may have enough dough to take off somewhere until things cool down. If that's the case, maybe we can get the FBI involved. I can't wait to tell Bill about this; he's gonna kill me."

Once everyone was gone, I managed to get Jenne to the bathroom with the help of her crutches. She was beginning to realize that the local that was numbing her repaired ankle was losing its power, and the pain was becoming unbearable.

"Hey, babe, do what you need to do in there, and then we'll get some of these pain meds into you. I know you'd rather not, but Anya said it would be important for at least a few days to get you over the hump."

"It hurts a lot, Kev."

I felt awful for her, knowing the worst was yet to come.

"I know, honey, I'm sorry. I'll fix up the sofa so you don't have to mess with the stairs. I'll stay here in the recliner in case you need something. Just take it slowly."

The three of us camped out in the family room for the night. It was a long one for all of us.

SIXTY-NINE

At eight the following day, Seth came by to pick up Emma. Jenne was sleeping soundly. Finally, the Vicodin was having its effect.

"Good luck down there, Seth; tell the boys to come by in a couple of hours. I'd like to let Jenne get some sleep; she had a rough night."

"Will do. Tell her we're thinking of her and give Alice a call if you need anything."

After he was gone, against my better judgment, I called Bill Owens.

"Hey."

"Hey yourself, why are you pestering me?" he asked.

"Thought I'd see if any progress was being made."

"I hadn't taken a hard look at MDV until after we last talked. It seems they own several lithium mines that are making big bucks with all the EVs coming out. There's a merger in the works that will make the shareholders wealthy. Whatever Robbins is into must have something to do with that."

I felt bad that I hadn't told Bill what this was about, but I told Seth I'd keep it quiet. I felt I had to tell him enough now so that he would know what was going on. He'd pass it to Matt, and that was okay too.

"Um, Bill?"

"Don't tell me, you have information that can help but you haven't told me yet. Am I close?"

"Well, a little…"

"You son of a bitch, why do you always get in the middle of shit?"

"I'm sorry, but this one was unavoidable. Before I tell you though, Jenne had an accident. She broke her ankle."

"She fall?"

"No, it was a car thing."

"Anyone else hurt?"

I felt like I'd been down this road before. "No. She was changing a tire and the car fell on her. And no, I wasn't home, so I could change it."

"The car *fell* on her?"

"Yes, but some guy lifted it off and he and his friend took her to the hospital."

"A guy *lifted* the car?"

"Um, he was big."

"Are you drunk?"

"No, not yet anyway. Look, I'll fill you in on all the gory—and they *are* gory—details later. I'm just telling you so you can let Shelly know. She'll probably want to visit but not for a week or so because of the surgery."

"Surgery?"

"It was a bad break."

"Jesus, Kevin, is she okay?"

"She will be. Now let me give you what I can. What Seth was working on will make lithium batteries obsolete. Baker's company won't be worth spit; that's why she needs to stop him."

"You knew this?"

"I did, but I had to swear not to say anything because of the trillions of dollars involved. Now, you can't either."

"Shit, it would've helped."

"I know, I'm sorry. Please pass it on to Matt. There's another thing."

"Tell me."

"The guys who set the fire and tried to get to Seth aren't doing it anymore."

"And you know this how?"

"I just know it."

"So he's safe?"

"Mostly."

"Kevin, what are you not telling me?"

"I gotta go, Jenne needs me; hi to Shelly. Talk to you later."

I hated doing that, he was my best friend, but I couldn't let Rhodes and Smitty get arrested.

SEVENTY

Baker was pissed. It had taken them three hours at the border crossing, and the camper ahead of them just *had* to chat endlessly with the Border Patrol. Some goddamn family with three kids, talk, talk, talk: probably from Alberta.

Traveling with Nakamura was almost as much fun as spending time with Rhodes and that huge goofy guy. The only difference was Kenji never said a word. He had some bullshit, new-age music playing and whenever she suggested another station, he gave her the stink eye.

Depending on traffic through Oak Harbor, they were still two or three hours away, so it looked like nothing would happen until the following day. At least they had Kenji's assistant make reservations for the night. Strangely enough, she managed to get the last two rooms at the Saratoga Inn. Damn, this island was a small place.

After dark, they reached Langley, checked in at the Saratoga, and walked to the Bistro for dinner. She would have preferred to eat alone; at least she could have talked to herself. She felt the need to review the plans for the next day and finally had to break the ice.

"Kenji, how should we do this tomorrow?"

After staring at his crab salad endlessly, seemingly searching for an answer, he looked up and addressed her. "You have tried to solve this problem using an axe instead of a scalpel. Tomorrow, I'll show you the proper way to negotiate. It should not be difficult. In the future, you may want to choose the more civilized approach."

Wow, she thought, *what a fun date*. If it didn't mean she would lose everything she had worked for, she almost hoped he'd flame out. She was looking forward to tomorrow's exchange.

SEVENTY-ONE

By the time Rhodes and his oversized buddy made it to our house, Jenne was awake and on her second cup of coffee. She'd mastered the skill of getting up with help, then using her crutches to get around. Although she was still in a great deal of pain, we managed to time the meds to ward off the worst of it.

She was smiling when the boys came in, albeit through occasionally gritted teeth. "Good morning. How was the night in the woods?"

"One of us slept well, right, Smitty?"

"Um, yes; I did. Randy says I snore. It must have been that lasagna you made; it was amazing."

"I'm glad you liked it. Here's the deal, you two need to lie low for a while, and I have an idea how you can make a lot of money without doing anything. What do you think?"

They both looked over at me, wondering how this could be. "Listen to her, boys, I think she has a good idea here."

They turned back to Jenne, obviously hoping she could deliver.

"How much do you two have?"

Rhodes thought for a minute, mentally doing some addition. "Let's see; I got twenty-five from Johnston, a hundred from Baker the first time, and then another forty."

"Thousand?"

"Yep."

"Wow, who said crime doesn't pay?"

"We're done with that now. Some of that was Smitty's, but after all that we've been through, I think we'll be splitting everything."

"Randy, really?"

"Smitty, we're partners. I know at first you were getting a third, but that doesn't seem fair. We're gonna be fifty-fifty from now on."

"You guys can save the love-fest until later. Listen up. Do you have this in a bank?" Jenne asked.

"Yes," said Rhodes. "I had Baker wire it."

"Okay, do you have a brokerage account?"

"No."

"Do this. Walk into a Merrill Lynch office anywhere in Seattle and tell them you want an account. Put everything in there; they'll put it in a money market or something. Wait a couple of days, then call and tell them you want to short MDV, Inc.; they'll tell you the symbol. Sell as many shares as you can borrow. It's trading around ninety-five bucks now, but they may have limits on how much you can sell."

"How do I sell them if I don't own them?"

"In a short sale, you 'borrow' shares, sell them at the current price, and then you buy them at a later time to replace what you've borrowed. After the shit hits the fan when Robbins's discovery comes out, the shares will be in the single digits. You'll be rich."

"Suppose you're wrong?"

"It's possible, I guess; the world could be hit by an asteroid too, but except for that, I think this is solid."

"Randy, she seems to know what she's talking about." Smitty looked hopeful.

"Well, it's half yours, so if you're good with it, let's do it."

I was considering doing the same thing, but we were a little too close to the information to be perfectly legal. "I think you should head for the ferry. There's no telling what will happen when Baker meets with Seth, and it's better if you're off the island. We've got your numbers, and you have ours, so we can text each other if anything happens. Lie low, maybe take a road trip somewhere, and watch the news. In a couple of weeks, everything will be different."

"Thanks for everything, Kevin, and you, Jenne, you've been very kind to us. We'll never forget."

"That goes for me too, Smitty; thank you to both of you," Randy chimed in.

"Hey, Kevin and I are the ones who should be saying that. I'm not sure I'd even be here without you two."

After hugs around, a tiny one for Jenne, they headed for the ferry terminal. I still couldn't wrap my arms around our new friendships with a couple of guys who burned down my wife's house.

I sure hoped things went well at the studio.

Seventy-two

Although Baker had seen the property on the satellite map, she was still surprised at the depth of the surrounding vegetation. They had just pulled into the former courtyard, the smell of gasoline and charred lumber still in the air.

"I can see why Rhodes missed the other building; you can't even see it from here," she said.

"Hmm."

The sooner this was over, the better. Nakamura made Rhodes and Smith look like entertainers of the year. "Come on; there's a path on the other side of that slab."

As soon as they set foot on the path, barking commenced from their headed direction.

"I guess Robbins has a dog."

"Hmm," Nakamura replied.

"Sheesh, let's get this over with."

Another hundred yards, and they were at the door of the shed-roofed story-and-a-half building. The barking was ferocious and loud. They knocked, and the door opened a crack.

"Yes?"

The barking was deafening now.

"Are you Mr. Robbins?" Apparently, Nakamura *could* form a sentence. "We represent MDV and would like to talk with you for a moment."

"I don't have the time.'

"It's essential, and we think it will be worth your while."

Seth appeared to consider it for a minute, then said, "Okay. You'll need to come in slowly with your hands at your side. Emma will bark and come up to you quickly, but just stand there; she won't hurt you."

At this, Nakamura's face betrayed a hint of concern. Baker suppressed a smile. She'd had shepherds as a kid and knew their style. It wasn't that she didn't have a healthy respect for what they could do, just that she knew the breed.

They did as they were told while Emma handled the inspection. Tiny bumps of perspiration dotted Nakamura's upper lip while he was sniffed and barked at. Eventually, Emma went to Seth's side, sat there, and observed. The MDV officer appeared only marginally more at ease.

"What do you want?" Seth asked.

Nakamura took over, "We know what you've been working on and how important it is. We respect that. Our company owns lithium mines, so I'm sure you know what your discovery will do to us."

"How do you know?"

"That isn't important; we do. As I said, lithium batteries will be obsolete once this gets out, as will MDV. We are not proposing that you destroy this discovery, only that you delay the announcement."

"Why would I want to do that?"

"If you do, we will be able to complete a merger that will make us very wealthy. That is to happen in four months. That's not very long, is it?"

"I'm sorry, I can't do that."

"If you do, we can compensate you."

"I don't think so. I'm not interested."

"Would half a million dollars interest you? For a four-month delay?"

Seth appeared to be shocked at the sum. "What?"

Nakamura conveyed a tiny, knowing smile, glancing over at Baker. "I said would half a million dollars interest you?"

"Man, that's a lot of money."

"Yes, it is. We can have half of it wired to your account this afternoon. The balance you'll get when the merger is completed."

"You're saying I can still release it, but I have to wait four months?"

"That's correct. We will advise you when the merger closes and we have realized our gains."

"What's to stop me from doing it after you've paid me?"

"Two things. We will expose you for taking money from a foreign company."

"Yes?"

"And should it come to that, and I hope it doesn't, we will hurt you and whoever you care for." Even Baker was shocked at the menace in Nakamura's voice. "You'll have nowhere to hide; I'll make sure of that. But let's not dwell on any negative issues now. You'll be a wealthy man, and your discovery will make you famous. Do we have a deal?"

"I, uh, I guess we do."

"Wonderful. Nikki will take down your banking information, and you'll see the deposit later this afternoon. Nikki?"

After taking the information, the couple left the studio, and Seth breathed a massive sigh of relief. "Well, Emma, was that fun or what?"

Once they got to the Discovery and made it back to the paved road, Nakamura turned to Baker. "*That* is how you negotiate, Baker; you make them an offer they can't refuse. How did you think I got this job—by being a pussy? If you had told me about this earlier, we could have saved a lot of grief. Fucking women."

The anxiety she now felt surprised her. She held her tongue and stared out the window, wishing that the merger could happen tomorrow.

Seventy-three

I was in the process of heating a bowl of soup for Jenne when the doorbell rang, followed immediately by Emma squealing because she was home. The look on Seth's face hinted that even if things had gone well, it had been a stressful experience.

"Talk to me; how'd it go?" I asked.

"Hey, Seth, glad you're still with us."

"Thanks, Jenne; how's the ankle?"

"Hurts like a son of a bitch. The only good thing is Kevin having to wait on me."

"Do you mind? Let's hear the man. Tell us what happened, Seth."

"It went better and worse than I expected."

"Did you get all of it?" I asked.

"All of it. That new voice recorder app worked perfectly. I've already sent you both the transcript."

"We can listen to it later; give us the gist."

"Baker came, but the one who did all the talking was a little guy who looked younger than I'm guessing he was. I'd bet he's high up in the company, certainly her senior."

"So, they offered to buy you off?"

"They did. Supposedly I'll have a quarter of a mill in the bank by the end of the day and the rest after the merger."

"Yikes, there's gotta be huge sums of money involved. Did you give them your material and the model?"

"They never even asked."

"How do they know you won't stiff them?" Jenne always considered the downside.

"They said if I do, they'll expose me, *and* they'll hurt, maybe kill, me and, I guess, Alice."

"That doesn't sound good."

"The guy seemed like a prick; I'm glad Emma was there, and I'm real glad we recorded him. He didn't want me to destroy anything, just delay the announcement until their merger went through. All I need to do is sit on it for a few months for five hundred grand."

"Would you consider it?"

"Nah, not my style. The money thing is no big deal; I can probably name my price and position once the announcement is made. The scary part is the threat; I'd die if anything were to happen to Alice."

"If we play our cards right, there should be no risk of that. I'll wait a few days for our friends to leave town; then I'll turn this over to Bill and the FBI agent. What are your plans?"

"I should have everything pulled together by Monday. Alice will take some time off so she can come to Richland with me, and I've alerted Whitely when we're coming. It'll likely take a week to vet everything, verify the calculations, and run the model through protocols. I'm confident everything will pass muster, and then it will be up to Jeremy to make it public. I dread the politics, but it's necessary in this case."

"It's good that you'll be away, although we shouldn't have any problems on our end. The MDV assholes likely won't move until the breaking news, but it's comforting to know you'll be at the PNNL, where there's plenty of security."

"Our thoughts exactly."

"Will you and Alice stop by before you leave?"

"Of course, Jenne. We're packing our things on Sunday, so okay if we come by late in the afternoon?"

"Perfect; see you then."

SEVENTY-FOUR

Seth and Alice stopped at our house before dinner on Sunday. Jenne was finally off the big drugs, and while the pain was still there, it was less so. She hated the fuzziness associated with the meds as well as the other more annoying side effects. Plus, we could now share an entire conversation without her dozing off.

They were happy to see her more aware and sad to be leaving her for a few weeks.

"Don't worry, Alice; Shelly texted me and said she'd be up to help out. By then, Kevin will have abandoned me and gone to the golf course anyway."

"Hey, you know I can hear you, don't you?"

"Oh, sorry, Kev, didn't see you there; you know, the drugs."

"Nice try." I turned to our friends and wished them well and would wait to see when the news broke. "Once the announcement is scheduled, Seth, would you give me a heads-up? I'd like to make sure the Feds are ready to move."

"You bet, as soon as I know."

We said our goodbyes and settled in for the Sunday Kraken game. Maybe they would win.

The text I received from Randy confirmed that he and Smitty were out of state. They took Jenne's advice and shorted MDV's stock, then hit the road. It seemed both of them had always wanted to visit Zion and Bryce Canyon parks, and this proved to be a perfect time.

Now that I felt they were safe from local and federal law enforcement, the dreaded day had arrived. I had to make the call to my best friend and apparently tormented Bill Owens. Shelly had spent the past week with us doing all manner of household chores, including the cooking.

After eight days, Jenne's condition had markedly improved. The swelling had subsided, and a cast had been fitted two days ago. She was getting around on crutches like she was born to them. There was even a hint that one-legged vacuuming was in her future.

I always made difficult or awkward calls from my truck. It was warm, quiet, and hands-free. Jenne had so gotten used to seeing me parked in the courtyard waving my hands and talking, she no longer questioned my actions. Besides, she knew Bill would explode.

"Yes?"

"Hey, Bill, it's me."

"I know, that's what this caller ID is for. What is it this time?"

"Does it *always* have to be something awful?" I thought idle chatter would delay the inevitable, but I was mistaken.

"It doesn't have to be, but with you, it always seems to be. Now, what do you want?"

"Do you remember our last conversation?"

"You mean the one where you told me things that if I had known them earlier, the FBI would have already closed the case?"

"I don't remember it quite like that, but yes, that one."

"Go on."

Here goes. I was already cringing. Thank God for the closed cab. "The lady, the Baker woman?"

"Yes?"

"She was here."

"WHAT?"

"She came to talk to Seth with another guy from MDV last week." *Maybe it will be less painful if I say it all really fast.* "They offered to give him half a million dollars to delay his announcement and said that they might kill him and Alice if he did not. We knew they were coming but couldn't tell you."

The truck was so quiet that I thought we had lost the connection. "Bill?"

"Yes?"

"Did you hear what I said?"

"I did."

"What do you think?" He had me worried.

"You know why I'm not talking?"

"Um, no."

"It's because I'm looking for my gun. I'm going to kill you."

"Come on; it's not that..."

"STOP. Stop talking. We have arsonists, extortionists, maybe even killers, and some are from other countries. ALL, and I mean *all* of these people, somehow have something to do with you. And now, *now* you tell me they were here, you knew they were coming, and still, *still,* you didn't read me in. What the fuck is wrong with you? Are you fucking insane?"

"I can explain it if you'll let me."

"I am so pissed I can't see straight. I'm hanging up now to get a drink somewhere. *If* I calm down, and that's a huge fucking if, I may call you back. Good-fucking-bye."

Now it was so quiet in the truck I shut it off and went back into the house.

"How'd it go with Bill?"

"Oh, you know, he was a little upset."

"What did he say about the recording?"

"I never got there. He, uh, kinda said goodbye; he was gonna go get a drink."

"A drink? It's eleven in the morning."

"Maybe he was slightly more than a little upset."

"I'm calling Shelly."

"Why, what for?"

"I'm going to tell her why we waited—so Randy and Smitty could get away. I'll tell her they saved my life, that the house they burned was useless anyway, that they didn't do anything to disrupt Seth's research. I've hinted at it as much anyway while she was here."

"How will that help?"

"Who does Bill listen to more than anyone?"

"Shelly."

"And who knows best when the right time to talk to him is?"

"Shelly."

"And who does he love more than you?"

"Shelly."

"Okay, so leave me alone, and I'll get her to intervene."

"Make sure she tells him we have a recording of the entire event."

"Yes, dear, I'm on it."

If women ruled the world, I thought it would most certainly be a better place.

Later in the evening, my phone buzzed; it was Bill Owens. "Hey."

"Hey... Shelly told me I was being an asshole and to call you. She explained things a little clearer and in more detail than you. She also clarified the depth to which your two friends went to save Jenne. Now I get it."

"Maybe that's because the guy I was talking to went ballistic."

"That's because the guy you were talking to doesn't understand how you can get into so much trouble by just being retired."

"What can I say? It finds me."

"That's enough. Shelly says you have a recording of what went down?"

"We do. I'll send it to you, and you can get it to Matt Steele. I don't know how he'll want to do this, but I have an idea."

"Well, hell, why wouldn't a seasoned FBI agent want to take advice in apprehending violent criminals from a retired interior designer? Do tell me, please."

"You said how it might be tough working with the Mounties up there, right?"

"*Could* be, I said *could* be."

"Once the news of Seth's discovery gets out, Baker and Nakamura will be broke *and* royally pissed. I think they'll come back here to take it out on Robbins. If you alert the Border Patrol to expect them, the FBI can apprehend them once they make it to the States."

Owens was quiet; I assumed he was considering my suggestion. He finally spoke. "It's not a totally stupid idea. I'll talk to Matt about it. By the way, I waited until I got home to have that drink—just so you know. Later."

I put the phone down and turned to Jenne. "You seem to know the best way to handle him, don't you?"

"Of course; I told you so."

SEVENTY-FIVE

The next ten days went by quickly. On a Sunday afternoon, Seth texted me that all was ready; there was a press conference on Tuesday morning. It would be a significant turning point in supplying energy to a world rapidly destroying itself by consuming hydrocarbons. The problem wasn't the availability of wind, solar, or hydro energy after all; it was finding a way to store the damn stuff until it was needed. Seth Robbins had found a way.

I immediately alerted Owens, and he, in turn, notified the FBI. He told me that my stupid, naïve idea was their plan for apprehending the MDV associates.

Whitely, as promised, made sure all the movers and shakers of public opinion were present at the presser. CNN, MSNBC, and FOX, as well as the network channels, were present. The major print and Internet press organizations were directed by their editors that something big was happening and needed to be in the small eastern Washington town of Richland on a Tuesday morning.

Since there were no rooms large enough to accommodate the crowds of media, a decision was made to set up the expansive lobby classroom style to do so.

At 11 a.m., every TV station in the United States, and many from around the world, broke for a news bulletin, the subject of which was unknown. It was inconceivable that Jeremy Whitely could keep the discovery under wraps while assembling such a representative gathering, and yet he had. When the president of the United States suggests that news organizations trust him, because if they don't, their White House credentials will be revoked, they submit.

At one minute past the hour, Secretary of Energy James Courcy walked up to the microphone amidst the bright lights, the whirring and clicking of cameras, and the progressively dying hushed whispers. He waited until he could hear the rain against the side of the lobby windows. Then, the Ivy League-educated, former titan of industry began his remarks.

"Members of the press, thank you for being here in Richland at the Pacific Northwest National Laboratory. Today marks the beginning of the end of the destruction we are doing to our planet." The assembled crowd quietly murmured their interest. "Our National Laboratory has perfected a system, a process, and a method for taking the energy produced from any environmentally conscious production process and storing it for an unlimited duration until it is needed.

"This means solar or wind production in third-world countries can be stored to be used during the rainy season or in times when the weather won't cooperate. This means charging an electric car for a few hours to travel a thousand miles. The savings in energy use alone will be monumental. The damage done to the earth by the savage ways we mine lithium will be eliminated. Our phones, computers, our tools, everything we use will require less energy." The room was unearthly quiet, so stunned was the audience.

"Ladies and gentlemen, this is the day we turn this goddamn ship around."

At once, the room erupted into shouted questions, yelling, and hand-waving.

Secretary Courcy raised his hands for quiet and waited. Eventually, the disruption subsided, and he continued. "Folks, I can imagine you'll have lots of questions; let me introduce Jeremy Whitely, whose job it is to run this place. He's far better equipped than I to handle those."

Whitely took the podium and began immediately. "Members of the press, let me thank you as well for being here. The secretary wasn't exactly accurate when he said I run this lab. My job is to assist the many scientists we employ. Nothing we discover or produce comes from me, only from the talented people working here.

"This discovery happened over many years, not days or months, through the persistence, dedication, and even bravery of one very talented scientist. His perseverance in the face of the many obstacles thrown in his way is how we arrived at this point. Let me introduce him for his remarks and your questions. Ladies and gentlemen, this is Seth Robbins, the inventor of the Waffle Storage Battery."

It was the only time since his first marriage that Seth was wearing a suit; Alice helped select it, of course. He was nervous but resolute, especially after Alice had told him she loved him and wanted to spend her life with him. As he walked to the podium, the room exploded once again, with cheers and hand-clapping everywhere. While waiting for quiet, he glanced to the back of the room, where three people sat. Two were smiling and clapping; one large one had a grin from ear to ear. It seemed Randy and Smitty had cut their trip to Utah short, joining Alice for the world-shaking announcement.

After several minutes more of cheering, Seth was able to speak. "Thanks, everyone. Everything Jeremy and the secretary had to say is true about this breakthrough. What he did not say is this is not my discovery alone. A remarkable, dedicated scientist for her entire life shares in this success. Without her, none of this could have been accomplished. With the finding and translation of her calculations and formulas, I was able to complete my work. Unfortunately, Sharon Waffle died a few months ago, but she'll be remembered forever because of her work.

"I'll take your questions now."

The questioning lasted over an hour and then only broke up because there were deadlines to make and interviews to do for the Eastern zone time slot. Such was the demand for Seth's time that Whitely stepped in to ration it to the major networks and two of the cable services. Somehow he didn't trust one of them to get the story straight. He didn't want the discovery mislabeled as an attempt by science to rule the world.

Jeremy was kind enough to reserve a small conference room at a nearby hotel for a private catered celebration dinner for Seth and Alice, along with their two odd friends. The publicity generated by the breakthrough would cement their funding for the foreseeable and the distant future.

After the day's hectic and nerve-wracking events, the quiet room and delicious meal were perfect. The food was even plentiful enough that Smitty seemed satisfied.

"Thanks for being there, you two; I'm flattered."

"Shit, Seth, we just wanted to see what had that Baker gal so interested."

"Hah, good one, Smitty, I wonder what will become of her. Hey, did you guys short the stock as Jenne told you to do?"

"We did. We sold it at ninety-five, and it was already at forty at the end of the news conference. CNBC said all the lithium stocks were tanking along with the oil companies. This is going to change everything."

"I guess so, Randy; we'll have to wait and see how things shake out."

SEVENTY-SIX

About the time the TV stations broke the news, Nikki Baker had just picked up a non-fat latte at the Starbucks located in the lobby of the MDV building. No one noticed a TV in the corner that was close-captioned to CNN. That was until someone shouted, "Holy shit, shut up, everybody; turn that up."

The thirty or so souls in the coffee shop were silent as the press conference played out. It was only another twenty seconds before Baker, her eyes wide, dropped her cup, yelled "Motherfucker," and bolted for the elevators.

Arriving at the executive floor, it was clear the news had broken. Nakamura was in Duffy's office getting an earful from his boss while administrative assistants were on their phones, frantically trying to sell any MDV stock still left in their 401(k)s. It was chaos.

She made it to her office at the same time Nakamura did. She sat at her desk as he closed her door. It was terrible timing, but the smug little fucker had been such an asshole to her, she couldn't resist. "So, Kenji, nice to see that you, the master negotiator, have this thing under control. Your buddy Robbins just jammed this vanadium so far up your ass, you're gonna gag on it. How's this working for ya, pal?"

With his nose flared and spittle flying from his mouth, he screamed, "It's your fault! You did this! We're ruined!"

"I don't think so, asshole; it was your show, remember?"

He leaned over her desk, his normally sallow complexion turning scarlet. "This is not over. I *will* kill that son of a bitch."

Then he turned, left the office, and left the building.

Baker instantly forgot about the little squirt. She pulled up her portfolio and saw lithium stocks were in freefall. An email informed her that the merger was off; Encel's stock was cratering. The entire industry would eventually disappear or be reduced to a fraction of its size.

All this because some goddamn scientist fucking *had* to find a way to make a better battery. Not just a little better, a fucking *waaay* better battery. There would be no riches, no merger, no job. There was nothing left, except maybe revenge on that prick on that island. He still had the 250,000 dollars they had wired him.

She had never killed anyone before, but right now, she felt like she could. She had no gun or weapon—it was Canada, after all. But maybe she could get one in the States; shit, everyone had guns there. The phones were jammed, the brokerage houses swamped, and the exchanges had closed due to technical issues. *Fuck it.*

The elevator took her to the fourth floor of the parking garage, where she exited, walked to her new Porsche Macan, and got behind the wheel. She loved this car, this car which she could no longer afford. Baker headed for the border, oblivious that Seth Robbins was still in Richland.

Seventy-seven

Special Agent Matt Steele had worked with Bill Owens on several high-profile cases. He trusted the detective implicitly and, strangely enough, even thought that O'Malley had a nose for finding solutions that were not so obvious.

The news conference was as riveting and impactful as Owens had suggested it would be. It wouldn't change a thing about his job or life, but it looked as though it would for many people.

Owens had clued him in on the timing of the release, and he, in turn, had alerted the Border Patrol. For once, the Mounties agreed to work with him and kept an eye on the two extortionists from MDV. They let him know as soon as Baker hit the road and headed south. Nakamura had not been seen; his Discovery was still parked in the MDV garage.

The Peace Arch backup was only an hour on Tuesday afternoon. It was still raining. When a hunter green Macan pulled up to the window of the Patrol station, the officer casually asked the attractive but harried driver to pull to the side. "Just need to check your vehicle, ma'am."

She dutifully moved over and shut the car off just as a good-looking man with short brown hair walked over and motioned for her to roll down her window. "Hi there, are you Nikki Baker?"

"Yes, I am. Why are you asking?"

"Could you step out of the car, please?" The man showed a badge of some kind.

When she complied, he said, "Because my name is Special Agent Matt Steele of the FBI, and you are under arrest for extortion." Another officer immediately grabbed her from behind and placed her in cuffs.

"You can't do this; I'm Canadian."

"Yes, ma'am, we know, but you're in the United States now. Welcome."

SEVENTY-EIGHT

The following eight months were comfortably dull, the sweet spot of life. Nikki Baker was brought to justice and spent time in a federal detention center. Even though she was a Canadian citizen, the officials declined to extradite, mentioning off the record that she got what she deserved.

Kenji Nakamura was never seen again. Some suspected suicide at some off-the-grid location; others suggested he fled the country because he couldn't cope with the demise of MDV. Jerry Duffy had assembled another group of investors and was looking into a vanadium battery manufacturing facility.

Bill and I patched things up and played golf whenever he could get away, while Jenne's ankle had finally healed. She, too, was spending time on the links.

On a beautiful, calm evening in late June, Jenne and I borrowed our neighbor's small runabout and puttered over the glass-like surface of the Saratoga Passage to a half-mile offshore. Jenne, through misty eyes, spread the contents of the urn. "She was a remarkable person, Kevin. I'm sorry she didn't get to see her work completed."

"I know, hon, I know. At least *we* understand, and so do Seth and Alice. Her name will never be forgotten; remember, it's the Waffle Battery.

We frequently heard from Randy and Smitty, who seemed to be spending a great deal of time together. My last text from Randy showed a picture of him and some big, tall, muscular fellow with a broad grin.

When I asked about him, he told me it was Chauncy. While on their trip to Utah, Smitty became exhausted after only a few short hikes and vowed to start eating better and get into shape. He'd lost ninety pounds and spent two hours a day at the gym. Randy also said his friend preferred to use his given name, Chauncy, going forward. I shared the picture with Jenne; she, too, was stunned at the transformation.

I was also informed that they were able to fill their short of MDV when it hit seven dollars and fifty cents, just before the company declared bankruptcy. The two men were millionaires and were discussing future living arrangements.

Since the announcement, the entire industrial complex had been revitalized. The stock market soared again, albeit with new start-ups and hundreds of new battery manufacturers. There were many casualties as some of the older energy companies refused to diversify by getting on board with the latest technology.

The oil reserves in the world held steady since usage had been cut in half, with greenhouse gases dramatically reduced. Some countries with questionable civil-rights policies even promised reform if allowed to use the new technology.

Seth Robbins was now a household name and would find a place in the history books. His income from patents alone was sufficient to see him through several lifetimes. In June, he and Alice were married, just after agreeing to take a position at the University of Washington in their science department. They were now both living in Alice's house in Wallingford.

They still longed to live on Whidbey but could not find a suitable property. They had joined us for dinner one night, when Jenne had a suggestion. "You know, the Waffle property is of no use to us. Why don't I sell it to you?"

Alice's eyes perked up. "What would we do with it?"

"You'd build a house. The septic system is already there, as is the well, the power, and cable. You could do it in half the time with a manufactured home."

"You mean like a trailer?"

Jenne shook her head and looked at me. "These youngsters don't get around much, do they?"

"I think Jenne's talking about modular construction. Quite a few companies build wonderful contemporary structures in factories and assemble them on site. They're beautiful. Check out Stillwater Dwellings and see what they offer. I'll bet you can cut construction time in half."

After doing a little research and talking to several companies, Seth and Alice selected one to work with. With minimal haggling, Jenne made them an offer they couldn't refuse on the property. They started in May, and the house was complete by October 1st. A housewarming party was planned for the second week of the month.

Because of his notoriety, Seth looked forward to moving to Whidbey Island. He and Alice planned to write and teach remotely, only going to campus occasionally when necessary. The house was everything they had hoped for. Jenne and I helped with many interior design elements, but the home required very few decorative details because of the wooded, natural setting. The concrete floors, expansive windows, and fir trim accents fit perfectly with the site, the native landscape treatments suggesting the home had been there for years.

The guest list was strictly for friends. Bill and Shelly, Chauncy and Randy, and Jenne and I were the only guests joining Seth and Alice. That was until Alice met Francis and Jake Early during a previous get-together at our house. The Earlys lived on the island, not too far from us, and were involved in a bizarre drug shootout that, somehow, we were involved in. They already knew the Owenses, and I was looking forward to introducing them to Randy and Chauncy.

There was still plenty of light until eightish in October, and it was warm for the evening. Seth and Alice had moved in the previous week, and the landscapers were still finishing up a few of the plantings. A half-dozen crew members were cleaning up when we arrived, their vehicles lined up on the driveway. Jenne promised we'd get there early to help Alice with the dinner prep. They had insisted Emma join in the festivities as well.

"Sorry about the traffic here," Seth explained, " They had to come back to do a few touch-up items; they're just finishing up outside."

"No worries. Where'd you get this crew? We always have a tough time finding help on the island." I was impressed by their work.

"They're from Oak Harbor. There was a card at the nursery, so I thought I'd give them a call."

"Looks like it worked out."

"They did a great job. That older fellow, Daniel, he's the owner. Most of the crew is either family or temporary, but Daniel runs the show. They'll be out of here shortly."

We busied ourselves inside and discussed the massive impact of the Waffle Battery. I accepted the offer of a glass of chardonnay and pulled up a seat at the kitchen island. "What about the studio out back?"

"For now, it's just storage, but there are a lot of memories back there." Seth seemed lost for a few seconds.

"I can imagine. Hey, look who's here." Emma's barking enthusiastically greeted the new arrivals.

"Sorry we're early; no traffic at the dock." Randy announced their arrival.

He and a much slimmer but more muscular Smitty, uh Chauncy, had arrived. To Chauncy's credit, he hesitated only slightly before gingerly approaching the dog and offering a hand.

"Geez, this is fabulous. Randy, you think we could do this?"

"Chauncy, let's table that discussion for at least while we're here." Randy shook his head and turned to us. "We got all this money, and he wants to spend it, sheesh."

Jenne guffawed. "I think you should, Chauncy. Talk to these two later, and they'll give you some names to call."

"Hey, Seth, will you go get the outdoor table we put in the studio. I'd like to use it for the hors d'oeuvres." Alice was making sure the food was presented properly.

"Sure. Hey Chauncy, wanna go see where you spent the night once?"

"Hell, yes." The two went off to fetch the table.

A few minutes later, Bill and Shelly arrived, followed shortly by the Earlys.

"Where's the famous scientist? I need an autograph." Shelly the kidder.

Alice answered, "They went back to the studio to get something. Kev, will you go see what's keeping them?"

"Sure, I'm on it."

As I headed out the door, I noticed the crew was gone, but one of their vehicles, a ten-year-old Toyota Corolla, was still parked on the side of the driveway.

Making my way through the brush, I arrived at the still, mostly hidden studio. It was quieter than I expected, especially since Seth and Chauncy had been out here for twenty minutes. The ground was soft underfoot, so I made very little noise. Before I got to the door, I heard a voice that didn't belong to either of my friends.

With the door slightly ajar, I could hear someone speaking. "I told you what would happen, didn't I? You ruined me *and* my company. I am nothing now, and your friend has to die as well."

"What will this accomplish? You're young; you can start over."

"I cannot show my face in this business ever again. You will have to pay."

I did not know the voice, but I recalled Seth telling me about the threats he received from the man with Baker. This sure as hell sounded like him. I was able to edge to the side of the door, where I could see through the crack. Both Seth and Chauncy were backed up against a workbench, where a very small landscape crew member—a cap pulled over his head—held a pistol on them. It was shaking in his hand.

Whoever it was, was nervous as hell, and I was curious why he hadn't already pulled the trigger. Maybe it just wasn't that easy to kill two people in cold blood. Still, he might do it.

I wished Bill were here, but he wasn't. The guy was little; maybe I could distract him, and Chauncy could make a move. Off to the side was a fir limb, like the one Chauncy had stepped on so long ago. This one was six feet long. I picked it up, stood as far from the door as I could, and shoved it open, with whatever force I could manage.

It swung inward and banged against the wall. There was a gasp, then a sound that must have been like when the limb snapped, then another, a sack of flour hitting the floor.

"You guys okay?"

"Yup," said Seth.

"What happened?"

"When the door slammed open, Chauncy grabbed one of those old electrodes I was messing with. He whacked this guy on the arm with it, then socked him in the head. I think he's out."

"Nice job, Chauncy."

"Yeah, thanks. Can we go eat now?"

"I thought you were on a diet."

"Not tonight. We're celebrating life, baby."

Yes, we were, just one thing left for me to do. I had to fetch my good buddy, Bill Owens, and tell him he had one more teensy weensy little something to clean up before we sat down to eat. Yippee, I couldn't wait!

ACKNOWLEDGMENTS

Juiced is a work of fiction. As always, the places are real, the people not so much. The names used may be the same or similar to those living or dead, but, rest assured, that is where the similarity ends. Thanks, once again, to my extremely tolerant wife for being the first read and editor, and thanks to my buddy Jeff Smith for help with the stock trading. I'm sure he'll let me know what I've screwed up.

There is no such thing as a solid-state vanadium flow battery, nor, from what I've read, is it possible. Vanadium redox flow batteries, however, *are* real, and the Pacific Northwest National Laboratory has and is continuing extensive research on them because of their enormous storage capabilities.

The lab, headquartered in Richland, WA, offers this blurb from their website:

> PNNL advances the frontiers of knowledge, taking on some of the world's greatest science and technology challenges. Distinctive strengths in chemistry, Earth sciences, biology, and data science are central to our scientific discovery mission. Our research lays a foundation for innovations that advance sustainable energy through decarbonization and energy storage and enhance national security through nuclear materials and threat analyses. PNNL collaborates with academia in fundamental research and with industry to transition technologies to market.
>
> We are a national lab with Pacific Northwest roots and global reach. Whether our researchers are unlocking the mysteries of Earth's climate, helping modernize the U.S. electric power grid, or safeguarding ports around the world from nuclear smuggling, we accept great challenges for one purpose: to create a world that is safer, cleaner, more prosperous, and more secure.

Made in the USA
Monee, IL
07 March 2023